KT-561-343

DANIELLE RAMSAY

The Last Cut

MULHOLLAND
BOOKS
HODDER

First published in Great Britain in 2017 by Mulholland Books
An imprint of Hodder & Stoughton
An Hachette UK company

1

Copyright © Danielle Ramsay 2017

The right of Danielle Ramsay to be identified as the Author
of the Work has been asserted by her in accordance with
the Copyright, Designs and Patents Act 1988.

All rights reserved. No part of this publication may be reproduced,
stored in a retrieval system, or transmitted, in any form or by
any means without the prior written permission of the publisher,
nor be otherwise circulated in any form of binding or cover
other than that in which it is published and without a similar
condition being imposed on the subsequent purchaser.

All characters in this publication are fictitious and any resemblance
to real persons, living or dead is purely coincidental.

A CIP catalogue record for this title is available from the British Library

Paperback ISBN 978 1 473 61150 4
eBook ISBN 978 1 473 61149 8

Typeset in Plantin Light by Hewer Text UK Ltd, Edinburgh
Printed and bound by CPI Group (UK) Ltd, Croydon, CR0 4YY

Hodder & Stoughton policy is to use papers that are natural, renewable
and recyclable products and made from wood grown in sustainable
forests. The logging and manufacturing processes are expected to
conform to the environmental regulations of the country of origin.

Hodder & Stoughton Ltd
Carmelite House
50 Victoria Embankment
London EC4Y 0DZ

www.hodder.co.uk

FIFE CULTURAL TRUST

HJ485194

Danielle Ramsay

Danielle Ramsay is a proud Scot living in a small seaside town in the North-East of England. Always a storyteller, it was only after initially following an academic career in literature that she found her place in life and began to write creatively full-time after being shortlisted for the CWA Debut Dagger in 2009 and 2010. She is the author of five novels in the Jack Brady series, *The Puppet Maker, Blood Reckoning, Blind Alley, Vanishing Point* and *Broken Silence.*

Always on the go, always passionate in what she is doing, Danielle fills her days with horse-riding, running and murder by proxy. An advocate against domestic violence for personal and political reasons, Danielle Ramsay is a patron for the charity SomeOne Cares, which counsels survivors of childhood abuse, rape and domestic violence.

To Elizabeth (Betty) Dand - for always believing.

FIFE COUNCIL LIBRARIES	
HJ485194	
Askews & Holts	06-Jun-2017
AF	£8.99
CRI	LO

Evil is always unspectacular and always human,
And shares our bed and eats at our own table.

W.H. Auden

CUT

Verb: make an opening, incision, or wound in (something) with a sharp-edged tool or object.
Synonyms: gash, slash, slit, pierce, penetrate, wound, injure, scratch, graze, nick. Snick, notch, incise, score, lance.

The Day Before

The scalpel lay on the stainless steel autopsy table next to the waiting body. It glinted with a hint of malice under the harsh overhead spotlight. The bulb spared nothing. Every small detail and imperfection on the body was laid bare below it.

The skin ...

She felt a wave of nausea hit her. She breathed in. Steadied herself. Forced herself to look at something else. She noted the identification tag tied to one of the toes. It documented the body as 'Subject A'; cause and time of death had been left blank.

She could feel her eyes starting to sting at the realisation of what had happened to her – to 'Subject A'.

Come on ... Pull yourself together. You can do this. If you don't, then ...

The waiting was making her uneasy. But it was a game. She had no choice. But he was making it difficult for her – intentionally so. She knew he would get a kick out of her being forced to remain down here alone.

Her eyes flitted from one shadowy corner of the damp basement room to another; anything to distract her from the naked body lying on the gleaming metal slab.

1

But she couldn't help it. Like the frantic fluttering of a doomed moth compelled to destroy itself against an electric light, her gaze returned to the table and its contents: the scalpel, the body and the ID tag.

She forced her attention away. It was the first time she had been down here. The high iron-barred windows had been blacked out so she couldn't tell whether it was day or night. She reminded herself that it was mid-afternoon, despite feeling as if it were the dead of night.

Compelled, she stared again at the body. At what had happened to it – *to her. Fuck! Who would recognise her now? That skin . . .*

She tried not to react. Not to allow herself to gag. She was here as a witness – nothing more. But she felt sickened by what she was looking at; the disgust overwhelming her. He had done that to her. *How? How could he do that to her?* He had damaged her beyond recognition. Her mouth was too dry to swallow when she caught sight of the needle and the black nylon that would be used to bind the skin together.

She focused on the ID tag again. The soles of the feet were cracked, discoloured with ingrained dirt. The yellowish nails were overgrown and split. She knew that the body on the table had been imprisoned against her will; subject to unspeakable acts of terror. Her skin hung in sagging folds from her starved body, spreading out over the edge of the metal table.

Why you? What attracted you to him? She stared hard at the gaunt, unresponsive face. At the bluish lips pulled back in a grimace, exposing teeth. The victim's mottled eyelids were closed against the intrusive glare of the spotlight. Her aquiline nose misshapen after being broken.

She noted the victim's long, straggly, over-bleached hair. An overwhelming sadness consumed her.

Again ... why you?

Heavy, deliberate footsteps bled into her dark thoughts. Readying herself, she looked across at the door and held her breath as it swung open, bringing with it a rush of cool air. It slapped her in the face; a sudden, cruel reminder of what lay beyond these impenetrable walls. Tense, she watched him as he walked purposefully towards the immobile body lying illuminated in the centre of the room. She waited for him to acknowledge her. For his eyes to turn in her direction. They didn't. Instead, he acted as if she did not exist.

She swallowed the anger and resentment she felt.

The white mask that covered his face accentuated his dark, intense eyes as they scrutinised what lay before him. There was a coldness within them; more than just a sense of professional detachment. She studied him with a sickened fascination as his gloved hands pulled the spotlight down, closer towards the body.

What is it that you see?

She watched with a feeling of dread as he picked up the victim's skin and stretched it out from the skeletal body. Satisfied, he turned his attention to the scalpel, scrutinising the blade under the light before bending

3

over the body. Then in one decisive move, he stretched the skin on the inside of the victim's left arm taut before slicing the scalpel cleanly through the tissue. Blood seeped out, pooling on the metal table.

Fuck . . . FUCK! She hadn't expected that.

Then something odd caught her attention. She frowned, narrowing her eyes, unsure whether it had actually happened. *Maybe she was wrong? Maybe she had imagined it? Oh fuck!* The body had moved again. There was no disputing it this time.

She tried to get his attention. To stop him. But it was futile. He was too focused on the body lying on the cutting slab to even notice that she was present. She attempted to shout out. Anything to get him to stop. But nothing happened. After all, her mouth had been sealed with duct tape and her body securely strapped to an old wooden wheelchair.

The kid was fourteen years old. Old enough to know better. He was scrawny and notably small for his age but despite his size, there was a dangerous, unpredictable edge to him. His chewed fingernails were encrusted with a lifetime of filth. She resisted the urge to tell him to stop gnawing on what was left of his raw and bleeding thumbnail. His flat, joyless eyes twitched from one corner of the room to the other like a cornered animal. There was a reason for his edginess – he was a murder suspect.

DS Harri Jacobs sat back, folded her arms and waited. One of them would break and it sure as hell wouldn't be her. She could feel her colleague, DC Robertson, bristling beside her. He, like the suspect, struggled in small, enclosed spaces. She knew that Robertson wanted to beat the crap out of the little scrote. Anything to move the stalemate on. But that would not bring forth a confession.

'Sarge?'

Harri simply responded by shaking her head. Her eyes were locked on the kid.

Suddenly, the stand-off was broken.

'What you waiting for, slit?' he asked, his rough voice heavy with disdain. After all, she was a copper – worse, she was a female copper. He made a point of eyeing her up. The look filled with a lustful malevolence.

Harri didn't drop her gaze. She knew his sort. She had looked long enough for him and his mates; had spent the past few days hunting them. She had found them hiding like rats in Elswick; an estate where the council tended to discard problem families. Poor education, poor role models and poverty resulted in a life of limited choices. She looked at the suspect. He was the product of his environment. Not that she felt sorry for him. No. She had seen what he had done to his victim – the smell of burnt flesh had still not left her.

Jason Tanner's vengeful gaze was locked on Harri. He looked more than ready to stick a knife in her. Or his cock. The leer in his eyes was enough to know that he was more than capable of sexual assault. The alcohol that she could smell on his sour breath would not have been the first time either. She knew of kids who had an alcohol addiction at the age of eight. Kids forgotten about on estates like Elswick or worse, Benwell; once referred to by a journalist as 'mini Beirut'. Kids with no choice but to grow up fast in a dystopian world of survival of the fittest.

However, Harri was not interested in Jason Tanner's background. It wasn't her job to give a shit about the reasons why this fourteen-year-old boy had murdered for sport. No; she would leave the social workers and psychologists to figure out what had gone wrong. As far as she was concerned, he was an evil little shit who needed to be locked up indefinitely. She was under no illusions; no amount of intervention or good intentions would alter this kid's psyche. Whatever naïve beliefs she'd had when she first started out had soon waned. The reality of the job had kicked them out of her. Her role now was to charge him. But first, she wanted a confession.

His clothes had been removed for forensic evaluation. She was certain that his expensive trainers would match the prints they had found at the crime scene. Then there was the evidence left by repeatedly stamping on the victim's head. Traces of blood could be seen on the sole, despite his attempt to bleach it out. However, Harri wanted more; she wanted an admission of guilt from Tanner's sneering lips – some kind of acknowledgement that what he had done was reprehensible.

'You know Darren Hodgson?'

He looked at her, eyes narrowing further as a flicker of unease flashed across them.

Harri dropped her gaze to the closed file in front of her. She shifted forward, opened it and took a moment to deliberate over its blank contents.

She could smell his discomfort. Stale and nauseating. The stench of his sweating body filled the room. Despite the hard act, she had rattled him. And she knew why. Darren was the weakest member of the gang and Jason had just confirmed it; he wasn't as smart as the rest of them, which meant he was a liability.

Harri looked at him and waited.

'Fuck you, slit!'

'From what Darren said, you're the one that likes to be fucked.'

He turned to his social worker by his side. 'You gonna let her get away with that shit?'

Harri didn't take her eyes off him, but she could feel the social worker's unease. She was new to the job. Consequently, she was out of her depth with the likes of Jason Tanner.

'Did you hear what I said or what, you frigid cunt?'

Flustered, the social worker turned first to DC Robertson and then to Harri. She found no support from either of them.

'Are you a mong or what? She can't talk to me like that!' Jason protested. 'I'm just a kid!'

'Shut the fuck up!' Harri said before the social worker had a meltdown. It worked; she now had his attention. 'Darren gave us a full statement. He said that you were the one who instigated the attack and it was you, and you alone, who assaulted the victim. You kicked him to the

7

ground and then stamped on his head until he was unconscious.' Harri paused to fully appreciate his reaction. It was clear that he wasn't used to being spoken to in this manner – at least not by people in authority. But Harri knew what kind of teenager she was dealing with: one who had respect for no one, not even his own mother, whom he had assaulted – often. This was a repeat young offender who had escalated from tying fireworks to cats' tails, to petty theft, followed by arson and finally, forcing a homeless man's beaten, unconscious body into a wheelie bin, dousing his body in petrol, setting him on fire and then watching as the victim burned to death.

'Do you have anything to say?' Harri asked.

'Yeah, fuck you! I did nowt. You know it. I know it and Darren fucking knows it! So why don't you do us both a favour and let me go?'

There was a loud rap at the door. Harri pushed her chair back and stood up. She had been waiting for this update. She nodded at Robertson and then over at the flushed social worker. 'Five minutes.'

'Hey, bitch? Get me a Coke and a Mars bar while you're at it!'

Harri replayed the film that had been posted on Darren Hodgson's Facebook page. Once the police had started asking questions he'd taken it down; exactly as she had expected. However, the post had already been shared repeatedly.

There had been a recent spate of gang members uploading mobile footage of their mates or themselves assaulting rival gangs or members of the public. Most were too narcissistic or stupid to realise that it could be incriminating. It had made Harri wonder whether the suspects had shared the murder on social media.

It hadn't taken long for Stuart, one of their forensic computer analysts, to trace it. It was even more than she had hoped for – conclusive evidence that Jason had assaulted the victim before setting him on fire. It was just as she had assumed. Not that she had found anything out from his friend Darren – he had refused to talk, as had the other four members of the group. It seemed they feared Jason more than the threat of spending time inside a secure children's home.

When the emergency services had been called out to the smouldering wheelie bin and its charred contents, no one on the Elswick estate would even answer their doors to uniform, let alone make a statement. Once the police presence had dispersed, an elderly resident had approached one of the SOCOs working the crime scene. He said that the attackers had been teenagers – well-known troublemakers who terrorised the residents. He hadn't named the culprits but it was enough for Harri to follow her hunch that Jason Tanner would be involved; his name was synonymous with trouble in the west end of the city. Then she had looked at his and his friends' social media accounts.

She checked the date and time on her phone: Thursday 31 March, 4:33 p.m. Ready, she walked back into the small interview room and sat down. The air felt stale and suffocating. She could feel Jason Tanner's hateful eyes on her.

'Where the fuck's my Coke?'

Harri resisted the urge to lean across the table and give him a good smack; attempting to teach him manners at this late stage would be futile. 'Were you aware that your friend, Darren Hodgson, filmed you assaulting the victim? The footage shows you and your mates throwing his body into the wheelie bin and then you setting him alight. You were then clearly filmed shouting obscenities about the victim as he burned to death.'

She could see his surprise, followed by rage, that the deleted film had been traced by the police.

'It was a post you "liked" and even commented on.'

'Naw! Wasn't like that! You've got your facts wrong! The bloke was coming at me, like. It was fucking self-defence.'

Harri nodded. 'Perhaps I need to watch the film again. I didn't quite catch that part.'

'Yeah? Maybe you fucking should!'

Harri stared at him – hard. 'So the petrol?'

His eyes shot towards the social worker for some kind of intervention. Her reaction was one of nervousness. He turned his glare back on Harri. 'What about it?'

'Was it coincidental that you had it at hand to pour over the victim?'

'Naw! Me and me mate had been like messing around on his dirt bike.'

'So it wasn't premeditated? You hadn't set out to assault a homeless person and set them on fire? It was, as you described, "self-defence"?'

'You thick or what, bitch? I already said that, didn't I?'

Harri studied him silently. His eyes glinted at her with menacing disdain. She was certain that they would cross paths again. He would be older, angrier and inevitably more dangerous. Locking him up with his own kind would only benefit him, not rehabilitate him. He was a kid with a psychopathic personality – someone whose amoral and antisocial behaviour would only escalate.

'Bit of advice, son, next time you murder someone, don't paste your intentions all over social media first.' Before he had a chance to come up with a retort, Harri turned to Robertson: 'Charge him.' She couldn't be bothered to waste any more energy.

'With what? I did you all a fucking favour! He was some homeless pisshead cunt that no one gave a fuck about!'

'He was ex-services, suffering from post-traumatic stress. He had a wife who reported him missing four months ago. He also had two young kids. You want to tell them how you poured petrol over their dad and set him alight? You going to tell them how the plastic from the bin melted into his flesh? After all the crap he had seen in the forces, he ends up dying at the hands of a pathetic little shit like you!'

Harri had expected to see a flicker of something other than coldness in the fourteen-year-old's eyes. But there was nothing. *No surprise ... or regret. Just an impenetrable blackness.*

She stood up. She had had enough.

'You fucking bitch! You wanna watch your back. Whoever slit you didn't do a good enough job.' His cold eyes lingered on the thick scar that disfigured her throat.

She didn't react. She was used to people staring. Some with pity, others with curiosity – most with repulsion.

Harri breathed out, relieved to be alone. The double doors of The Bacchus Bar on High Bridge in the city centre swung closed behind her, silencing the revelry; primarily Robertson's drunken booming voice as he regaled the rest of the team with another infamous anecdote. Harri had heard most of them before – they all had. She had decided to call it a night. No one had noticed her leave, which was her plan. She wanted to let the team enjoy themselves. After all, they had nailed the investigation. Jason Tanner had been charged late that afternoon with the murder of the ex-services father of two. But Harri still had a bitter taste in her mouth. Maybe it was the suspect's attitude towards the charges. She might have caught the perpetrator but it didn't lessen the horror of what had been done to the victim; a man who had fought for his country and survived, only to be so pointlessly murdered. Life was arbitrary – no one knew that more than her.

'You got a light?'

Harri turned to see that Stuart, the computer analyst, had followed her. She didn't remember inviting him and assumed someone else on the team must have suggested it. Not that she could complain; it was Stuart's forensic IT skills that had found the deleted mobile phone footage.

It had been an impromptu celebratory drink at the end of their shift. Harri had felt the need to go – just for a couple – to show team solidarity. Not that she felt any; not yet. Nor did she feel much like celebrating. She had simply forced herself to go through the motions.

She looked at Stuart's expectant face. 'Gave up,' she replied, realising he thought she'd come out for a cigarette.

'I keep promising myself that I will and then shit happens and . . .' He shrugged, patting down his jacket in search of a light. Eventually finding it, he lit up.

Harri watched, envying him that first exhilarating drag. Nothing compared to that heady feeling of intoxication. Nothing.

Comparatively relaxed, he smiled at her. 'Want one? Promise I won't tell.'

She shook her head.

He shot her a look that suggested it was her loss.

She shivered as she pulled her jacket collar up. 'Right. I'm off.'

'Really?'

Harri heard the disappointment in his voice. It took her by surprise. She had been single for so long that she had forgotten how to tell if someone was into her. She suddenly felt awkward. Stuart was late twenties, tall, with dark hair twisted back in a bun. Physically, he was her type. Or at least used to be.

As if reading her thoughts, he smiled at her. Relaxed, suggestive even.

She had forgotten what it was like …

'Anyway,' her tone was suddenly cool. Professional. 'Thanks for all your help.' She could see his flicker of surprise at her abruptness. She didn't give him a chance to reply. Instead, she turned and started walking away. As she did so she heard another member of the team come out and join him. Then laughter. It cut through her like a knife. But it was the words that followed that hit her – hard.

You've got no chance, mate! Not with her. She's seriously off-limits. You know what happened to her, right?

Restless, Harri sighed and turned over. The words were still replaying in her head. Minutes passed before she started to drift off again. Then she heard it. Something creaked. Her eyes shot open. But she couldn't make anything out. The room was filled with shadows. Some familiar. Some not so familiar. She cursed herself for not leaving the hall light on, held her breath and listened. Nothing; apart from the reassuring whir of the refrigerator in the kitchen. It was then that she realised that her bedroom door was partially open. She was sure she had closed it. *Hadn't she?*

She lay perfectly still, every sense in her body screaming at her that something was wrong. Then she realised why. It took her a moment to register it. Breathing. Raspy. Adrenalin surged.

Someone was in her bedroom. Waiting . . . Watching her.

He came out of nowhere. Forcibly holding her down. A gloved hand covered her nose and mouth. She struggled. Tried to bite. To scream. But it was futile. He retaliated by pushing down so hard she couldn't breathe. Before she had a chance to react, he flipped her over, ramming her head deep into the pillow. He grabbed her arms and pinned them against her back. There was an explosion of pain.

Fuck . . . Fuck . . .

She suddenly felt light-headed.

'Scream and I slice your throat open. Understand?'

She froze. The agonising pain was drowned out by his words.

He's going to kill you . . .

'Do you understand me?'

She didn't answer. Her only thought was that she didn't want to die. *Not like this.*

He kneed her in the back, hard. 'Do you understand?'

The pain jolted her. If she wanted to survive this, she needed to play along. She attempted to nod.

'Good girl. You keep quiet and do as I say and then maybe . . . just maybe, I will let you live.'

She felt him snap handcuffs around her wrists.

Think. Come on . . . think!

But panic had overwhelmed her. She didn't know what she could do.

He grabbed a fistful of her hair while his other hand forced her head back. 'You like to play games, don't you?'

She didn't respond. Couldn't.

Her mind was racing.

'Let's see how you like me fucking with you for a change.'

He suddenly released her hair. But the other hand still held her head. She felt something touch her neck. It took a second for her to understand there was a knife pressed against her throat. The tip of the blade, ice cold. Teasing. Threatening. Her mind filled with images of what was about to happen. She, better than anyone, knew how this would end.

'You like this?'

She felt the knife trail up her cheek until it reached the soft skin below her right eye. He pressed the tip of the blade into the flesh. Terror exploded inside her. She struggled, but his weight on her back pinned her down. She attempted to scream. To beg. Nothing. His hand muffled any protest she tried to make.

DON'T! Please don't do it …

Her body was rigid. She squeezed her eyes shut as she waited for the knife to cut in. It didn't. *He didn't.*

Relief flooded. Then she felt the lick of the blade caress its way back down her neck. It stopped. He deliberated for a moment before digging the edge of the blade against her throat. Hard. Cold.

She didn't feel anything at first. Too adrenalised for pain to register as the blade sliced across her neck.

Surprise, followed by panic, coursed through her like an electric shock. She didn't want to die. She knew that if she didn't do something – *anything* – he was going to kill her. But she was paralysed. Terrified, she remained still as he bent down close to her ear; savouring her fear. Breathing in her pain. Her horror.

She didn't need to see his lips to know that he was smiling; enjoying the power he had over her. Nor did she need to see his eyes to know that they would be filled with contempt.

'You're so fucking perfect.' His voice muffled. 'But you know it, don't you?'

He pressed his own face against hers. Held it there for a moment. 'You know how much I have wanted you, Harri . . . wanted this. I have waited so long to touch you . . .'

He knew her name. How the fuck did he know her name?

Her mind struggled to find a connection. She didn't recognise his voice. *Or did she? She couldn't be sure. But he knew her . . . How?*

The voice was distorted too much for her to be certain. Fear snaked its way through her body, coiling itself in a tight knot in her stomach.

'I've watched you. Watched you fucking around. Watched you with other men. Flaunting yourself. You'll never fuck around again after I'm done with you. Will you? WILL YOU?'

She tried to shake her head. Couldn't. She tried to recognise him. His voice. The weight of his body. His height. She felt sick. *Fuck, no . . . Not you . . . NO!*

She attempted to struggle. To fight back. But he had her completely. She couldn't breathe ... couldn't scream ... couldn't think.

Then she felt him ... felt his hardness against her. She knew what was coming next.

'Did you really think you could tease me and get away with it? You fucking owe me this,' he hissed.

No ... NO!

Gasping for breath, Harri sat bolt upright. Drenched in sweat, her T-shirt clung to her body. She was deafened by pounding blood as her heart beat furiously. It took her a moment to realise that she was awake and alone. She tried to breathe. Short gasps of air at first. Then deeper breaths. Slower, less frantic. Less ... *terrified.*

It's over with ... it's over ...

She clenched her hands in resistance. Bit her lip. Hard. Fought the tears spilling down her face. In that moment she hated herself. Hated feeling pathetic. Feeling weak.

Stop crying! You hear? You're fucking done crying!

She was done being a victim. She had survived. She had moved on. It was over. All she had to do was keep telling herself that. Until eventually she believed it.

It's over. It's over ... He can't get you now ...

She rubbed the truculent tears away, then looked at the radio alarm clock. It was only 11:51 p.m. Still shaken, she switched on the lamp on the floor next to her. Just in case. She looked around the vault-like space. There was nowhere to hide. No other adjacent rooms. It was one sparse, open-plan room. The kitchen and the bathroom were less than basic. But it was hers and she knew every inch of it.

She fought the urge to check that no one was in the empty building below – paranoia wasn't her thing. Instead, she turned angrily onto her side and tried to block out the recurring nightmare by looking across at the windows opposite. She stared blankly out at the zig-zagging headlights of cars as they passed across the Tyne Bridge. Her eyes drifted away from the River Tyne towards Gateshead. The embankment was shrouded in blackness. Oppressive. She shivered involuntarily. It felt as if someone was watching her apartment.

Don't be ridiculous!

She rolled over on the double mattress, turning away. She had positioned it opposite one of the four original windows that dominated the sixty foot by sixty foot space. When she went to bed she would lie watching the yellow and orange lights that danced and flashed across the river. It gave her a sense of security. That she was not alone.

She had used the money she had made from the sale of her flat in London to buy this space on the fifth floor of a derelict building just off the Quayside. As soon as she had seen it, she knew it would suit her. It had been sold as a 'project' – but even that description was too optimistic. There were no commodities to speak of – nothing that made it habitable. Most of the wood floor-ing had been infected by woodworm and needed to be renewed. The exposed brickwork, shabby and partially covered in lead paint, needed sandblasting and repointing. The original beams required treating and, in some cases, replacing.

But she still bought it. The reason was simple: no one could enter it without her knowing. She was on the top floor with one way in. One way out. The windows that flooded the space with light during the day could not be opened. Which was exactly what she wanted. She had made herself a prison – a box where she could shut herself away from the outside world.

It was simply a place to eat, sleep and shower. That was all she needed – a safe room where she could lock everything else out.

To lock out people like Stuart . . .

The words that she had overheard earlier stung her. After what happened to her, she had accepted that life would never be the same again.

She stared over at her kitchen space, trying to distract herself. She had made the best use possible of the space. On the wall opposite the windows, a Sixties-style fridge stood beside a wooden table with drawers that functioned as a kitchen worktop; on it were a kettle, microwave and a dish rack filled with some china and utensils. Next to the table was a chipped and stained Belfast sink that had seen better days, but it was one of the original fittings that had come with the apartment.

The bathroom was as basic as the kitchen space, housing only a white enamel sink and toilet. Both had been hidden behind a stud wall at one end of the room. As soon as she had bought the apartment, she had knocked the wall down, wanting every part of the space exposed. She had then plumbed in a basic shower cubicle – her only luxury. It had taken her two days to assemble and connect it. Not that she had any hot water. But at least she could shower. And while she showered, she would be able to see every part of the flat; most importantly, the door.

She scanned the large room, looking for a hint that something was out of place. The room was spartan. She could see into every corner. There was no place to hide here. No shadows for a rapist to lurk in.

A vintage leather tan couch sat underneath a window, opposite the kitchen space. An old wooden tea chest, covered in newspapers and books, was in front of it. A threadbare Persian rug lay under the tea chest. Beside the couch were the only possessions she had allowed herself to bring from her old life; a record player and an eclectic vinyl collection. If she had to disappear again, they were the only things she would take – the only tangible thing she had left of her father.

She refused to think about her life then. It had gone and there was nothing else to show for it. Her eyes drifted up to the exposed beams overhead. She had wired and positioned four speakers at each corner of the room. Since she was the only resident in the building, she could blast music as loud as she wanted. *For now.* At some point the floors beneath her would be sold off and turned into luxury apartments or offices.

Hanging from the rafters in the middle of the room was an old red punching bag. She had taken kickboxing lessons after her assault and had trained every day since.

Harri looked towards the large metal door. She was checking that it was still bolted. That no one had managed to break in while she was asleep. She knew she was being ridiculous. It was impossible. There was no way in from the outside – no fire escape. The only way up to the fifth floor was either by the stairs or the decrepit Thirties lift, which made more noise than actual movement.

She remained lying on her side, rigid, willing herself back to sleep. But she couldn't relax. She held the baseball bat that she kept under the patchwork quilt to her body. She had spent time planning. Psyching herself up for his return. Next time she would be ready. Next time, she would kill him.

She waited to unwind. But she was too wired. Annoyed, she resigned herself to getting up. She needed to burn off the adrenalin coursing through her body.

She pulled her T-shirt off and looked for her running clothes. As she did so she caught sight of herself in the mirror that leaned against the wall next to her clothes rail. She instinctively recoiled at the ugly crisscross scar on her left breast and the jagged line that ran across her neck. Both scars were still raw – the flesh not quite healed.

She turned away, sickened by the image. She tried not to look at herself naked – too much a reminder of what had happened. Soon it would be exactly a year to the hour of her attack. She had survived. What angered her was the way he had marked her. She would live every day of her life with permanent reminders.

But she was fooling herself if she thought the scars were only physical. He had left her with the promise that he would come when she least expected it; finish what he had started.

For what he wanted was to kill her.

DAY ONE
FRIDAY: 1st APRIL

Chapter One

The chemicals he had used stung her eyes. But she couldn't close them. She was too scared of what would happen. He had left her strapped in the old-fashioned wheelchair down in the basement – alone – staring at the cutting slab in the centre of the room.

Her body . . . *Oh God* . . .

Tears slipped silently down her pale cheeks, seeping over the black duct tape. She was terrified by what she had seen. It was beyond anything she could ever have imagined. There was no logic behind what he had done to 'Subject A'.

Or maybe in his head it made sense? For he never hesitated . . . Not once. He just concentrated on . . . on altering her.

He had left her lying there, bleeding, barely alive, for hours and hours before returning to complete his transformation.

He was gone now – with her.

Where did he take you?

He was a perfectionist. She knew that; had witnessed it first-hand. It burned like a raging fever in his eyes.

She stared hard at what was left on the metal autopsy

table. The skin, blood and— She did not want to think about the rest.

No ... don't think about what he did to her afterwards ...

Her face felt cold. Her tears were filled with remorse – though there was nothing that she could have done to help. There were only three of them left now.

He had promised her – them – that he would find a cure for their ailments. He said that they were all infected with the same disease; a disorder of structure that he was charged with curing. It was his *obsession*. His life role. And he had selected them individually – had sought them out from so many potential candidates. His intention was to physically change them. To make them unrecognisable. She understood that now. He had bleached Subject A's dark brown hair blonde, covered her eyes with bright green contact lenses, altered her body and finally her face.

The thought of the end result terrified her. *He* terrified her.

She strained to hear something – anything. But all she could hear was a deathly silence that bounced back at her off the thick stone walls. She was scared. But she couldn't call out for help.

Then she heard the music. It was faint but she could still make out the crackling and static from the old vinyl on the gramophone. It was the third movement from Debussy's *Suite Bergamasque*. The hairs on the back of her neck stood up as a feeling of disquiet unfurled itself in the pit of her stomach. She knew that something was wrong. That one of the other patients must have been distressed. The music was only played to help induce a state of calm in the sanatorium. That was what he called it – *the sanatorium*. He had told her that the old building was built to accommodate tuberculosis patients. It had all made sense to her then – the rows of old-fashioned wrought-iron beds, the large, white-washed ward and the countless empty wheelchairs lined up sinisterly in the hallways.

She thought about what could have upset the patient – or patients; for there were two of them left up there. *No . . . He wouldn't have?*

Paralysed, she had watched as he had wheeled 'Subject A' out of the basement room. He had never once looked at her. It was as if he had forgotten that she even existed. She tried to ignore the panic that was starting to build. Sometimes he would be gone for what felt like days at a time as they lay in their hospital beds, unable to move. Waiting. Always waiting for him to come back. Sometimes he left them in their wheelchairs facing the windows; all in a regimented line. He said it was good for their constitution – the biting fresh air. He would forget that the cold and rain could drive through the large open windows, burrowing into their sickly flesh as it clung to their protruding bones. He would forget that they were immobile; unable to move or speak until he returned. All they could do was watch and wait. Prisoners in their own bodies.

She wondered whether he had taken 'Subject A's' body upstairs to the ward.

*Oh my God ... Has he put her back in her bed? NO ...
Surely not like that ... Not after he had altered her ...*

She blinked back the tears as the music seeped into the basement. It was loud now. Too loud. This was atypical. She knew something was wrong. That someone was very distressed.

She tried to swallow down the bile that had risen to the back of her throat. She didn't want to choke to death. Not alone. Not like this. She could feel her body begin to spasm. Shock was starting to set in. The reality of her situation too horrific. She now knew what he planned to do to her. After all, she had witnessed 'Subject A's' transformation first-hand.

But whatever he had attempted to do had not worked. That was what he had said. That 'Subject A' was not nearly as perfect as '*her*'. She had wondered who he was referring to. All she knew was that this woman – *his obsession* – had long blonde hair and bright green eyes. He had attempted to alter 'Subject A' to look like her – *and failed*.

Chapter Two

Her breathing was hard and fast. Her head hurt. A dull throb waiting to explode. But she refused to stop. Too angry, too defiant to give in. Her eyes filled with dogged determination as she forced herself to continue.

Fuck it!

A New England Patriots baseball cap was pulled down low over her face, giving her the anonymity she needed. Her hair was pulled back in a tight ponytail. She pulverised the dark pavement as she pushed every muscle in her to keep running.

She could feel the pain of the past catching up; feeding off the injustice she felt.

Stop it, Harri! Stop being a fucking victim!

Filled with pent-up fury, she sprinted past the warm glow of the Pitcher and Piano as the bar started to close. Midnight and the place was surprisingly full of revellers spilling out onto the Quayside, taking in the hypnotic blue lights of the Millennium Bridge as it arched over the River Tyne – a poetic feat of balance and modern-day engineering. The dazzling lights reflected off the menacing water below momentarily calmed her. A brief respite from the resentment she felt.

31

She had already run for twenty minutes. But it wasn't enough. Not yet, no matter how much her body objected. Her pain was too raw and if she was to get any sleep she needed to burn it off. Two more miles and then she would head back. Physically and, hopefully, mentally exhausted.

Instinct made her turn and look across the black river towards Gateshead and the car parks and industrial sites to the left of the Baltic Flour Mill and the Sage. All she could make out were the garish yellow glow of disappearing car headlights and the burnished orange of streetlights.

An icy sliver of unease stirred within. It was a familiar, unwelcome guest. She hated feeling this way. Annoyed at herself, she headed for the steps leading up to the Free Trade pub.

She reached the top and stopped. Bent over and panting, Harri raised her head and looked out across the Tyne, taking in the breathtaking view. At night it was magical – vibrant and alive, lit up in every direction. The place was always buzzing and that was what she craved. People, noise, lights – anything to distract her.

She usually felt safe here. Hidden amongst the chaos.

But tonight was different. She felt on edge. *As if someone was watching her.* She knew it was irrational but she couldn't shake the feeling. She put it down to the fact that it was a year ago to the night when it had happened. When her life had changed.

She breathed out. Steadied herself. She had a new life here. One that she had to make work. There was no going back.

She let go of the railing and ran down the steps, and continued on for another mile or so before checking her watch: 12:29 a.m. It was time to turn back and head for home. She passed the Baltic Chambers and turned into a side alley. She fumbled for her keys when she reached the hidden doorway. But as she did so she heard a noise behind her. She spun around as a hooded figure stepped out from the shadows. Six foot two. Athletic.

Wary, she took in his presence. She may have been petite in comparison but she knew how to use his height and weight against him. She had a choice; headbutting the bones of his nose up into his skull – an unexpected, sudden movement involving bringing his face down in a hard whiplash movement straight into the crown of her head. Or, she could come at him with a roundhouse kick; heel to the jaw knocking him straight to the ground – and out. Both would work.

But he was gone before he gave her a chance to make a choice, as if she had imagined him. She was all too aware that she could seriously injure someone, even kill them, without a second's hesitation. *Rather that, than ...*

She blocked the thought. She had spent months rebuilding herself. Counselling had been obligatory. And it had worked. Without the doctor's help, she would not have been able to continue, let alone work as a copper. He had made her understand how to survive; what she needed to do to get her life back. And she had; she had learned to fight. When she had come to this conclusion he ended the counselling sessions. He explained that he had done everything he could for her.

His fear was that she would become overly dependent on him. And so confident that she could cope without him, he had cut her loose. It had been a painful transition at the time and a major influence in her decision to transfer to the Northumbrian force. After all, there was nothing left for her in London. She had sent him a text informing him of her decision and he had wished her well.

Stepping inside the old Victorian building, she took in the silence. The stillness. It was hidden off the Quayside. She liked the fact that it overlooked the River Tyne. Simply because it meant that no one could watch her. Stalk her. *Like before.*

Switching the overhead light on, she noticed the take-away leaflets on the ground and other junk. Stuff she had stepped over countless times. When Harri had relocated, she had set up a PO Box so that her whereabouts remained private.

She picked them up with the intention of binning them, then ran – two steps at a time – up the stairs, hitting the light switches on each floor as she went. Heart thundering, muscles objecting, she finally reached the top floor. She opened the heavy door to her apartment and then locked and bolted it behind herself.

Harri did what she always did and checked that there were no unexpected surprises waiting. Everything was as she had left it. She threw the junk mail in the bin and looked out at the Tyne Bridge. She still couldn't shake the irrational feeling that someone out there was watching her. She headed for the shower.

Turning it on, Harri steeled herself for the initial shock of the ice-cold water, scrubbed at her body with a rough sponge. Once out, she brusquely towelled herself dry, found her T-shirt dumped on top of the mattress and, shivering, hurriedly pulled it on.

She froze. Out of the corner of her eye she saw an A4 envelope on the floor by the bin. She realised it must have been hidden amongst the free weekly newspapers.

Curious, she walked over and picked it up. The envelope was blank. She ripped it open. Inside was an A4 photograph. She pulled it out. *No . . . no . . .*

She automatically turned away.

Fucking look at it, Harri!

She forced herself to look back down at the familiar image. After all, it was her face staring back at her. Swollen. Eyes bloodied. Her nose broken. Unrecognisable. Her blonde hair tangled and covered in blood.

She attempted to swallow. But her mouth was too dry.

Her eyes took in the ugly sutures across her savaged neck. Sickened, she scrunched the photograph up into a tight ball and threw it into the bin.

Shit . . .

She recognised the photograph as one of many that had been taken after her assault. The bastard had rung 999 and reported her attack from her own mobile. She assumed that he had called the emergency services to guarantee that she would survive.

He had promised her he would find her again and when he did he would . . .

She stopped. Tried to breathe. Forced herself to block out the words. *His words.* His promise. She had always known this moment would come. She had discussed it in counselling. But now it had become a reality.

She pulled out the baseball bat from under the bed covers. Gripping it, she walked over to the door and sat cross-legged on the floor with her back against it. The only way in or out of the apartment was through this door. Also from this vantage point she could see the whole of her flat.

An accepting calmness descended. There was only one thought going through her mind: *he was coming back to finish what he had started.* She looked out the window into the blackness, filled with a resolute determination. She had always known this day would come.

But this time, I will be ready for you ...

Chapter Three

He took a mouthful of single malt scotch; savoured the subtle smoothness as he stared out of the floor-to-ceiling wall of glass at the vast city spread out below. It was late. Not that it made a difference to him. He turned his attention to the computer screen. He rested his head back against the leather chair as he studied the crime scene photographs of his ex-patient – Harri Jacobs.

One image dominated the screen; it was an enlargement of her bloody and swollen face, taken hours after her ordeal. The thick black sutures left by the surgeon zig-zagged their way across her neck, brutally binding the cut flesh together. He took another warming mouthful as he absorbed the carnage that had been enacted. The slit throat. The crisscross stabbing on her chest – inches from her heart. But these were just the physical wounds. Injuries that would heal over time. Then there was the psychological trauma she had suffered. Her attacker had left her barely alive with the promise that he would return. It had been his job to make her face this possibility and prepare for it. She had wavered on the edge of falling beyond his reach – beyond anyone's help.

He looked at the time on the screen: 1:11 a.m. – exactly a year since her rapist had made his presence known. He knew that sleep would be the last thing on her mind. The last time he had seen her was over five months ago. She had left London shortly after their final session. He could not help her any more. Not when she had finally accepted that only *she* could bring closure – no one else.

He thought of the way she had looked in their last meeting together. She had looked resolute. Determined. So different from the woman he had first met. The one who could barely answer, let alone look him in the eye. *Did he feel a pang of pride? Of accomplishment? After all, she had been one of his most difficult cases. And here she was ready to come face to face with her demons – the man who wanted to kill her.*

In that moment he wanted her here; with him.

He took another mouthful of scotch as he settled for second best and clicked on an audio recording of one of their sessions. He had spent hours with her after her attack. Initially, she didn't talk. But slowly, ever so slowly, she had started to trust him. All he had to do was be patient.

He leaned his head back and closed his eyes and waited for her voice to fill the room. She had piqued his interest from the moment he had first heard about her. Then when he had finally met her, he understood why she was so special. Why someone had been obsessed to the extent that they had entered her ground floor flat and watched, as she slept, before making their presence known. Then at precisely 1:11 a.m. on 1st April, they had made their presence known.

'What do you want me to say?'

He smiled at those reticent words. Her voice was punctuated with sadness, but there was an unmistakable undercurrent of anger. Defiance. Revenge even. How long he had waited for her to come to this realisation – this decision?

He listened to the silence. *His silence.* He had not answered her question. For it had been a rhetorical one. She knew exactly what he wanted her to say – *but she had to say it.* It had to be *her* decision; her own realisation.

He heard her soft intake of breath on the tape as she acknowledged that he was not going to provide her with the answer. He wasn't going to make it easy for her. It had to come from her.

'You don't honestly expect me to share with you what I want?' she asked.

Silence.

He remembered that moment. Recalled how he gently cocked his head to the side as he waited. It was not his job to condone or judge. His role was to remain neutral. He had watched as she defiantly shook her head, not wanting to admit her true desire.

Then she sighed; a gesture of acceptance.

A flicker of a smile played at the corner of his mouth as he remembered the dark look she had given him at the time. Her intensely melancholic green eyes had suddenly come back to life, fuelled with anger and resentment at him for attempting to drag her from the depths to which she had fallen. She had struggled with whether she wanted to be saved; more importantly, whether she wanted to save herself. He, better than anyone, understood the debilitating pain she felt; so intense to begin with that she could see only one way out. The absolute fear of her rapist's final promise too great. So that had been his role. To guide her. To provide her with an out. A way of reclaiming her life.

He exhaled. Slowly. Waited for her response on the tape. He had listened to this session repeatedly. He knew each pause, each subtle nuance, as if he had breathed life into them himself.

'All right . . . You really want to know?'

Silence.

He could visualise himself studying her. His countenance may have been inscrutable, but inside he felt a tumult of emotions. After all, he had yearned for so long to hear those words. But he reined in his excitement and waited for her to explain herself.

'I . . . want him to come back.'

He remembered how her eyes suddenly flashed with threatening intent. He had shifted towards her. A subtle nod that she had his confidence – his understanding. He knew why she wanted her rapist to return. He had spent hours and hours trying to get her to realise that there were only two options available – *kill or be killed*.

'Why?'

His voice was low and disarmingly gentle. He surprised himself.

'I just do.'

He felt a wave of pleasure course through his body as he listened to those emotionless words.

'And when you do, what do you think the outcome will be?'

He recalled how she looked at him, as if surprised by his need to ask the question. There was no warmth in her expression when she finally answered. No joy. Just a resolute glint in her eye.

'I will be able to move on.'

Silence.

He listened, still with his eyes closed. He could feel his heart rate increase with anticipation. He knew every word – he had orchestrated them.

'I want to end it. Before he kills me.'

He recalled how he had simply nodded. How he had savoured those delectable words. After all, it had taken an incredible amount of perseverance and guidance to get her to reach this conclusion.

He knew the next question. He had had no choice but to ask it. He had to be certain.

'You are sure that this is what you want?'

Listening to the audio, he could almost feel her eyes on him again, as if she were in front of him. There had been no hesitation, no doubt. Only a desire for it to happen.

'Yes.'

The word hung in the air.

Finally, he broke the silence between them.

'How do you intend to find him?'

'Through my job. I'm not quitting.'

'And if you can't find him?'

'Then I will make sure I am ready for him if he returns.'

Silence.

'*When* he returns,' she corrected.

'Harri . . .'

She had frowned at him then.

'Will it end it for you? Facing him again?'

'Yes.'

There was no going back.

He waited as the tape ended. That was their last session. There was no point in continuing to counsel her. She knew what she needed to do. He had done his part.

He opened his eyes. Looked at the time: 1:33 a.m. He swilled what was left in his glass before draining it. Exactly a year ago, Harri Jacobs had been subject to one of the most brutal assaults he had dealt with. But she had found a way forward. A means of claiming her life back. Or at least, that was what she wanted to believe. He resisted the urge to call her. To hear her voice one last time. That was against the rules. It was too late anyway. It was already 1st April: the day had already begun.

Chapter Four

Harri wasn't sure how long she had been sitting with her back against the door. She pulled the quilt around her shoulders as she stared at her mobile phone. Across her knee lay the baseball bat. She was waiting for him. *Unlike before . . .*

She listened. Nothing. She steeled herself to make a move. Her eyes automatically looked across at the windows. She realised that somewhere out there, on the opposite bank of the river, he could have been watching her every move. All it would take was a telescopic lens.

Shit!

She thought of the hooded figure lurking in the alley when she had returned from her run. He had been there for a second. Then he had gone. She wondered if that had been him. Had he posted the envelope?

Harri looked down at her phone, staring at the date: Friday 1 April. It was a day she would never be able to forget: April Fools' Day. A year ago, she had been attacked.

She would like nothing better than to think the picture that had been slipped through her door was some sick April Fools' joke, played on her by a resentful colleague.

She thought of DC Robertson and her run-in with him before they had interviewed Tanner. She would give anything for him to have been responsible for the photograph – anyone within the police could have gained access to her victim report and printed off a copy. But no matter how much she tried to convince herself, she knew it couldn't possibly be him. After all, none of her fellow officers knew her address. *Or did they? Had someone followed her home after the pub?*

She wasn't so sure. She realised that she might have to talk to her boss, Detective Inspector Tony Douglas. But the last thing she wanted was for him to think of her as a victim – an easy target. She had already walked that walk in the Met and she definitely wasn't going to repeat the same mistake here. Admittedly, the scar across her neck had not gone unnoticed. She was acutely conscious of the stolen glances from her colleagues. That awkward moment when she met someone for the first time. They couldn't help but stare. But she refused to be ashamed, or feel pressurised into covering it up. She knew that they wanted to ask about it. It was human instinct. But no one had the nerve. She was certain that people talked – who wouldn't? After all, her attack had made national headlines. Her name had been omitted from the news reports; unlike her occupation. It wouldn't have taken much for her colleagues to make the connection. She thought back to the laughter at the pub followed by the razor-sharp words: *You've got no chance, mate! Not with her. She's seriously off-limits. You know what happened to her, right?*

44

Harri would be the first to admit that she was an anomaly. She didn't socialise with the team after work, or even during office hours. She kept herself pretty much to herself, which so far hadn't won her any favours. *Or friends.*

She had no choice but to sort this out herself.

She scrolled down her phone. There was one person whose whereabouts she needed to check: Mac. She hit dial when she found his landline number. She knew if he checked the phone number he would not recognise it. She had changed her number when she left London. She waited as his phone rang. And rang. She acknowledged that it was 3:45 a.m. However, she knew him well enough to know that if he was there, he would answer. He didn't. It cut to voicemail. His voice: deep, assertive, authoritative.

She disconnected the call, took a deep breath. Tried to think. She had to consider all possibilities.

The photograph, the date, it all pointed to someone who knew the details of that night. Crucially, it pointed to someone in the job; to someone who had access to every detail of the assault. The photo, retrieved from the bin and now lying on the floor beside her in a sealed plastic bag, had been taken shortly after she had come out of surgery, for evidence. She thought about her assailant. He had had keys to her flat. It backed up her theory that her attacker had access to her locker at work. The suspicion that her rapist was a colleague in the Met was one she had not been able to dispel. And now the photograph lying in front of her added weight to that belief. She thought of Mac: DI Mac O'Connor.

Without hesitation, she answered the call. She was still sitting with her back to the front door, one hand resting on the baseball bat, phone in the other. It was Douglas. Her boss. It was 5:17 a.m., which meant that something serious had been called in.

She paused: 'Sir?'

'Have I woken you?'

For some reason the sound of Douglas' deep Geordie inflection, one that he refused to soften, caught her off guard. In that instant he reminded Harri of her father. She breathed in deeply, trying to rein in the tumult. Now wasn't the time to get emotional. But in that moment, Douglas was the closest person to her.

'Something like that, sir,' Harri replied, clearing her throat.

'A suspicious death has been called in. Can you be ready in fifteen minutes?'

'Yes, sir.'

'Good. I'll pick you up shortly.'

Harri listened as the phone went dead.

She looked down at the baseball bat she was still clutching and weighed up her choices. She could lock herself away from the world in this high glass prison, or she could get dressed and get on with her life. There was potentially a murdered body lying somewhere waiting for her attention. She could feel a twist of excitement at the prospect. This was why she did the job; to turn chaos into order. To do what she had not been able to do for herself; protect others from the heinous crimes that some people felt compelled – *or chose* – to commit.

Harri picked up the plastic bag containing the photograph. She decided that she would have it sent off to the lab. She had already contaminated it. But if she was lucky, there might still be prints. Her attacker had worn gloves, a ski mask and a condom the night he had assaulted her. DNA evidence had been retrieved from the crime scene, and then discounted. Understandably. *Conveniently.* After all, it belonged to another copper; one who had forced his way into the crime scene. Her old boss – Mac.

Chapter Five

She heard the click of a lock.

Her eyes shot open. Blackness choked her. She held her breath as fear kicked in. Paralysing her.

She forced herself to look at the alarm clock on the bedside cabinet: 5:33 a.m.

She listened hard. Strained to hear something. Nothing. No one was there. He hadn't returned. Not yet. But she knew he would; he always did.

The reality of her life struck her. She was fully awake now. Alive – still. Nothing had changed. The freedom of sleep too fleeting. She could still taste the other world she had inhabited for those few hours, where she could be herself. Where she could escape. *From him. His presence. His control.*

Her eyes started to burn. Stabbing repeatedly, like angry wasps stinging her. Then she remembered why they hurt. The lenses had dried onto her eyes. He despised her blue eyes. To please him, she had agreed to wear green contact lenses, even when she slept. Some nights she would be forced awake, wide-eyed in terror, to a torch being shone in her face. He would tell her it was necessary to check. So she suffered the pain – all to stop him from hurting her. If she didn't do as he wanted, he would get angry. He insisted that when she first opened her eyes, they had to be green. *Like 'hers'*.

She knew he would never love her the way he loved this other woman – the one with the real green eyes. The woman he wanted her to become. *And hadn't she? Hadn't she done enough to her body? But it hadn't been enough.*

She felt sad and pathetic. And alone. So so alone. She switched the bedside lamp on. Then turned over and tightly hugged his pillow. As she did so she caught sight of a clump of her hair. She picked it up. It felt bristly and dry. She rubbed it between her fingers and watched as it turned to fine, golden, dusty fragments. She then ran her fingers through what was left. She could feel patches now – bald spots – where it had gone permanently. The skin was sore and blistered where the hair had stopped growing. She hadn't been to the doctor's about it. He wouldn't allow it. The hydrogen peroxide that he forced her to use had destroyed her hair and scalp. He insisted that it was applied every other day to avoid even the slightest hint of roots.

She tried to loosen the knot in her hair with her fingers. But they had got stuck in a gnarled, tight ball of frizz. She pulled, hard. Angrily. Felt the strands of hair come away with her freed fingers. Tears flowed freely. The sadness she felt was overwhelming.

It's not a surprise he doesn't want you any more. Look at you. You're disgusting now. So disgusting he doesn't even look at you. Not properly. Not the way he used to. He can't stomach your sagging skin.

She thought about what had happened to her. *To him.* When it had all started to change. She had met him on an online dating website. She had been his 'type' – that was what he had said when he had read her profile and seen her photo. Petite, blonde with blue eyes. He had said she was beautiful. Too beautiful for him. At least he had in the beginning. But then he had started wanting to change her, to 'enhance her natural beauty'. Her long hair had not been quite blonde enough for him. Not curly enough. Her eyes had not been the right colour. Her weight, too heavy. So she had allowed him to alter her – to improve her. After all, he loved her. First he had dyed her hair, to make it more striking. Then he had asked her to wear bright green contact lenses to emphasise her prettiness. Finally, he had starved her – for her own good.

She licked the hot salty tears from her top lip. She hated him. Hated him for turning her into this *hideous, ugly ... thing.* She hated him most of all for making her hate herself. If she could, she would go. Not that she had any place to go to. And even if she somehow managed to get to the police, what would they do? Laugh at her? Tell her she was '*fucked in the head.*' How often had he told her that?

Enough for her to believe it.

She thought about the other woman. The woman he obsessed about. He had told her that only two per cent of the human population had green eyes, which made them all the more unique. Or it made *her* all the more unique – the woman he had tried to turn her into. She had seen the photo he had of her. The one he carried in his wallet.

The one he did not realise she had found. And she was . . . so naturally beautiful. Something she herself could never be; regardless of how much he tried to change her.

Tears soaked the pillow she was desperately clutching. She hated herself for crying. For letting it hurt her. She hated him. But then why did it hurt so much? She could feel the ache deep inside her. The fear of rejection. The knowledge that no one cared whether she lived or died. At least he *had* cared, once. He had cared enough about her to threaten that if she ever left him, he would find her and kill her. But now . . . she wasn't so sure. She festered away, locked up inside this five-bedroomed detached mausoleum. But she knew that her existence was becoming an inconvenience to him. More so now he had tracked *her* down. The woman he had tried to change her into; the one with the penetrating green eyes and curly blonde hair. *The one in the photo.*

Chapter Six

Dressed in black biker boots, black skinny jeans, a long-sleeved white T-shirt and a black Diesel L-Edge leather jacket, Harri waited outside the Baltic Chambers building for DI Douglas to show. She never altered her dress code when at work and only varied it when off-duty by wearing faded blue jeans and a black T-shirt.

Her hair was loosely tied up. She never wore it down when she was on the job – not since her transfer from the Met. Nor did she wear make-up now, either on or off the job. Her life had radically changed since she had been attacked. Before that night, Harri had been certain she was being stalked. But she had played it down, not wanting to report it at work. Too afraid her unfounded suspicion would compromise her job, or at least compromise how her colleagues treated her. It was one decision she regretted. Someone had been watching her. Stalking her, and had even had the audacity to let her know about it. He had somehow got hold of her number and would ring her repeatedly. She would block the number, only for him to use another unregistered mobile. Her failing was not taking it seriously. Harri had never once thought he would come into her home. Whether he had entered her flat before the night he raped and assaulted her, she couldn't say, but during the weeks before the attack she had felt uneasy whenever she returned home. It was as if objects had been moved, ever so slightly. Drawers opened and contents handled and then replaced, but not quite as she imagined she had left them. She had put it down to exhaustion and work-related stress. It had never occurred to her that someone had keys to her flat.

Ironically, as a copper she had dealt with countless scenarios similar to her own. Perhaps for him, making her too scared to stay on the job was the intention. Which led her to believe that it was personal. Whoever had attacked her wanted to scare her out of the force. *And he had succeeded – at least where the Met was concerned.*

Determined that he wouldn't destroy her or her career, Harri had gone from being a Detective Constable in the Met to a Detective Sergeant for one of the four Murder Investigation Teams in the Northumbrian force. Two Murder Investigation Teams – otherwise known as MITs – worked north of the river, and the other two south of the river. Harri worked on one of the north teams, under Detective Inspector Tony Douglas. He was the Senior Investigating Officer. He made a good boss and Harri was quietly grateful that she had been assigned to his team.

She watched as a sleek black saloon car pulled up in front of her, assuming that this was the hire car Douglas had said he was getting. They had an ongoing case, a 'runner'; a serial rapist who been targeting young women in Newcastle for over a year. They needed the assurance that they could undertake surveillance without being noticed – the pool cars CID used were a dead giveaway. Douglas was the kind of boss who liked to get his hands dirty. His plan, assisted by Harri, had been to stake out the clubs and pubs in town this weekend. The rapist's cooling off period was lessening and it was highly likely he would strike again. Whatever success she had felt at charging the teenager with murder late yesterday afternoon had quickly evaporated. The reality of a serial rapist was a harsh reminder that there were plenty more Jason Tanners out there.

Harri walked round to the passenger side and opened the door.

'Sir,' she said as she climbed in.

The first thing that hit her was cigarette smoke, combined with Douglas's aftershave. Second, that he was impeccably dressed in a smart grey suit and white shirt. His short, black hair was messily gelled and his jaw was covered in a five o'clock shadow instead of his usual beard. He was only forty years old but the etched lines on his forehead and jowls added years to him.

Douglas gave her a concerned look.

Harri made a point of ignoring it.

'You all right?'

'I'm fine sir. Just couldn't sleep,' she answered. 'What do we have on the victim?'

'Not a lot.'

Harri looked at Douglas.

He inhaled deeply on his cigarette. 'White female. Early twenties . . . If that,' he added, shrugging. 'That's as much as I know, apart from the fact that it's a gruesome one.'

'Was she raped?'

Douglas threw the cigarette butt out the window and then pulled off.

'Sir?'

He shrugged. 'Can't say yet. Let's see what we find when we get there, shall we?'

Harri stared at him. It was clear that Douglas wasn't in the mood for talking.

She accepted the silence and sat back as he drove away from the Quayside, heading towards the crime scene. Traffic passed in a blur as Douglas zig-zagged at breakneck speed. She had known him for just under five months; appointed to him when she first transferred from the Met, Harri had spent the first two months shadowing him before she got promoted. She had been placed under his watch. It was his job to decide whether or not she was up to the role of DS.

Douglas wasn't threatened by the fact that she was driven. She wanted his job and had plans to be a DI by the time she reached thirty-five, which gave her five years to prove herself. Nor was Douglas intimidated by the fact that she was a post-graduate with a degree and MSc in psychology from Bristol University. Not that it had done her much good. She was great at meting out psychological advice to others, but when it came to herself, it was an entirely different matter. There was also the legacy of her father – Detective Superintendent Inspector George Jacobs. Douglas had never once mentioned the connection – unlike some of her colleagues on the team.

That was how things worked between her and Douglas. Their relationship was solely focused on the job. Anything else was off-bounds. Harri had heard talk about Douglas' personal life and knew not to ask. And he never questioned her reasons for transferring from the Met; exactly how Harri liked it. He was her boss and that was a line she never wanted to cross. After being forced to cut all contact with her past, Harri had vowed never to let anyone get close to her. She couldn't take a chance again. She was convinced that she knew the person who had attacked her. The fact that it could have been one of her own, another copper, was one of the reasons she had transferred. Not that Harri had spoken to anyone about her suspicions. How could she? After all, she had no proof.

'You look like shit,' Douglas commented, breaking the silence.

Harri looked at him. She wanted to able to off-load to someone about the photograph delivered to her apartment building. But this wasn't someone, this was Douglas. He was the only person in her life she trusted. But she couldn't tell him. Instead, she remained silent.

'Your disappearance last night didn't go unnoticed,' he continued.

Harri tried to rein in the irritation she felt. 'I was tired. I had just worked eighteen-hour shifts for six days straight. What do you expect of me?'

'To make more of an effort with the team. Your team.'

She turned to face him. 'You can't fault me. Didn't we get a result yesterday?'

'I can't fault you professionally. But you need to open up a bit more with them. Show them that there is more to you than just the job.'

Harri sucked in air through gritted teeth. The last thing she wanted was to get personally involved with anyone – colleagues or otherwise. She trusted no one. *The job was all she had now. And she needed it more than ever.*

'For fuck's sake, Harri!' He took his eyes off the road. 'Last night was about relaxing, kicking back and having a laugh with the team after the hours they had put in to nail that little bastard. There's more to running a team than just showing up and handing out orders. They have to know that they can depend on you to cover their backs and vice versa. Both professionally and personally.'

'Maybe they prefer me to have a professional distance?' Harri threw back.

'Is this to do with DC Robertson?' he asked, scowling at the car crawling ahead.

Robertson was the least of her concerns. She had dealt with him in the only language a testosterone-driven jerk like him understood. But it was clear that her run-in with him had not gone unnoticed.

'He deserved it.'

'Seriously?'

She didn't need to look at him to sense the disappointment in his eyes.

'Why the fuck would you follow him into the Gents? If

you have a problem with a colleague, you deal with it through the proper channels.'

Harri didn't answer. Douglas knew why she had followed Robertson into the toilets or they wouldn't be having this conversation at five fifty-six in the morning.

'Explain to me why you couldn't let the man take a slash in private? Instead, you go in after him and wait until he's having a piss to talk to him.'

'It won't happen again.'

'You're damned right it won't. He was having a slash for fuck's sake!' Douglas muttered as he slammed the brakes on as the traffic lights suddenly turned red. 'You do know he could make an official complaint against you?'

Harri was certain Robertson wouldn't take any action against her. Not considering the events leading up to her confronting him in the toilets. Shortly before she was due to interview Jason Tanner she had gone looking for Robertson only to find him mouthing off about her being crap at her job. It wasn't atypical where Robertson was concerned, but he had crossed the line. He had been speculating about whether she had been promoted above him because she was shagging Douglas. That he had heard she had a proven track record for sleeping her way to the top, which was the reason she had been forced out of the Met. She had cornered him and asked to have a private word. He had blatantly blanked her and walked off to the Gents. So she had followed him into the toilets. He had made a point of turning his back on her to have a piss, saying that maybe she should take the hint. When she didn't leave, he had muttered: 'There's a reason someone would want to slit your fucking throat.' Her blood had chilled in her veins when she had heard those words. She had asked him to repeat it. He ignored her. So she had shoved him, demanding that he answer her; hard enough to throw him off balance. Enough that he slipped in his own piss. While he lay on the floor, she had looked down at him and told him that if he had something to say about her he should have the fucking balls to say it to her face.

Harri didn't respond to Douglas' question. Instead she kept quiet. She didn't regret the way she had tackled Robertson's lack of respect towards her. In fact, she wouldn't hesitate to do it again.

'Look . . . I know DC Robertson is fucked off because he missed out on a promotion. All right? I know he reckons you walked straight into what should have been his job when you transferred from the Met. But if he was giving you cause for concern you should have come to me.'

'I will make sure I do that in future, sir,' she responded.

Douglas roughly ran a hand over his stubble.

She was certain that Douglas had heard the stuff Robertson had been saying. Everyone at the station had heard it. But her boss had chosen to ignore it and she was sure he had hoped that Harri would have done the same. Douglas had warned Harri that joining a team filled with more testosterone and muscle than Newcastle United wouldn't be easy. It was a given that as the only female on the team she would be in for a hard time, that some of the lads wouldn't take too kindly to having a woman calling the shots. She just had to get on with it. And if it became too intolerable, to go to him. But she had taken it into her own hands and had dealt with it. Worse, she had failed to report her actions.

Harri was capable of handling herself; she had wanted the rest of the team to understand that. And that was what she had done when Robertson had publicly ridiculed her. As a woman, she was an easy target in a team comprised mainly of home-bred Geordie lads whose banter would make Vinnie Jones blush. There was also an edge of resentment. In their eyes, she hadn't earned the right to be their senior officer. She had transferred from the Met, walking into a promotion that should have gone to Robertson; rumour had it that she had not earned the right to be a DS, that in her case it had been *who* you know, not *what* you know – out-and-out nepotism. After all, her father had been a legend here. Officers still talked about Detective Superintendent Inspector George Jacobs as the hero that he had been and assumed his daughter had used his name and reputation to get appointed to DS. Nothing could have been further from the truth; Harri had worked damned hard to pass the exams, a fact wasted on some of her colleagues.

She could feel Douglas studying her, so she focused on another driver as he pulled alongside them at the traffic lights. Her face was hard. There was no disputing it, there was an edge to her this morning and it was clear that Douglas felt it. She knew he would be assessing her. Wondering whether she could be a team player or not.

'Promise me one thing, then?'

She didn't react.

'Harri?'

She forced herself to look at him.

'Walk away next time. Because there will be a next time, I guarantee it. All you've done is show the lads that they can have some fun at your expense.' With that, Douglas put his foot to the floor as the lights changed.

Harri remained silent. She needed a moment to compose herself. It was the first time he had ever pulled rank on her. And to be fair, it was the first time he had ever needed to. He knew she was wilful, but she also had an eye for detail that most people missed and a doggedness that would drive another boss to distraction. But not him. He knew she always came through in the end. He must be at a loss with her right now. Ordinarily, she would have fought back and given her reasons for behaving the way she had done with Robertson, but she had clammed up on him. In the past, she had always been open with Douglas when it came to the job. If she had doubts or questions, she wasn't afraid to ask. He was her only ally on the force and the last thing she wanted was to lose him.

They sped out of the city centre towards the suburbs of Jesmond in silence. Suddenly Douglas pulled off Jesmond Road and took a sharp left onto Osbourne Road. He then snaked his way onto Clayton Road and then turned onto a tree-lined street dominated by imposing Victorian houses with top-of-the-range sports BMWs or 4x4 flash white Range Rovers parked outside. Some of the houses were used for student lets, but a lot of the properties were still occupied by the wealthy classes of the North East – it explained the need for private schools in the area, including Church House School, which they had just passed.

She cast a quick glance at Douglas as he pulled into Eskdale Terrace – the scene of the crime; the multiple flashing police lights ahead a giveaway. She recognised the area from her school days when she had attended Church House School. She had grown up here. Harri blocked the memory. She didn't want to go there. *Too many memories of her father.*

She focused on the present. The sky overhead gave an eerie feel to the cordoned-off area. The emerging day threatened to be ominous and oppressive. Blue and white police tape flapped in the chilly breeze. Ahead of them, countless police cars with flashing blue lights blocked the street. She noted the large white mobile incident van parked up, confirming that James Munroe the Crime Scene Manager and his team were busy dealing with the scene.

Douglas abruptly ground to a halt, jolting her forward. She shot him a look.

He ignored it. Instead, he checked his phone: 'Give me a minute, will you? I need to make a call.'

Harri got out of the car and shut the door. She shivered in the cold early-morning air and folded her arms tight across her chest for warmth. It was now 6:02 a.m. Lights blazed in the majority of the houses. Friday morning and people were waking up to another day. Same routine for most of them. Apart from one unidentified female who was currently lying at a crime scene, not far away.

Uniform milled around, some casually chatting as if this was an everyday occurrence. A couple of residents were gathered by the police tape, coats hurriedly thrown over pyjamas as they tried to second-guess what was going on. The unusual amount of activity and noise in this typically quiet suburb had started to attract attention. Harri knew that the numbers of on-lookers would soon increase. Some unfortunate residents would wake up to the news that they would not be able to drive, regardless of the crucial school run or journey to work. Whatever vehicles were parked in the cordoned-off street would remain behind police tape until forensics had finished searching the area surrounding the Metro station.

The Metro line ran between the coastal towns of Whitley Bay and Tynemouth connecting the residents to Newcastle city centre and then south across the River Tyne to Gateshead and finally Sunderland. In less than an hour the scene would be swamped by early morning commuters and school children making their way to the station. Jesmond Metro was also popular with residents who lived out at the coast. They would drive the eight miles or so along the coast road and park in Jesmond, using the Metro to get into Newcastle. It was far easier than trying to park in the city, and cheaper.

She noticed a professional couple, each carrying a coffee bought from some local deli, talking to one of the uniformed officers. Disappointment followed as they were informed that the Metro station had been closed. The nearest one was West Jesmond, which might have been inconvenient, but not as awkward as it would be if Douglas had decided to have the whole line shut down.

Harri turned towards the crime scene, hidden from view by the Metro station. The harsh spotlights burned brightly, illuminating the shadowy pathway and hedgerows. She imagined that there wouldn't be a lot of space amongst the bushes and trees to set up a forensics tent without disturbing evidence, so a screen blocking the crime scene would have been used.

She saw two male SOCOs clad from head to foot in white forensic suits walk out from the pathway. Both pulled down their face masks to talk freely. One of them was carrying a plastic evidence bag. He held it away from his body as he heatedly replied to something his colleague had said. Harri wondered what they were talking about. And what was in the evidence bag.

Harri turned as DI Douglas got out the car. He clicked the alarm on and threw away what was left of his cigarette, clearly ready to make a move.

'Come on. The sooner we get this over with, the sooner you get breakfast. It's your shout by the way,' Douglas reminded her.

'As if I could forget,' Harri replied as they headed towards the two uniformed officers blocking the entrance.

'DI Douglas and DS Jacobs,' Douglas informed the two uniforms.

He waited until one of them recorded their names in the crime scene log before entering the area.

Harri nodded at both officers as she followed Douglas past the perimeter into the cordoned-off crime scene. The log list would stay active until the last person left, typically Munroe, the Crime Scene Manager.

'Who called it in?' Harri asked as she followed Douglas.

'PC Johnson. He did what he could until back-up arrived,' he answered. 'Not that he was able to do much for the victim. From his account, the witness who found the body had also tried his best to help her, not realising that she was already dead.'

'Has a statement been taken from the witness?'

'Not yet. He's not making a lot of sense.'

Harri looked at him.

'He's still drunk and in a state of shock. He found her body as he was making his way home from a party.'

The fact they had a witness was a positive, but Harri wasn't sure his statement would be credible.

'Let's see what we have, shall we?' Douglas suggested.

She had to quicken her pace to keep up with him as he headed towards the mobile incident van where he had spotted James Munroe. He and Douglas were good mates on and off the job, as both were keen cyclists. Munroe had a dark sense of humour, something that came in handy when dealing with some of the unpalatable jobs he was given. He also loved his job, which was a bonus. Nothing excited him more than a call in the early hours telling him that his team were needed to attend a suspicious death. But he wasn't that different from the rest of them. Whenever a call came in, they would all be lying if they didn't admit to feeling the same surge of excitement and anticipation. The only exception was when a suspicious death involved a child. In those situations every copper felt a sense of dread. Regardless of how often you dealt with a serious crime like that you never got used to it.

Munroe cracked a warm smile in their direction as they walked over to him. Harri had worked with him on numerous cases and of all the head SOCOs he was by far her favourite. He was easy-going, affable and always had time for questions. Some of the Crime Scene Managers she had worked with made it quite clear that they didn't like coppers near their crime scene – regardless of whether they were the Senior Investigating Officers.

'You two want to take a look at the body then?' Munroe greeted them.

'That's why I am here,' Douglas said.

'Hope you haven't had breakfast,' Munroe replied, ignoring the sourness in Douglas' voice. 'It's a particularly unpleasant one.'

'Show me a murder that *is* pleasant.'

Munroe shook his head at Douglas. 'Anyone told you that you're shit to work with first thing in the morning?'

Douglas shot him a threatening look. 'Nobody would dare.'

'You're an arse. You know that?'

Harri watched as Munroe then bent down and reached into a metal case, pulling out two sealed plastic bags. He checked the sizes before throwing one to her and the other one to Douglas.

'Here you go. Get suited first.'

'It better be the right size this time,' Douglas warned him.

'I told you, we only had small. It's not my problem that you're built like a bloody All Blacks player!'

'Still had to wear it while you pissed your pants laughing, you bastard!' Douglas retaliated.

'I have to get my kicks some way,' Munroe smiled. 'Especially if I have to put up with your bad-tempered face this early in the morning.'

Munroe turned to Harri. 'Present company excluded, of course,' he added.

Harri didn't respond. She let Douglas and Munroe continue to take the piss out of one another while she got suited up. She was keen to see exactly what they had on their hands.

'When you're ready, make your way to the crime scene across the forensic platforms on the grass. I don't want anyone going near that end of the path. Understand?'

Harri nodded. She could see that Munroe's team had placed three-foot plastic A-frame evidence markers along the path that led out onto Eslington Terrace. Satisfied that they knew which route to take, Munroe left them to it.

She looked down the secluded pathway.

'Ready yet?' Douglas asked.

She quickly finished suiting up.

'Come on then. Let's get this over with,' he answered. 'Better warn you, if Munroe says it's bad then it's going to be bloody ugly.'

'Sure I've seen worse,' Harri replied, thinking of the photograph of herself in her jacket pocket.

Douglas' phone rang. He fumbled around inside the white forensic suit to try to get it out of his jacket. Finally retrieving it, he checked who was calling.

'You go ahead, I'll catch you up.'

'Don't you want me to wait for you?'

'Just do as I asked, will you?'

Surprised by the tone of his voice, she did as ordered and ducked under the police tape. She shot Douglas a backwards glance, and watched as he answered his phone in a strained, hushed voice. He had a pained expression on his face as he listened. An imposing figure of a man, Douglas clearly looked after his body and was physically fit; ironic, given his twenty-a-day habit. He also wasn't ashamed to have it known that he put in long, hard hours working out at the gym or cycling. Even though his body would be the envy of any thirty-year-old, his face was a different story. It had been beaten up by years of working the job and a crap personal life.

He rubbed his face with his left hand as he nodded at whatever was being said. He met Harri's eye and then turned away. Embarrassed at feeling as if she had been caught watching him, she headed off alone towards the crime scene.

Harri forced herself to stay. To look. To be objective. To not react at what was lying in front of her. She had no choice but to fight the feeling that stirred in her stomach. She now understood why Munroe had warned them.

What had been done to the victim was far beyond anything Harri had seen as a copper.

She turned away from the body and bent over. She needed to take in slow, deep gulps of air to stop herself from puking. Her body was trembling. She knew it was a natural reaction to something so horrific that she was struggling to process what had happened.

Why? Why would someone do that to you?

Chapter Seven

The music had stopped hours ago but she was still sitting in the old, wooden wheelchair facing the metal table. The oppressive silence scared her more than the crackling and static sound of the gramophone high above her. When the music finished she heard the distinct slamming of a car boot, followed by car tyres crunching and kicking up gravel as it pulled away. She assumed he had taken 'Subject A's' body somewhere. After all, he had 'failed' her. *No . . . He had . . .* murdered *her. Cruelly . . .*

Or, had he gone looking for *her*? His obsession: the blonde-haired woman with bright green eyes? The one he had attempted to change 'Subject A' into? She couldn't silence these thoughts. The questions that plagued her down here, alone in the dark. She was so scared. Terrified that she would be left to die in this basement. When she had heard his car leave panic had raged through her body, tortured her mind. It had taken all her strength to fight it. To stop herself either hyperventilating or choking to death on bile. For he had left her gagged.

But he hadn't forgotten her. He came back for her – eventually. She couldn't move her head to look up at him. To turn to him as he pushed her out of that dark room and slowly pulled the wheelchair back up the stairs. To tell him she was grateful that he had come back for her. But her eyes had said it all. He would know the gratitude and relief she felt. She had heard of the psychological phenomenon known as Stockholm Syndrome, where a victim begins to identify with their abuser. She had discounted it when she had studied it in her first year of psychology at Uni. But now . . . Now she understood the bond. Especially in such an extreme situation as the one she had found herself in. She needed him. Without him, she would die. And . . . she wanted to please him. For him not to see her as a threat, as some-thing – *someone* – that he needed to destroy. This was about surviving. About living and not ending up like 'Subject A'. She knew she was special to him; he had chosen *her*. Not the others. It was her that he had taken to the basement room to witness his transformation of 'Subject A' – no one else.

The thought of her – the body on the cutting slab – made her uneasy. She had not known her real name. 'Subject A' had ceased to talk before she had arrived. The other two had mumbled to her that 'Subject A' had been there the longest and had once talked to them. Their barely audible voices had been filled with fear, but also rebellion. But if they had told her 'Subject A's' name, she had long since forgotten it. Just as the other two had long since forgotten to want to survive. To her, they had already given up and had chosen death as their escape – *from him and this . . . sanatorium.*

The cool air brushed against her body, reminding her

that she was still alive. The sensation was heightened after being left in the airtight room. At the top of the stairs, he turned her round and started wheeling her along the large hallway. She was on the ground floor now. The only other time she had seen it was when he had first brought her here. But it had passed in a blurred daze as he wheeled her up to the ward on the first floor. She had lost all sense of how long she had been kept here. Time had become an unknown quantity. A concept that belonged to a previous life. But what she did know was that her body had changed. The difference was not as radical as it was with the others. But then they had been here longer than her.

There were so many rooms leading off from the hall-way that it felt like a maze. But all the doors were closed, locking her out from whatever secrets they held. She wondered if there were others like her behind those sealed doors. As he pushed the wheelchair around a corner she caught her breath in surprise. The ornate double doors that led out into the grounds had been thrown open. The cool morning air suddenly enveloped her, kissing and teasing her bare skin. She breathed in the smell of the outside world. It was so close that she could almost touch it and yet it whispered of another life, one that she had left behind when she had come to him. He allowed her a moment to breathe in what she had given up before turn-ing her away.

Tears stung her eyes as she now faced the large shad-owy hallway. She forced herself to commit it to memory – *just in case* ... The peeling wallpaper, Persian rugs, portraits, china ornaments and stained glass lampshades all belonged to a time that had long since ceased to exist. She drank in the many pieces of Victorian objets d'art gloomily lit by antiquated lamps as they passed her eyes as they moved towards the ramp leading up to the first floor.

No ... NO!

She was tired of staring at the same cracked ceiling above her hospital bed. Or the grounds outside. The grounds where the dead had been buried; the countless unmarked graves that she stared at and wondered if they held her predecessors. Had they been subject to his obsession with altering women; perhaps 'Subject A' wasn't the first? Or were those graves for the original occupants of the sanatorium? The ones who had not survived tuberculosis as it ravaged their lungs, bones and nervous systems, despite the fresh air and open space.

She felt a cold hand touch her shoulder. *His hand.* A ghostly reminder of 'Subject A'. She shivered. It was involuntary. *Everything was, now.*

Before she realised it, they had reached the first floor. The corrosive smell of disinfectant assaulted her senses. Then the colour white blinded her. The bare walls, doors; everything was startlingly neutral. The doors to the ward were thrown open wide – waiting for her return. She felt a sudden sense of panic; sadness even, that he was returning her to them.

Then she heard them, despite the creaking noise of the old floorboards: *the others.* It was *just* discernible – their breathing, so fragile and yet so laboured. She wanted to say something, but her mouth was still sealed with tape. She caught sight of the row of six beds lined up against the white-washed wall. Two had never been used – *at least, not yet*. One had been stripped; 'Subject A's' bed. Another – hers – had been turned down, ready for her return.

Then there were the other two beds and their occupants. Shocked, she held her breath. *How long has it been since you last saw them properly?* Their ashen, sunken faces were positioned so they could greet her. But their unfocused eyes stared at nothing. He had sat them up, supported and bolstered by pillows, for there was nothing to their bodies now. Neither one moved. Or said anything. He had no need to seal their mouths. Whatever words they once had were lost; shrivelled up and taken by the wind and rain.

Like her, both had a saline drip in their bony arms fed from a mobile IV pole and stand.

She wanted to cry at what was left of them. But she couldn't. He had arranged this for her. He had wanted them to greet her. *Oh God ... how I wish he hadn't let me see them ... they are dying, right before my eyes.*

Their once-beautiful bodies had disappeared and all that was left were the folds upon folds of sallow skin that seemed to melt away from their skeletal frames. He was altering them.

If she had not been gagged she would have screamed and screamed. The picture of what he had done to 'Subject A' suddenly unleashed itself – a prophecy of what was to come. In the background the crackling sound of the third movement from Debussy's *Suite Bergamasque* began to play. But she didn't hear the music – not any more. All she could hear was the sound of the scalpel as it scraped against the metal table, slicing through excess skin.

Chapter Eight

The body was harshly exposed under the bright spot-lights, naked and splayed out on the cold ground. Harri could see that she had not died here. She had been dumped. Someone had carried her horrifically altered body and left her here for the early commuters to see.

Her face . . . or lack of it. Oh God . . . what did he do?

For that was what struck her first; the face. Harri took a deep breath. Had to, otherwise she would have retched. Someone had thrown highly corrosive liquid over her. It had hit her face. Her neck. Her chest. Some of which had melted to nothing. The liquid had burned its way through the victim's flesh. Her teeth were exposed. Partially dissolved. The acid had liquefied any surrounding tissue, penetrating its way to the bone.

She turned away. She needed a moment to process what had happened. Time to absorb the horrific nature of her death. She focused on her breathing as she stead-ied herself.

She looked back at the victim's head. Even though the disfiguring injuries were horrific, it was the eyes that made Harri feel nauseous. They seemed to stare straight at her; through her. The eyelids and surrounding tissue had melted, leaving behind bright green eyes that glinted uncannily.

Suddenly an image came to mind. It was the first body she had ever seen on the job and it was something that she would never forget. It was a suicide – an ugly, unnecessary death. But it wasn't the body hanging from the old farmhouse kitchen's wooden rafters that had disturbed her, or the swollen legs where the blood had pooled to the lowest part of the dead body. It was the bulging eyes. Eyes so badly damaged by asphyxiation that they looked to be filled with blood red vengeance, and pure hatred as they seemed to stare straight at her.

Harri shuddered at the memory.

'You all right?' James Munroe asked as he joined her.

He may have been ten years older than her, but like Douglas, what he had seen on the job had aged him. Perhaps not physically, but he had the air of someone who had experienced more than most. She absentmindedly touched her cheek, pushing a stray curl back from her face.

Munroe gave her a sympathetic grin.

'Don't worry about it. I have days where I'm sick to the stomach at having to deal with other people's shit.'

Harri looked at him, surprised.

'Seriously. Sometimes there's the odd one that gets to you. I can't say why, but it just does. I love the job but there are times when I question why I do it.'

Harri nodded. She had experienced more days than she cared to remember that made her ask herself why she had become a copper. But the answer was simple – it was all she knew.

'Yeah . . . but could you ever imagine not doing this?'

Munroe looked back at the body as he considered Harri's question.

'No,' he answered.

Harri simply nodded. She couldn't imagine doing anything else with her life. Her father had been in the force until the day had he had been killed. She assumed that it would be the same for her; the only way she would be forced out before retirement would be in a body bag. Her mind turned to the photograph hidden in her jacket, and to the man who had sent it; the man who wanted to fulfil his promise to kill her.

'You sure you're all right?'

Harri nodded. 'I'm fine.' She could see that he wasn't buying it. Not that she blamed him. The statement couldn't have been further from the truth.

'Listen, I know Douglas has been really off-hand lately, but it has nothing to do with you. I can guarantee that. He's going through a really difficult time. I don't know if you're aware, but it was around this time of year that his wife died.'

She looked at Munroe. She had no idea. Then again, why would she? He was her boss, not a personal friend. 'I didn't know . . .'

'Just so you know to cut him some slack. That's all.'

'Thanks,' Harri muttered. She couldn't help but wonder whether his abrupt manner and private phone calls were connected to his wife, or something else entirely.

'So what do you think?' Munroe asked, changing the subject as he jerked his head towards the body.

'We've got some sick bastard out there,' Harri said, relieved to be focused on the job again, instead of her boss.

'You're right there,' Munroe agreed. 'I've photographed the burn wounds to the face and upper body. Christ knows why someone would do that to her. Poor young lass didn't stand a chance. And then . . . there's what has happened to her body. Her skin . . .' He shook his head. 'I've got an eight-year-old daughter and it doesn't bear thinking about that someone could do that to . . .' He was unable to finish.

Harri simply stared down at her. There was nothing she could say. The crime against this young woman had rendered her silent. No words could make sense of the atrocities that had been carried out.

She hoped that the victim had been dead before she had been doused in sulphuric acid. That her killer had shown her some mercy. But Harri's gut feeling told her this wasn't the case. That her killer had intended her to feel everything he did to her. After all, from the state of the body, it appeared as if he had been torturing her long before the acid attack.

Blood was splattered in various places. The ground was covered in smeared foot and handprints. Harri imagined that the drunken student who had had the misfortune to discover the victim must have knelt down beside her. Perhaps tried to help. She was sure that some of the blood-smeared hand and footprints could be attributed to him. He would have been covered in it.

She forced herself to look at the woman. Her age was difficult to discern. She was definitely post-pubescent.

But her body was so underweight it was hard to tell whether she was in her teens or early twenties. Harri had noticed immediately that what was left of her hair had been bleached. Very recently. And it looked odd. It was brittle and frizzy, as if the colour treatment had been left on too long. There were no roots visible. And if there had been, they would have been the same colour as the black hair underneath her armpits and over her groin.

Harri waited until Munroe walked off to talk to one of his team before crouching down to get a closer look. She tried not to react to what was left of the victim's face as she leaned over to sniff the clump of remaining hair. If it had just been bleached, then it would still have that residual smell of hydrogen peroxide. She realised that it might be more difficult to tell given the corrosive liquid that had been poured over the victim's face. She picked up a handful of the long blonde hair and inhaled. There was a definite trace of bleaching chemicals. Something didn't seem right. She wondered whether the victim had bleached her hair or whether her killer had. And if it had been the killer, why? Why go to so much effort . . .

It hit her. *He was altering her.*

Harri surprised herself with this thought.

The victim's skin had an unnatural pallor, as if she hadn't been in daylight for a significant length of time.

She heard voices approaching from behind and quickly stood up, stepping back from the body just in time.

'I bloody hate death! And more so at six in the fucking

morning!' a female voice with a hard Dundonian accent complained.

It must be Eleanor Blake; one of four Home Office pathologists who worked for the Northumbrian force and the only woman. Harri had not actually met her, but she had heard her described as barking mad. Then again, every pathologist Harri had met had been madder than a box of frogs in one way or another. She supposed it went with the territory. They dealt with the kinds of death that your average person couldn't possibly imagine. They evaluated it, dissected it, diagnosed the cause of death and then put it back together, ready for the next one.

Harri turned to see Douglas come round the forensic screen positioned to hide the body, accompanied by Eleanor Blake.

She was an androgynously handsome woman in her late thirties. Tall, well-built and dressed in the same attire as the rest of them – a white forensics suit. Her short black hair was heavily gelled in a retro punk style. Her angular features suited the edgy haircut. Harri caught sight of the six silver studs that Blake was wearing in both ears as they glinted under the bright lights. She had a nose ring in and a piercing above her lip. This surprised her. Harri didn't know what she expected of a pathologist, but it wasn't Eleanor Blake.

'Well, someone clearly didn't like her,' Blake said as she took stock of the victim. 'Odd . . .'

Harri resisted the urge to ask her what she meant. Instead, she kept quiet and watched as Blake bent down and assessed the body. Not a muscle moved on her face as her sharp brown eyes moved from the body to the surrounding area.

Then Harri realised what the pathologist had found so odd – the identity tag tied to the victim's right foot.

'Have you ever seen anything like this before?' Blake asked Douglas as she pointed to it.

'No. Never,' Douglas answered.

Blake examined the tag. 'Someone clearly has a bloody sense of humour. This identifies the victim as 'Subject A. D.O.D.: 1 April C.O.D.: Starvation'. She turned and looked at Douglas. 'This is one sick April Fools' prank.' Not expecting a reply, she turned her attention back to the victim. She took her phone out, pressed record and started muttering into it, her voice too low and heavily accented for Harri to understand what she was detailing. Crouching, with the phone held as steady as possible, the pathologist scrutinised the victim's injuries.

Finished, Blake took a notepad out of her suit and proceeded to make a sketch of the body and its position in relation to the crime scene.

Harri assumed that Munroe or another member of his team would have already drawn their own rough sketch of the victim. She was aware that sketches could show scales and dimensions in a way that photographs couldn't, although the first thing his team would have done would have been to photograph and film before anything was disturbed. Then they would have begun the arduous job of collecting evidence.

The pathologist's gloved hands deftly made notes as she detailed, without touching the body, the alterations that the killer had made.

Harri could see that the victim had not put up a fight – there were no defensive wounds on the hands. No evidence that the victim had struggled to protect herself. *Why?*

She watched as James Munroe came back over to them. He had done an exceptional job of preserving the area. Plastic platforms had been placed where they were standing and along the grass verge that snaked out from behind Jesmond Metro towards Eslington Terrace.

Directly behind the Metro the pathway veered off steeply, leading to the subway under the A1508. Allegedly, this was the route the witness who had made the 999 call had taken on his way home. If the witness had continued it would have led him out onto Eslington Terrace. Harri thought about the three-foot plastic yellow A-frame evidence markers she had seen along the path and wondered whether the killer had left by that route.

'You've already taken temperatures?' the pathologist asked as Munroe approached.

'Yes,' Munroe replied, his answer abrupt.

Harri assumed he had been slighted by the pathologist's rhetorical question. After all, he had overseen countless suspicious and natural deaths and understood what was expected of him.

Harri watched the pathologist examine the body. They were waiting to walk through the homicide scene with Munroe before heading back to the station. It was crucial that they got an idea of exactly what had happened before starting their own enquiries. Munroe had years of experience as a SOCO and would already have pieced together a version of events from the evidence he had collated.

However, some Crime Scene Managers didn't like the police hanging around. They saw the crime scene as belonging to them. It was their job to make sure that the victim was delivered to the morgue with as little disturbance as possible, which meant keeping contact with the body to a minimum. Harri wasn't allowed near the body – she was supposed to view it from a distance. She was acutely aware that she had broken that rule and it would have cost her if she had been caught.

If she wanted to get up close and personal, then she would have to analyse the film footage and photographs that Munroe's team would take. It both mildly irritated and amused her the way homicide detectives were represented on TV. The rules simply didn't apply. They never wore a forensics suit and they always handled the body and trampled over the crime scene.

She turned to Douglas. It was clear that he was preoccupied with making his own mental notes of the scene. His face was grave as he cast his eye over the badly deformed body. Harri turned her attention back to the victim. To her, the attack was too frenzied for it not to be personal. There were obvious signs of overkill. Primarily the victim's face.

'Did you find any ID?' Harri asked Munroe.

Irritated, Blake cleared her throat, insinuating Harri had broken her concentration.

'I did a preliminary check but didn't find anything. We'll have a more thorough look when we've bagged her up.'

'I'm not sure this was a random attack, sir,' Harri said to Douglas quietly, so Munroe and Blake couldn't hear her.

Douglas looked at her, waiting for an explanation.

'This was a personal attack,' Harri whispered. 'Someone wanted to hurt her so badly that they didn't just want to kill her. They wanted to destroy her face. To take away her individuality. Make her unidentifiable.'

Douglas didn't argue. The evidence was lying in front of them.

'This isn't a typical acid attack either. I've seen a few in the past couple of years at the Met but they tended to be male victims. Corrosive substances like sulphuric acid are being used more and more in gang-related attacks. It is seen as an extreme mark of dominance. Letting the victim know, *I didn't kill you but I have marked your face so everyone knows*. But what has happened to her . . .' Harri paused for a moment as she tried to comprehend who would do something like this. She knew this type of crime existed, where the intention was to kill the woman, but she had not seen it in the UK. 'Whoever did this to her did not just want to disfigure her, they wanted to torture and kill her. The amount of acid is more than your typical offender would carry around in a bottle or a cup to throw at someone. This has penetrated through to the bone.' Harri paused as she shook her head. 'It's more reminiscent of hate crimes committed against women and children, but it predominantly occurs across Southeast Asia, Sub-Saharan Africa, the West Indies and the Middle East.'

'First things first, let's see if we can get an ID on the victim and then start from there,' Douglas said. 'If you're right, we need to have a look at everyone connected to her. Family, friends and colleagues.'

'If we can identify her,' Harri stated as she looked back at the victim. 'The extensive damage to the victim's head suggests that the killer didn't want her identified.'

Douglas didn't reply.

But Harri knew she was right. Even if they had her dental records, they would not match. Not now. The acid had dissolved part of the bone in her upper jaw.

'Have you finished with the body?' Blake asked.

Harri realised it was directed at Munroe.

Munroe nodded.

'Confirm the lividity with me?'

Munroe did as instructed and bent down beside Blake. They rolled the body onto its side, exposing the victim's back.

'You've already photographed this?' Blake asked.

'Yes,' Munroe answered.

Harri detected a slight edge in Munroe's otherwise easy-going manner. She assumed that he didn't like his ability to do his job efficiently being questioned. She wasn't sure whether Dr Eleanor Blake's abrupt manner was intentional or whether she was so caught up in the job that she was oblivious as to how she came across.

'Post-mortem lividity,' Blake determined, examining the deep bluish-purple discolouration covering the front of the body. Her voice cold. Clinical.

Munroe didn't answer. Not that Blake had expected one. It was a rhetorical statement.

Harri studied the discoloured flesh where the blood, once the heart had stopped pumping, had pooled to the lowest portions of the victim's body. It suggested to her that the victim had either died face-down, or had been turned onto her stomach shortly after death. Which meant that she had been dumped here. Whoever had done this had attacked her somewhere else. Then they had brought her here and laid her out on her back for the world to see.

Harri watched as the pathologist pressed the skin to see whether it blanched. If it did it would indicate that the body was in the early stages of lividity, which meant she had been dead for less than four hours.

Blake pressed down hard, but the skin didn't change colour. She'd been dead for longer than four hours. It was now after 7:00 a.m. and the 999 call reporting the suspicious death had come in at 4:01 a.m.

The pathologist rested the body back in position. She looked up at Douglas.

'She definitely died somewhere else.'

Douglas nodded.

'The body is stiff, which means rigor has started to set in. The air temperature is cool, which could have slowed down the process but given the state of livor mortis and the fact that rigor has already worked its way past the face and neck I would suggest the victim's been dead between eight and twelve hours.'

'You can't be more precise can you?' Douglas asked, hopeful.

'No. That's as good as you're going to get for now. I'll analyse stomach contents when I do the PM and check for any signs of insect infestation. I can't see any activity around the mouth or the other orifices, but I'll have a closer look later. I'll also check the change in body temperature. I might be able to narrow it down by a couple of hours but don't hold your breath.'

Douglas nodded. He understood the score. It was still impossible for pathologists to discern the exact time of death, contrary to public perception.

'Poor girl! Right, I've seen enough for now. If you've finished let's get this show on the road,' Blake said as she turned her attention back to Munroe.

Munroe's team would have already taken tape lifts from the hands and what there was of the face. If they were lucky, the assailant would have left some forensic evidence.

'When is she being delivered to the morgue?' Blake asked.

'Funeral directors should be here soon,' Munroe answered.

'You have contacted the Coroner's office to make sure that the morgue will be open?' Blake asked, her voice as hard and cutting as her expression.

'Yes,' Douglas answered.

'Good . . . good. Right, I've got better things to do than stand around here chatting over a dead body. So if you'll excuse me, I'll see you all later. And you,' Blake said, pointing at Munroe. 'Make sure those Crime Scene Officers of yours haven't had any breakfast will you? I don't like regurgitated food anywhere near my morgue, unless it's stomach contents that I've personally removed!'

'Yes, Dr Blake,' Munroe answered.

Harri was aware that at a post-mortem of this nature it was expected that the Crime Scene Manager and a couple of SOCOs would attend.

'Drop the bloody "Dr", Munroe! You know it irritates the fuck out of me. Can't stand that kind of crap.'

Blake cast a last cursory glance at the crime scene and then the body.

'You need to get the bastard who did that to her, Tony,' she said. 'I don't like what I am seeing here. And a killer with a sense of humour is a dangerous one in my books.'

Harri was surprised to hear Blake talk to her boss like that. But then she didn't know anything about her relationship with Douglas.

Blake turned to Munroe.

'How long do you think you'll be?'

'I reckon another two hours,' Munroe answered.

Munroe was thorough. A successful crime investigation depended upon his and his team's skills at collecting various kinds of evidence, which would be analysed at the lab. The SOCOs would be searching for physical and biological evidence. The physical would come from fingerprints, footprints and fibres left behind by the unknown suspect. The biological evidence included blood stains and DNA.

Munroe's acumen and eye for the slightest detail could make all the difference to the outcome of the murder investigation.

'Just let me know when you get there,' Blake instructed. 'I've got a couple of appointments I'll put back so I can get started on the PM later this morning.'

Blake glanced at Douglas. 'Does that suit you?' she asked.

He nodded.

'Great. Right, see you lot later,' Blake concluded before turning to leave.

She shot Harri a stern look.

'Try and get your boss to quit smoking. I don't want to be dissecting his lungs in front of a roomful of med students,' she ordered.

'Hypocrite!' Douglas retaliated.

'At least I quit! Maybe you should check yourself into rehab before you end up on my cutting slab, eh?'

'Haven't you heard? Rehab is for quitters!'

Harri watched as the flicker of a smile crossed Blake's otherwise hard face.

'You keep selling yourself that same old bullshit, Tony!'

Without another word she strode past Harri, forcing her to move out of the way.

Harri watched Blake disappear. If she was honest she was surprised that Douglas was on such good terms with her. It slightly jarred. Maybe it was because Blake had made it quite clear that she didn't have time for Harri. Or was it that Harri felt mildly jealous? It was clear that she hadn't been invited to attend the post-mortem. Whether she did would be down to Douglas.

Harri turned to Douglas to ask him but he had already walked over to Munroe and started taking the piss by mimicking his behaviour around the pathologist. Munroe gave as good back. The murdered body was briefly forgotten while the two of them mocked one another. She was familiar with this kind of talk; coppers and SOCOs were known for their dark sense of humour. She had heard banter thrown backwards and forwards between investigating officers that would have made the dead blush if it had been possible. But she knew better than anyone that this was the way they dealt with the horror of the job. Cruel, sick jokes over a couple of pints was the natural end to a difficult day. Coppers and SOCOs were both offered counselling through the force if a crime scene was particularly gruesome. But she didn't know of one person who had gone down this avenue; most got it out of their system by adopting a hard, macabre sense of humour and a healthy thirst.

'All right Munroe, run me through what you think happened here,' Douglas said, ending the light-hearted banter between them.

'Right, we've found impression marks from two types of shoes on the ground around the body. One set we believe to be from the witness who found the victim. But we also found impression marks from what look like trainers. Roughly size eleven and male. Unfortunately for us though, they appear to be new. I didn't see any damage to the sole of the trainer from the impressions.'

'Shit!' Douglas muttered.

Impression marks could be crucial physical evidence. A print taken from a relatively new shoe would only tell them the make, style and size. If the trainer had been worn for a period of time it would have what forensics called 'individualising evidence', specific to the person who wore the trainer – equal in its uniqueness to a fingerprint. No one person walked the same way. Over time, shoe prints became individualising evidence as the soles changed due to the wearer's gait, or the ground they trod on.

The fact that the suspect's trainers were new troubled Harri. She doubted it was coincidence. It told her that he'd had no intention of leaving any identifiable evidence at the crime scene.

'Have you ascertained which route the suspect used?' Douglas questioned.

Munroe pointed down the pathway where the A-frame markers were dotted around. 'We recovered traces of blood forty feet away from the body suggesting that she was carried from that direction along the path to where she was dumped here.'

'Was there only one assailant?' Harri asked.

'From what I can gather, yes. I established three consistent sets of footprints on the path. Two belonging to the witness and the attending officer and the other to the assailant, presumably. All three were contaminated by the blood from the victim.'

Harri immediately thought of the witness they had held in custody and PC Johnson who had radioed in the suspicious death.

Douglas nodded. 'Thanks Munroe.'

'Sure.'

'Come on. Let's head back,' Douglas said to Harri.

She gave the victim one last glance. Something about this didn't feel right. She couldn't put her finger on why. She agreed with Blake that the killer was playing with them. The identity tag on the deceased victim was worrying. She pushed her hair back from her face as she looked up at the emerging dawn. The sky was a mute, gunmetal grey. Someone, somewhere would be missing the victim. At least, she hoped so. Whether she believed it was a different matter entirely. Hopefully there would be some news waiting for them back at the station. Ideally, a missing person's report would have been filed. The victim was young. Too young to just disappear without anyone noticing. *Surely?*

Harri felt her mobile vibrate. It was a work phone and the only one in her possession. She had no need for a personal phone now. She took it out of her inside jacket pocket. A text. The mobile number unknown. Curious, she clicked it open.

Do you know who I am, Harri? For I know you – intimately

She felt sick; as if she had just been punched in the gut. She did her best to keep her expression blank. She looked up. But no one was watching her. *How ... How did he have her work number?*

She reread the text: *I know you – intimately*. She knew without a doubt that this was the man who had slit her

93

throat and raped her. Who had hand-delivered the crime evidence photograph early this morning to her apartment building. But he had upped the game – *his game*. She shivered involuntarily as the murder victim came to mind. What were the odds of a killer dumping a body that he had physically altered to have blonde hair and green eyes – identical to her own – on April Fools'; exactly a year to the day when her rapist had promised to return to and, finally, kill her?

Chapter Nine

She heard the low growl of the car. Immediately she felt that sickening feeling in her stomach. She waited to hear the crunch of tyres as the car swung into the driveway. Nothing. She felt her body relax as the car faded into the morning.

She had remained in bed since she had first awoken at 5:33 a.m. He hadn't returned. So she had lain there staring into the blackness, wondering when he would come back. Sometimes he would disappear for days. She had been hoping that he would be away for another day at least. Lately his absences had become more and more frequent and lasted longer than usual. Not that he ever told her why; never had. Simply that his business was not her business. She hoped that when he did return he would be in a good mood. His mood swings had worsened. Nothing she ever did now pleased him. If anything, just the sight of her angered him. Tears pricked her eyes again. She felt so sad and pathetic. And alone. *So so alone*. Tears flowed freely; the sadness she felt at what had become of her overwhelming.

She had spent the last few hours wondering when it

had all changed. They had met two years ago. It had been so intense and all-consuming. He had possessed her from the moment he saw her. And she had never doubted him. Why would she? Nor did she question his obsessiveness. Instead, she allowed herself to believe he truly loved her. In that time she had lost all contact with her parents and friends. It had not taken long before he had ostracised her. A matter of months. Her family and friends didn't have her 'best interests' in mind; whereas he did. So when they criticised her for allowing him to change her, he had argued he was improving her and that they didn't like it because they were jealous. *Of her . . . Of him . . . Of them.* And she had believed him. At least she had then. The changes had been so gradual. Too subtle for her to notice. A drip, drip, drip effect, until eventually he had completely anaesthetised her.

When he had met her she had had a job. A good one. She had been a newly qualified nurse working at King's College Hospital. It wasn't long before he had made it known that he didn't like her working shifts; especially night shifts. He soon started accusing her of having an affair. Of sleeping with other men while she said she was at work. He drove her everywhere, never letting her out of his sight. But it wasn't enough to appease him. To prove her love for him. Her unerring faithfulness. He had finally insisted that she choose: him or her career. She had chosen him of course – had to, as he had beaten her up so badly that night, refusing to believe that she hadn't slept with one of her colleagues, that she couldn't go into work the next day – or the next week – even if she had wanted to. And by that stage, there was no one left to help her.

The first time he had ever assaulted her was on their wedding night. She had spent it in hospital. Naturally, she had lied. How could she tell the colleagues attending her that the charismatic man she had just married, the one sitting vigilantly by her bed, had done this to her? It was easier to lie. Less humiliating and shaming to pretend that she had tripped over the hem of her wedding dress and fallen down the stairs. No one questioned her statement. *Why would they* ...

They had married within three months of meeting; against her family and friends' advice. She hadn't listened to them. Too blinded by his charisma to see him for what he actually was – a controlling abuser. She had trusted him. What was there not to trust?

He had taken her phone the night of their wedding; checking for any messages of objection from her family, her friends. She had none. He didn't believe her. He had accused her of deleting them. Not that she had, but she had paid a price for his distrust of her. He had smashed her phone first, before dealing with her. She had never been allowed to replace it.

She hated him. Hated him for turning her into this hideous, ugly ... *thing*. But she couldn't leave even if she dared to. He had told her that if she ever left him he would kill her. And she believed him.

She could only leave the house if accompanied by him.

But those occasions had lessened and lessened. He wanted her to stay inside with the wooden blinds closed and the windows locked – always. She didn't have the keys to open either the front or back door, or the windows. He kept them on his person at all times. So when he did disappear for days on end, he would forget that she couldn't leave. That when the food ran out, she had no way of getting any. And she had no one to call for help. For nobody on the outside knew what was happening to her.

She turned over and stared at the feeble early morning light filtering through the blinds. She had always feared he might kill her. But the way things were escalating it was not a just a possibility, it was inevitable. His violent outbursts were constant now. She wondered if he was having an affair. *With her. The woman in the photograph that he kept in his wallet. The one he obsessed about.* It was a thought that had dominated her lately. But if he was, why wouldn't he leave her? Or even let her go? But she knew the answer: it was all about control. He controlled every minute detail about her life now. *Everything.* What she ate – or didn't. What she wore. And what sickened her to her core was that he got a kick out of it.

The pillow felt damp against her skin. She hadn't realised that she was still crying. Not that it mattered; tears were pointless. They wouldn't save her. Nothing could; apart from herself. She had to fight back. *Somehow.* Physically she was no match for him. He was six foot two with a powerful body; she had no chance.

No one could help her. Not even the police. They wouldn't believe her. No one would believe – that was what he repeatedly told her. *Who would believe her over someone like him?*

Chapter Ten

Douglas was unusually silent on the drive back to the station. The good-natured banter that he had been throwing around with Munroe had evaporated as soon they had returned to the car. She wondered what was going on but knew that she had no right to ask. It was simple – he was her boss. She thought of the phone call he had taken after they had got suited up. He had been unusually abrupt with her, making it quite clear he didn't want her around when he answered. She thought about what Munroe had said to her earlier about Douglas' personal life as the early morning traffic passed in a blur.

Before she realised it, they were turning up onto Forth Banks where Newcastle City Centre Police Station was located. Not that she should have been surprised, given how Douglas drove. The new station had been opened in 2014, replacing Market Street Station as Northumbria Police's headquarters. It was the operational base for 600 Northumbria police officers and staff working in Newcastle and Gateshead. At the time of its official opening it had been hailed as a high-tech police station with its fifty modern custody suites and 180 CCTV cameras covering the cell complex, electronic finger-print scanners and the technology on-site to process DNA testing.

The area was deserted apart from the council's street cleaners who patrolled the streets in the early mornings, making way for a new day of discarded rubbish. Harri could just make out the shadowy figures under the multiple archways of the bridge ahead, trying their best to sleep despite the cold; hidden by grubby quilts and sleeping bags. Soon enough they would be gone, disappearing as if an illusion, only to return when darkness fell.

Douglas swung into the station's car park, pulling up behind a marked police car.

'I want details of every CCTV camera located around the crime scene. We're looking for a perpetrator arriving with the victim and then leaving between 12:00 p.m. and 4:00 a.m.,' Douglas instructed as he got out the car. 'Passengers from the Metro would have used the pathway until midnight, making it impossible for the killer to have left the victim there before that. The likelihood of getting caught was too high.'

'Yes sir,' Harri answered, following him out. 'I'll get on to it straight away.'

'I want something on my desk before we attend the PM. Understand?'

'What about breakfast?' Harri asked.

Douglas distractedly shook his head.

'No . . . no, nothing for me,' he said before locking the car and walking off towards the station.

Harri watched him. This wasn't like him. He had a voracious appetite. Something was wrong, that much she was sure of, but she had no idea what it could possibly be. She was certain it had nothing to do with the investigation. Douglas had seen a lot worse in his time. All she could do was make sure she gave him one less thing to worry about by getting on with her job. The last thing she wanted was him thinking that she couldn't cope. A sliver of unease crept in.

The photograph delivered in the early hours of the morning. But this wasn't just any morning – this was 1st April; a year to the day she was attacked. Then there was the text she had received at the murder scene where the victim's body had been physically altered to look like her; green eyes, blonde hair . . .

She blocked the thoughts. *Not now. Keep focused on the job, Harri. He can't do anything while you're surrounded by other coppers.*

The last thing she wanted was for Douglas, or anyone else on the murder team, to know that the man who had raped and threatened to come back to kill her had returned. That the murder victim had been killed and physically altered – *to look like her* – by the same assailant who had attacked her. She was in no doubt that her rapist and their killer were one and the same. She knew that she was breaking every rule by withholding the photograph and text. However, if the team found out, Douglas would have no choice but to remove her from the investigation. She was under no illusions; she was the killer's primary target.

She breathed out. She had to focus. She had been waiting for him to return. And now he had, she had only one option – to hunt him down before he got to her.

The station was in chaos. Uniform were dealing with the typical drunks from the Bigg Market the night before; as well as an alleged rape and a couple of domestics. But they had it under control. It was Douglas' team who were running around, trying to collate as much information as they could to piece together what exactly had happened during the hours leading up to the murder.

Harri made her way to the women's toilets. The text had thrown her and she needed a moment to compose herself before facing the team. Once inside and certain that she was alone, she went over to the sink and turned the cold tap on. As the water gushed out she let the tears that she had fought so hard against flow down her cheeks. She would allow herself to feel the fear, the pain, just this once; then she had to start acting – not reacting. Shaking, she tried to compose herself. She raised her head and looked in the mirror. It was a sobering sight. Douglas was right, she did look like shit.

She threw cold water over her pale face. It had the desired effect. She pulled out some paper towels and dried herself off. She needed to make a call. Sort this out.

Her eyes dropped down to her neck. To the brutal scar that *he* had left across her throat.

If you want to play games with me, you bastard, then I'm ready for you.

Harri braced herself as she scrolled down her contacts list. She was sitting in a toilet cubicle; the only guaranteed private space away from her colleagues.

She pressed call. Waited as her phone connected to the other mobile – his personal number. Her heart thundered as she listened to it ring.

Why, Harri? Why?

But she knew why. She couldn't shake off her suspicion that he was her rapist and so she needed to see if he would answer. She needed to know his whereabouts. If he was in London, then she could eliminate him. There was a reason she had put so much distance between herself and the Met. And that reason was Mac O'Connor: her ex-boss, the man who had broken every rule in the book when he had forced his way into a crime scene – her flat. If she was forced to think about that night, it was not only terror, but shame and humiliation that coursed through her.

She listened as she held her breath. She had no idea what she would say. Or what exactly it was that she expected from him. But maybe it would finally give her the answer she needed – that DI Mac O'Connor had raped her; that he had slit her throat and left her with the promise he would return to finally kill her. And now . . . Harri thought of the young, unidentified murder victim who had been physically altered to look like her.

Christ, Harri . . . what are you thinking? This is Mac for fuck's sake! Do you really believe he is capable of murder?

She thought back to when she had worked on his team. She had initially been flattered by the unsolicited attention. After all, who wouldn't be? He was her boss. A senior ranking officer who had decided that she, a young DC, was worthy of his attention. He was in his early forties, with traits that she couldn't help but find attractive; he was tall, dark and good-looking. But it was more than that; he had something about him. Some inexplicable quality that made people like him, want to be around him. He had leadership qualities that his team and superiors admired. A quality that Mac used to his own gain, as Harri would find out.

She was the only one on the team who didn't trust him. She had done to begin with. After all, he was handsome, charismatic, with an edge of arrogance about him that women and men – herself included – liked. Then after a late-night session in the pub when the rest of the team had left, Mac had offered to see her back to her flat. She had had too much to drink to think straight so against her better judgement, she had agreed. But she had trusted him. And even though she found him attractive, she still had enough wits about her to refuse his sudden advances: aggressive, lustful and unwanted. After all, he was her boss, and she wasn't a fool. She had worked hard to get accepted into the Met. And she had big plans. So no matter how drunk she was, she didn't want to be tarnished with the reputation of having slept her way to the top. She respected herself too much for that. Had worked too hard to live up to the memory of her father.

So when she had struggled and he had not listened, she had struck out at him to leave her alone. Had screamed for him to get out. Which he did. *Finally*. He had not apologised for his actions, and instead blamed her. Angry that she had teased him, led him on. That she had been flirting with him from the moment she had been assigned to his team. Then he had left, not before telling her he wanted her off his team. That if she didn't leave voluntarily, he would force her out.

And he did. Two months after he had promised he would make her leave, she had been raped and assaulted.

She had worried about the consequences of refusing his advances, and she had been right to. After that night, he rarely addressed her at work. And if he did, then it was in a clipped manner. Still professional – just. Then through the course of the following days and weeks, one by one, her colleagues started distancing themselves.

It was about a month after Mac had demanded that she quit the team that she had the disquieting feeling that she was being stalked. That someone was watching her. Calling her landline but not leaving a message, or hanging up when she did answer. Random texts would come through – sexually inappropriate ones – from numbers she didn't recognise. She had ignored it. Hoped it would go away. After all, she had enough to contend with at work. Her professional life was hanging in the balance. She needed to be part of the team, but it was becoming more and more apparent that she was being pushed out to the periphery. But she wouldn't transfer. She had decided to wait it out. It took her being sexually assaulted for her to call it quits. Five months after her attack Mac won: she left the Met.

It was personal – he knew her name; had keys to her flat. Was it Mac? She couldn't say for definite. From what she was able to ascertain, the attacker was the same height and build as Mac. But no one would have believed her even if she had been brave enough to articulate her darkest fears about her boss: that he had entered into her flat, attacked her and then left with the promise he would return again, to kill her. Over the months after the attack she had thought about why someone of Mac O'Connor's professional ranking and status would jeopardise everything to terrorise her. But then again, if it had been him, he hadn't risked anything; a respected DI, his explanation for forcing his way into the crime scene had been accepted and his DNA, which had been recovered, had automatically been dismissed. After all, he was her boss and on hearing the 999 call come in had reacted without thinking, racing to the crime scene. As far as she knew, he had not informed anyone that he had been in her flat a couple of months prior to her attack.

His phone cut to voicemail. She listened as Mac O'Connor instructed the caller to leave a message. That he would get back to them as soon as he could. She disconnected the call. Sat for a moment, staring at the screen, trying to figure out her next move. She decided to call him at work. She needed to know for her own sanity that she was wrong – that he had nothing to do with either her assault or the murder victim. That he was not responsible for sending the photo or the text. That he was currently in London. She clicked on 'contacts' and rang his work number, not giving herself time to back out.

His office phone rang and rang. Harri realised with sinking clarity that he wasn't there. She heard it 'click' as it was transferred.

'DC Jackson,' answered a voice that Harri immediately recognised.

A wave of nausea hit her. 'Anna?'

'Yes?'

'It's . . . Harri . . .'

For an awkward moment DC Jackson did not reply.

'Yeah . . . Harri. Of course. How are you?'

Oh shit . . . Why did it have to cut through to you?

She already felt stupid for calling. But she felt even worse now. She had not heard from anyone at the Met since she had transferred to the North East. Which was what she had wanted. She had made it clear that she was starting over; which meant cutting all ties – especially with Anna.

She had been close to Anna back then. Before the question of loyalty had become an issue. It was mainly because of Mac that Harri had started to distance herself from Anna. Or to be precise, that Anna had started disassociating herself from Harri. Anna had known about their boss's obsession with Harri. It was something they had laughed about. But soon the laughter had stopped. Anna had started making excuses not to meet up with her after work for a drink. Then even the phone calls and texts stopped. Eventually Anna found reasons not to be partnered with her. She would do anything, including working opposite shifts, to avoid seeing Harri. It didn't take Harri long to know that Anna had distanced herself from her: for professional reasons of course; she had a career and wanted to keep it that way. But Anna wasn't the only one to act this way towards her. The rest of her colleagues soon followed and Harri found herself isolated at work.

So when she was subject to the attack, she was already a social pariah. The team had all but ostracised her. The reason – Mac.

'Harri? Are you still there?'

Her voice jolted her back to the present. 'Yeah . . .'

'Look, I don't mean to be rude or anything, but why have you called? I haven't heard from you in nearly a year.'

Harri bit down on her lip. Hard. Stopped herself from saying something she would regret. 'Yeah . . . Sorry. Life, you know? New job. New location. It's hard to find the time to fit everything in.'

'I tried calling you but your phone was disconnected.'

Harri was caught off guard by the statement. She resisted the urge to ask why not call her when she had really needed her? 'I got a new contract with a different company. Better deal and all that. I'm sure I sent you a text with my new number . . .' It was a blatant lie. But she felt forced into it.

'Right.' Anna's voice was hard. Indifferent. *Hurt?*

Harri willed herself to speak. She hadn't expected this. She had psyched herself up to talk to Mac. To confront him. But she was unprepared for talking to Anna. Even more unprepared to hear her say that she had tried calling her. *Why? Why were you calling me?* She couldn't bring herself to ask the question.

'So how's things?' She knew it was an inane question, but it was the best she had.

'Busy.'

'Same here.'

'Look Harri, I've got to go. I'm expected in a meeting in five.'

'Wait! I just wanted to know if Mac was around. I need to talk to him.'

Harri heard her intake of breath.

'Is it to do with what happened to you?' Anna asked. Her voice had changed. There was a sympathetic tone to it now.

Harri felt herself recoil. She couldn't stand pity. Especially from someone who had betrayed her trust. She willed the right words out of her mouth. 'Something like that.'

'OK. Well, I'm afraid he's not here. Can I take a message or pass you on to someone connected with the case?'

'No . . . It's fine. I'll call him back later.'

'Oh . . . I should have said that he's on leave.'

'Since when?' asked Harri, surprised. Coincidence? She doubted it.

'From yesterday. Why?'

There was a suspicious edge to Anna's voice. 'I was just wondering when he would be back so I could ring him then.'

'Oh . . . right. As far as I know he's on leave for two weeks.'

'Do you know where he's gone?'

'No! And if I did, I couldn't tell you, Harri. You should know that.'

'Of course. I wasn't thinking. I'll call back in a couple of weeks.'

'Are you sure?'

'Yeah. Look, it was great talking to you, Anna.'

'You too. Keep in touch. My number's still the same.'

'Will do,' Harri replied, despite having no intention of ever calling her. They were dancing around each other with politeness. Both had an edge of insincerity to their voices.

She cut the call and exhaled slowly. She could feel her skin crawling with discomfort. The last person she'd wanted to talk to was Anna. She had shared with Anna what had happened and Harri was certain Anna had told the other team members about Mac's unwanted advances that night. However, she seriously doubted that Anna had repeated verbatim Harri's version of events. She'd heard the malicious rumours – that she had thrown herself at her boss. Shamelessly flaunted herself, repeatedly. That he had politely declined. Consequently, she had forced herself on him that night. The story was that she was so focused on the job she would use anyone to get promoted. And Harri was no fool; she knew that her colleagues assumed she had slept with him. But these were all rumours whispered behind her back. Nothing was ever officially cited. She had been left with her professional ethics in question and reduced to the same status as the main protagonist in Nathaniel Hawthorne's 1850 novel, *The Scarlet Letter*. However, unlike Hester Prynne's scarlet 'A' for adulteress that she was condemned to wear until her death, Harri wore hers as a metaphorical stigma – after all, Mac O'Connor was also a married man.

She thought about what Anna had told her; that Mac had taken two weeks' leave effective as of yesterday.

What are you up to, Mac?

She had a bad feeling about it. She didn't trust him. And she didn't believe in coincidences. The fact that he had taken leave a year to the day she was raped and assaulted only added to her suspicion that he was responsible. *But did that make him a murderer?*

He had watched as the team – his team – ostracised her. Mac could have silenced the rumours about her. Challenged and corrected them. But he didn't. Why would he? He had made it clear that he wanted her out. And for what? Being an attractive young woman with ambition? Or was it the fact she had rejected him? Maybe she was one of many young women who had caught his eye. The only difference was that she had fought back; had refused to be bullied. Would do it again without hesitation, despite the consequences.

Harri lightly touched the gnarled scar across her neck. Whoever had done this to her had silenced her. *Altered her. Scarred her – physically and mentally.*

Numb, she stared at his name on her list of contacts. She was certain that Mac wasn't in London. That he was in Newcastle. It was more than a feeling. *She just knew.*

Harri walked into the large room that operated as a shared office for the murder team. The room was empty, apart from DC Robertson at his desk with his back to her. He turned to see who had walked in. The expression on his face said it all.

Shit ... Harri watched as Robertson pushed his chair back and stood up to leave.

'Can I get you a coffee?' Harri tried.

She could see the muscles in his face tighten as he forced himself to acknowledge her. He was six foot tall with overly pumped muscles. Harri hated to admit it, but even she had to concede that he was exceptionally good-looking. Watching him, she could understand why women were so attracted to him. He had short black hair and a rugged, handsome face. His olive-coloured skin was the perfect combination with his deep, dark brown eyes. He even had eyelashes that would be the envy of any woman. But that was where it ended and his personality bypass took over. He would often boast about the women he was shagging to the other lads on the team. Harri had heard him tell how he had 'tagged' some model and a couple of the *Geordie Shore* lasses. It was the first time Harri had heard the colloquialism used in reference to shagging a woman, but it hadn't been the last. Initially, she had put it down to wishful thinking, but over the course of the past five months she had seen the way women reacted around him. Whether it was other female coppers or civilians, they all seemed to fall for his good looks.

'No, thanks,' Robertson flatly answered.

Helpless, she watched as he packed up what he needed. Douglas was right, she should have gone to him first instead of taking matters into her own hands. It seemed infantile now. She had made a point. But at what expense?

'I'd appreciate your help interviewing the witness later,' Harri said as he walked towards the door.

But Robertson didn't respond. He was clearly pissed off with her. And she had to agree that he had every right to be. She was his boss and had humiliated him. Not a good move. She needed as many members of the team as possible on her side right now. Admittedly she had been provoked. But whether or not he had implied she deserved to have her throat slit, she should have handled it better. After all, she was his superior.

'Excuse me, Sarge,' he said, gesturing towards the door.

Harri stepped out of his way. 'Look, Robertson ... about yesterday morning ...'

'Forget it. I have.' Without waiting for a response he walked out of the office, leaving the door wide open.

The sarcastic tone in his voice was like a slap; countless times she had instructed him to call her

'Harri', to no avail. She watched as he caught up with his colleague, DC John Michaels, who was walking down the corridor. She couldn't make out what he said to Michaels, but it was clear he was still angry. Harri watched as the two DCs walked away. Michaels was in his mid-thirties. He was the same height and build as Robertson, but that was where the similarities ended. He had dark blonde curly hair that, no matter what he did to it, always looked too long and unruly. He was exceptionally pale with gentle blue eyes and an unfortunate Roman nose that dominated his face. Out of all the men on the team, he was the least testosterone driven. Michaels was also the one who gave her the least trouble and always completed his duties. Harri was acutely aware that maybe that was why she liked Michaels – he didn't challenge her authority.

She was annoyed with herself. Her actions yesterday had made the situation even worse. But at this moment in time Robertson was the least of her concerns. She was confident she could sort the situation.

Unlike the photograph that had been hand-delivered. The anonymous text. Someone was targeting her, which made her a victim. Then there was the murdered body discovered early this morning. A young, female victim whose physical traits had been altered to resemble Harri's blonde hair and green eyes. She knew the protocol – if Douglas had the slightest inclination of the link between the victim and herself, she would be removed from the investigation.

She couldn't allow that to happen. She had access to resources that would be beyond her reach as a civilian. If she wanted to track who'd sent her the photograph and text, then she needed to stay on the job. If she found out the identity of the person who had sent them, she would find her attacker.

She closed the office door and leaned against it for a moment. She thought about the question: *Do you know who I am, Harri? For I know you – intimately*

She was certain it was Mac O'Connor. More so after finding out that he had taken two weeks' leave. That he had effectively disappeared.

She distractedly looked over at her workstation and noticed a brown envelope on her desk. It threw her back to the one that had been delivered to her apartment building, containing the photograph.

Shit . . .

Her mouth suddenly felt dry as a clammy sweat embraced her. She forced herself to walk over to it, despite the fact that her legs felt like lead. She reached her desk and tentatively picked the envelope up. Unlike the other one, this was addressed to her: Detective Sergeant Harriet Jacobs. Postmarked London. She realised she was overreacting. It would be some work-related issue. She tore it open. A photograph was wedged inside.

She pulled it out – facedown.

Come on, Harri. It can't be any worse than what you got this morning.

She steeled herself. Willed it to be nothing. At least nothing that could hurt her.

One . . . Two . . . Three . . .

She turned it over and then stared in disbelief. It took her a moment to comprehend what she was looking at.

SHIT!

Chapter Eleven

'Watch where you're going will you!' Harri exploded as a young DC ran into her, making her spill the coffee she was carrying.

Surprised by her outburst, he moved out of her way.

'Sorry, Sarge.'

'Do you know where I can find Douglas?' she asked, making a point of shaking dripping coffee off her hand.

Irritation flashed across her face when he didn't immediately respond.

'He's in his office,' he answered, his face now flushed. 'We've got a development with the witness, I was told to find you.'

'It will have to wait,' Harri dismissed him. She knew the drunken student wasn't responsible for the young woman's death. She had the evidence in her hand. Evidence that she had to take to Douglas.

She handed the DC the half-empty cup of coffee and left him standing there as she ran for the stairs. He looked as taken aback at her explosion as if she had just thrown a punch at him. But right now she wasn't bothered about what he thought. Or the rest of the station for that matter. Her only concern was getting this information to Douglas.

Harri knocked on Douglas' door. Her mind was racing.

Think of the consequences first. If you tell Douglas about the photograph and text, then you risk losing everything: no chance to get hold of the bastard who raped you and then sliced your throat open. He's playing with you, so let yourself be the bait, Harri. Let him come to you. But you can't do that if you get removed from the investigation.

She knew what she had to do – she had no choice.

'Come in!' Douglas shouted.

She mentally prepared herself as she opened the door.

Douglas looked weary. Worried even. She had no idea what was going on and didn't feel it was her place to ask. Also she had her own troubles – ones that she couldn't share with him for fear of being removed from the investigation. She needed to be objective and professional, despite the fact that some sick bastard was out there taunting her, and she needed to be in a position where she could retaliate. She needed to stay on the job.

'Sit down,' Douglas instructed.

The concern in his eyes unnerved her.

'Here, sir.' Harri handed the photograph and the envelope over as she sat down. 'It was on my desk.'

She watched. Waited. But Douglas put the envelope down.

'Sir?' she asked, unable to hide her surprise.

'In a minute.'

Harri resisted the urge to question his unusual

behaviour. Instead she remained impassive, despite the sudden tension she felt.

'There is no other way of saying this . . .' Douglas looked at her. 'I had a call from the Met earlier. From a member of your old team—'

'Who?' Harri interrupted without thinking. 'DI O'Connor?'

A sickening feeling stirred in the pit of her stomach, followed by suspicion. 'What did he want?'

Douglas studied her for a moment. What composure she had had at first was gone. She knew that the shock would have registered. If not on her face, definitely in her eyes.

'I'm sorry. I didn't mean to make you uncomfortable, Harri.'

The tension in the now claustrophobic room was palpable. She wasn't sure exactly what was happening here. She didn't trust Mac. And she definitely didn't trust him to be talking to Douglas.

'I'm fine.' It was a lie. She felt anything but fine. But he was the last person she would admit that to.

'I'm pleased to hear that. Especially considering the relevance of today.'

Harri flinched. It was an involuntary reaction and she despised herself for it. 'I can assure you that it is very much in my past, sir.'

Douglas nodded sympathetically. But she wasn't sure whether the sentiment was sincere. A gut feeling told her that Douglas had heard something about her; something that made him seem distant right now – guarded, even.

'I'm sorry, I can understand that my bringing this up must make you feel uncomfortable. But it was DC Anna Jackson's concern for you that brought it to my attention, not DI O'Connor. Your ex-colleague's just called me. I hadn't realised that it was exactly a year ago.'

She forced herself to remain emotionless as she stared at him. Inside, she was furious. *Fuck you, Anna! Fuck you for interfering.*

'It is of no significance to me. And nor should it be to you.' She knew it was a bold statement to make – combative even. But the last thing she wanted to show him was any sign of weakness. More so if Anna had been talking to him.

'Well, I think it is relevant. And so did DC Jackson, which was why she reminded me of the date.'

Harri sat perfectly still, acutely aware that Douglas had no intention of ending the conversation, regardless of her opposition.

'She asked me to pass on her best and to tell you that you are sorely missed.'

Again, Harri did not respond. It was a blatant lie. Anna Jackson had made her life intolerable. They all had – they had followed DI Mac O'Connor in his bid to get her off his team. He had wanted her out and didn't care how he achieved it. *And he had won – finally.*

'I was aware from your records that you had had a time of absence before you transferred here.'

'It was sick leave, sir.' She felt the need to be factual, not vague.

Douglas cleared his throat. Dropped his eyes briefly

from her cold stare. 'Yes, of course. I meant sick leave. What I am trying to say is I had not realised it was exactly a year ago that you were attacked. And . . . I just want you to know that I understand if you would like to take some time off.'

'Starting from when?' Harri asked, aware that Douglas had momentarily taken in the savage scar on her neck.

'I was thinking effective now,' he said, now looking her in the eye.

'And what would I do?'

Douglas looked awkward.

'Sit around and think about what happened to me? I would rather be occupied at work.'

'I understand. I was trying to be—'

'What else did Anna say about me?' She couldn't help herself.

'Just that she was worried about how you would be coping, given the date. I then realised that your unprofessional behaviour yesterday with Robertson could have been connected to . . .' Douglas faltered, unsure of how to phrase it.

'I can assure you that my disciplining of Robertson had no bearing on what had happened to me a year ago. If it had, then Robertson would still be on the floor lying in his own piss.'

Douglas ignored her statement. Or at least, he did not react to it.

'Is that all she said?' She was worried that Anna had informed Douglas that she had been checking up on DI Mac O'Connor. She had been foolish enough to have confided in Anna when she had visited her in hospital after her assault that she suspected it had been Mac. The look on Anna's face had been enough to silence her. It was evident that Anna thought Harri had gone too far with her obsession over Mac's behaviour towards her after she refused to sleep with him. Anna had made some excuse and had left shortly afterwards. It had been the last time Harri had seen her.

She felt a wave of anger flush through her. Anna had no right to contact Douglas. She waited for him to mention DI Mac O'Connor.

'It has also come to my attention that there are rumours going around regarding the reasons you left the Met.'

Surprised by this statement, Harri forced herself to keep quiet, wondering exactly where this was leading.

'If you want me to deal with it, then I would be more than happy to,' Douglas said.

Harri instinctively breathed in. Held her breath for a moment, then released it. It was a technique her counsellor had taught her for moments where she felt out of control or overwhelmed. She took her time before answering. 'Thank you, but no. Just so you are aware, the rumours are unfounded—'

Douglas raised his hand to stop her. 'I didn't believe they were anything other than unfounded. That is not what I am establishing here.'

She held his gaze. Tried to get a measure of whether that was true. She could feel her face burning. The rumours that she had slept with her boss – with Mac – must have followed her from London. She wondered whether Anna Jackson had disclosed this rumour to Douglas. She was bristling at the idea of her personal life being discussed by someone who was feigning concern. 'It doesn't matter to people whether the rumours are factual or not, sir. People talk. They like to create scandal. Arguing against it would make it worse. But if you were worried about how it was affecting my ability to work, you don't need to. It doesn't bother me.'

Douglas did not respond.

'Just for clarity, it was the rumour that I left the Met because I had an affair with a commanding officer that was unfounded. Obviously the others, about me being assaulted and my father being in the force here in Newcastle as a DSI, are correct. As I am sure you know.'

Douglas nodded. 'Your father was a very well-regarded man, Harri. Anyone who was privileged enough to work with him only had the greatest respect for him. I . . . I am sorry about what happened.'

'Thank you,' Harri said quietly. She had heard that Douglas had known her father. Not that he had ever mentioned him to her until now. She was relieved that he hadn't and hoped it would never be mentioned again. Harri had her own reasons for wanting to forget her past. The pain she still felt at his untimely loss was as intense as if it had only happened yesterday. She dealt with it the only way she knew how – by forgetting. Or at least trying to.

Harri sat back and waited. She had nothing else to say and as far as she was concerned, there was nothing else that Douglas needed to ask. Her eyes dropped down to the envelope. The real reason she was here. She had curbed her impatience at not being able to raise it immediately. She knew that once he opened it, any questions about her dark past and professional ability would dissipate. And fast.

Douglas looked at the photo again. He swallowed. Stared. Harri wondered what was going through his mind. He turned it over. Read what was neatly typed on the back.

He shook his head.

'It doesn't make sense. Why would it have been addressed to you?'

'I . . .' Harri hesitated for a moment. Composed herself. She had struggled with this question until she had an answer she could offer Douglas, for she knew it had to do with her attack a year ago. She didn't believe in coincidences.

He is playing with you, Harri. The question is, how long do you have before Douglas and the team realise? Before they understand why the killer physically altered the victim to look like . . . you?

She reined her thoughts in. Shrugged. 'I can only assume whoever has done this knows I am the only female member of the murder team. Maybe they thought it would have a greater impact on me.'

Harri ignored Douglas's frown. It was clear that he was struggling to accept her interpretation. She willed herself not to react. *Because if he thinks this is connected to you and your past, then it's over with . . .*

Douglas dropped his gaze back down to the postmark on the envelope. 'It was sent first class yesterday. It was intended to reach us – you – today. The same day as . . .' He faltered. Shook his head as his eyes rested on the photograph of the victim the killer had named, 'Subject A'.

'Precisely, sir. This has been planned.' Harri wanted to say that the killer was 'playing' with them. But couldn't. Simply because she was worried that Douglas might put two and two together and realise that the killer's intention was to unnerve Harri. Scare her. Remind her of what had happened to her this day, last year – *of his promise to return.*

Douglas sighed heavily and ran a large hand over his bristly chin. 'London . . . Is that to confuse us? To make us think he isn't local?'

'I don't know.' Initially she had immediately thought of her attacker. After all, she had been living in London when it had happened.

Douglas pushed the stark black and white photograph in front of Harri. 'It's already too late. He's killed her. So why send a photograph of her hours or days before he killed her?'

Harri didn't respond. Instead, she stared at the disturbing image. There was no disputing that this was the victim. The significant difference was that she was still alive when the photograph had been taken.

The emaciated young woman – girl – was wearing a long gown, lying on a hospital bed. The identity tag that had been found attached to her body was tied around her right big toe. Harri felt nauseous when she looked at the victim's sunken face. Her dull, flat eyes stared blankly at the ceiling. She was already dead – mentally. In her right arm was an IV drip attached to a stand by the bed.

On the back of it the killer had typed: *Subject A: Experiment Failed.* The words were too chilling to contemplate.

'What do you think he did to her? He's suggesting he experimented on her.'

Douglas shook his head. 'I have no idea. Let's hope that Dr Blake can give us some indication of what he means.'

Harri turned the photograph back over and studied the victim. She felt sick at the realisation that her death could be because of her. She thought of Mac. *Could he possibly be responsible for this? She had been certain he had raped her. But this . . .*

Whoever was responsible would have needed time to plan such a crime. She wondered whether Mac could have possibly continued working in the Met and abducted and starved this victim. She felt sickened by the answer. It was possible. *Anything was possible. And Mac was on leave . . .*

'We need to check all hospitals and hospices to see whether any patients matching our victim have been removed,' Douglas instructed.

'Sir,' Harri agreed. Not that she expected that to be the case. She had a feeling that the killer had kept her in an unknown location. She also had an uneasy feeling that the victim was not ill – despite the suggestion.

She studied the photograph again, her eyes taking in what surrounded the victim. Anything to give her a clue to where it was. She looked up at Douglas. 'Sir? Here . . .'

He nodded. His expression grim. He had already spotted it – *her*.

In the far corner of the room there was a mirror and in it a reflection of the victim lying on the bed. But beyond that something else. *Someone else?* Harri narrowed her eyes as she focused on the miniscule detail.

Shit . . .

'The reflection in the mirror . . .' Harri looked up from the photograph. 'There's someone else in that room. Potentially another victim.'

Douglas' expression said it all. He looked as sickened as Harri felt.

She looked back down at the image. The other woman seemed to be sitting in some sort of old-fashioned wheelchair. She needed to get the image enlarged but she was certain that the person in the wheelchair was staring not at the body, but straight at the camera. *Or . . . at the killer.*

Chapter Twelve

Harri tried her best to breathe through her mouth. She glanced at the clock; it was nearly midday. Anything to distract her. The smell always got to her. But this was worse somehow, beyond anything she had ever experienced – or ever wanted to experience again. Not that she was the only one sickened by what they were witnessing. The two unlucky SOCOs that James Munroe had brought with him looked more than ready for a bolt to the loos. She couldn't blame them. The way she was feeling, she wouldn't be far behind.

Douglas' cool composure did not go unnoticed by Harri, nor did Munroe's relaxed manner. She, on the other hand, was struggling to keep down the breakfast she had eaten on the way to the Royal Victoria Infirmary. She should have heeded the warning Blake had given at the crime scene and waited until after the post-mortem.

Eleanor Blake looked across at Harri, catching her off guard, as if aware of her discomfort. She swore that the pathologist's unnerving gaze had dropped to the ugly scar across her neck for a moment; a constant reminder that she too could have ended up on an autopsy slab. If it did, then Blake swiftly moved on as she turned to Douglas and continued in her dispassionate matter-of-fact tone: 'No sign of trauma around or in the vagina and anus. I have taken swabs for traces of sperm or any type of spermicide or lubricant of course, but to my eye, this lass has not been sexually assaulted. However, I think the bastard did more than enough. Don't you?'

The rhetorical question was left unanswered.

Harri was relieved for the victim's sake that she hadn't been raped. She knew all too well the physical and mental trauma. But at least she was here, still breathing, unlike the unidentified body cut open in front of her.

Blake shook her head as she looked at the body. 'Poor lass. You've got one evil bastard out there, Tony. He has significantly changed her physical appearance. You wouldn't place her as an eighteen- or nineteen-year-old. Not with the trauma her body has endured. Her hair was dyed hours before her death. Sulphuric acid was poured over her face, resulting in extreme damage to the skin, tissue and, in parts, bone. She has no recognisable facial features, or teeth. This isn't a random murder. This was premeditated. It took months to get her to this state.'

Harri had silently watched Blake's every move as she examined the outside of the body first, using a scalpel that had a ruler marked on the blade so she could accurately detail her findings. After opening the skull, she had made a Y-shaped incision from the shoulders to mid-chest and down to the pubic region and then used rib cutters to open the chest cavity. Then began the method-ical process of examining, documenting and weighing the internal organs. The stomach had contained no traces of food. Something that had not come as a surprise to anyone.

Now Blake had finished with the body, the two mortuary technicians busied themselves with the process of replacing everything that had been removed – including the brain.

There were no niceties in death; and there had been none in this victim's last few months of life. However, Blake's manner, and that of the two technicians, had been respectful as well as curious. There was no joking or piss-taking, as there had been at the crime scene. This was a suspicious death and Blake's job was crucial – she had the medical background to see any anomalies that would link the body to the killer; indiscretions that could otherwise go undetected.

There was a fierceness about her and she clearly didn't suffer fools gladly. But Harri could see that Blake had earned her reputation for being one of the best in her profession; someone who not only lectured at Newcastle University but throughout the UK and abroad.

Harri's eyes drifted to the sign above the door: *Hic Locus Est Ubi Mors Gaudet Succurrere Viate*. In other words, *This is the place where death rejoices to help those who live*. She hoped that was the case. They now knew that the killer of this young woman had another victim kept in a similarly debilitating condition. In other words, slowly starving to death.

'The eyes were an interesting touch,' Blake casually noted.

Harri looked across at them on the examination table. Placing green glass eyeballs into what was left of the victim's eye sockets was indeed an 'interesting touch' – and a sick one.

'So was the cause of death poisoning?' Douglas asked.

Harri had also assumed this, from the significant internal scarring and damage to the oesophagus and trachea, and the traces of sulphuric acid in her stomach.

Blake shook her head. 'Sorry, I should have made myself clearer. No. Cause of death was heart failure due to starvation. Her organs would have failed within the next twenty-four hours so the shock of the acid attack was the catalyst for her going into cardiac arrest. From the excess folds of skin covering the body, I would say that she has lost over sixty per cent of her body weight. That is a staggering amount to lose in such a short time and if I am honest, I am surprised she survived for as long as she did. She was suffering from extreme catabolysis, which is when the body breaks down its own muscles and tissues to survive.'

'How long would it take for an adult to starve to death?' Harri asked.

'I would surmise that it has taken this victim approximately twelve weeks. Eight to twelve weeks is the average, but there are some instances of it taking up to twenty-four weeks. The key is hydration and we know from the needle wound and bruising that an IV line was fed into her arm. Whoever did this to her, wanted her to starve to death slowly and painfully. Which is exactly what she did.'

Harri looked at the folds upon folds of excess skin that spread over the autopsy table. She couldn't help being drawn back to the barbaric black stitches that knitted together the insides of both arms – it was here that the killer had taken a knife to the victim to remove her excess flesh and then stitched the skin back together. Even in death, the puckered skin still looked raw and angry.

'And this,' Blake said, gesturing at the black sutures, 'is worrying. I don't like this at all. If her heart hadn't given out, then it wouldn't have taken long before septicaemia killed her. The flesh around those stitches was seriously infected. Let's see what the blood results from the lab tell us, but I doubt he anaesthetised her first.'

Harri silently agreed. She didn't believe the killer would have been interested in whether the victim was in pain. That wasn't what this was about. She assumed that the victim had been conscious when the acid had been poured over her face, as it was clear that she had swallowed some of it. She wondered if in the shock of the acid hitting her skin, the victim had unintentionally both swallowed and breathed it in.

'You've got one twisted fucker here, Tony. I don't envy you your job.'

Douglas gestured at the bloody carnage on the table. 'I don't envy you yours either.'

Harri looked at her one last time. It was beyond comprehension. The fact that the murderer had called it an 'experiment' – 'a failed experiment' – scared Harri more than she wanted to acknowledge. She and Douglas knew that there was a second victim. The photograph that the murderer had sent had been enlarged, confirming that there was another person in a wheelchair in the room alongside 'Subject A'.

'Seriously, Tony, this guy has just got started. He's got a taste for this and I can promise you that if you don't find him, she won't be the last.' Blake shook her head as she stared down at the killer's handiwork. 'He's in the process of perfecting his procedure. The question you need to ask yourself is, *what is he trying to achieve here? Who was he trying to turn her into?* For that was what he was doing. Starving her to half her original body weight, dyeing the hair blonde, eradicating the features and placing green eyeballs in the sockets . . .'

Douglas caught Harri's eye. It was clear that he was as concerned as she was about the other woman in the photograph, and the likelihood that she, too, would end up on the autopsy table.

If Blake was right that the killer was just getting started, what did he plan to do to his next victim?

Chapter Thirteen

Samuel Riley had his head bent low as he was led out the interview room. He looked exhausted. His clothes had been removed. The custody officer had given him whatever he had at hand – a white T-shirt, grey jogging bottoms. Harri had refused to let him sleep himself sober for fear that he would forget something crucial; that it would be lost in a drunken haze. She had made him take a shower to sober up.

He looked barely twenty. He lifted his head and looked at Harri as he passed her. Fear filled his eyes – still. She assumed he had never been in trouble with the police before, let alone been interviewed in relation to a murder enquiry. She felt sorry for him. Sorry for the horrific scene he had inadvertently stumbled upon on his way home from a student party. This would change him. She was certain of that.

He was now being released. She had spent the past hour or so interviewing him with DC Robertson. She had wanted to make sure that she had gleaned every miniscule detail. Given that Samuel Riley was their only witness, it made his statement crucial. In that time his alibi had also been verified. He had left the party when he had said and twenty minutes later was recorded reporting what he had found to the emergency services. Harri had listened to the 999 call. It was clear that he was drunk. Scared. Confused. It was also evident that he wasn't sure whether the victim was alive or dead. That he didn't know what to do to help her. However, Eleanor Blake had clearly stated the victim had been dead for over eight hours. She'd been dead when Samuel Riley found her, ruling him out as a suspect. But he had not just found the body, he had inadvertently stumbled upon the killer. Riley had witnessed him leaning over the body on the ground. Noticing Riley approaching, he had straightened up and said something to him before turning and heading down the path towards the parked white transit van. Whatever the killer had said had been lost on the drunken student. However, he had managed to give them a description of their suspect – six foot two, athletic, dressed in black with a black ski mask covering his face. Her own assailant had been tall, athletic and had worn a ski mask. *What were the odds?*

The witness had also said that the unknown suspect had an accent – a London one. It correlated with the London postmark on the envelope with the photograph of the victim.

Details of the white transit van the witness had seen the suspect leave in had already been released to the public, asking the driver to come forward to help with the investigation, or any witnesses who saw the vehicle. But so far, nothing. This worried her – a lot.

The killer was one step ahead of them; he already had another victim ready to kill, one whose physical condition was similar to the murdered teenager. Which meant that they didn't have long to find her; to find *him*.

Harri felt sick.

What he had done to the victim was so horrific, she couldn't bring herself to think about what he was doing to the girl in the wheelchair.

She exhaled slowly. There was one fact that she could not discount. The envelope had been addressed to her – the only female on the team. It had arrived on April Fools' Day; a year to the day she was attacked. *A coincidence? No. She knew there were no such things as coincidences in her job.*

Harri looked around the Incident Room. Situated on the first floor, it was one of the largest conference rooms in the station. Desks, computers and phone lines had been brought in for the team. Every detail connected to the case would be brought back there. The room would now be the team's home for the duration of the investigation. There were roughly twenty officers waiting for the briefing to start. She noted that Robertson was absent. She presumed he was still matching their victim's details with the countless missing person's reports on file. In the previous year alone over 300,000 calls were made to the police reporting someone missing and almost half of the people who did go missing were between fifteen and twenty-one. It made Robertson's job time-consuming, if not impossible.

She looked at Douglas, waiting for him to begin. He was furiously scribbling in his policy book. Every decision that Douglas made as the Senior Investigating Officer had to be written down, dated and timed. Gone were the days of making up the rules as you went along. Now every detail had to be committed to paper so that it could be examined later. The problem was, sometimes decisions would have to be made on a hunch rather than anything conclusive. Given how fluid a case could be, the SIO could end up writing their own resignation when a decision turned out to be critically wrong.

She waited as the room filled with silence. As she did so she turned to the interactive whiteboard. Felt sickened. But there wasn't one person in the room who did not feel physically sick when they looked at the crime scene photos of the victim. Brutal. Gory. Inhumane.

This was someone's unidentified daughter.

Harri had seen gruesome deaths in her time with the police, but this was a first. Harri turned to Douglas as he stood up and addressed the room: 'The post-mortem has shown that the victim was still alive when sulphuric acid was poured over her. The quantity used was enough to partially dissolve her skull and brain tissue. She also ingested and inhaled the substance, which caused her to vomit up blood. Ultimately, the shock sent her into cardiac arrest. At this stage we have only one eye witness who saw the suspect leaving the victim on the path before driving off in a white transit van. He described him as six foot two, athletic build, wearing black clothes and a black ski mask. He heard him say something. Unfortunately, he can't remember what since he was intoxicated at the time, but he did say he had a Southern accent which sounded London based.'

'We haven't seen anything like this before, have we?' someone asked.

Douglas looked at Harri. 'I think DS Jacobs might be better equipped to answer that.'

'No, not like this,' Harri said, standing up. 'Or at least not to this degree. Acid attacks are on the increase in the UK. The figures last year show that the number of admissions into hospital as a result of attacks using a corrosive substance has almost doubled in ten years.'

'How easy is it to buy this stuff? Surely we'd be able to track him down by checking with suppliers of sulphuric acid?'

It was a valid point but one that she had already checked. 'I wish it was that simple. I've already had a look and it's incredibly easy to buy this chemical online.'

She still could not comprehend the acid attack. It was cruel, unjust and barbaric. It was at times like this that such extreme examples of the perverse nature of humanity left her numb. She turned to look at the photographs of the victim on the interactive board behind her, shook her head as she looked at the gruesome carnage that was the victim's head and face. Her eyes then took in the photograph next to it. The one the killer had sent. Gaunt, skeletal, lying on a hospital bed, staring blankly at the ceiling.

'Don't most hate crimes like acid attacks stem from an emotional involvement of some sort with the victim? And aren't the injuries she sustained to her face suggestive of overkill?' asked DC Michaels.

He had a point. Harri had suggested as much to Douglas at the crime scene; that the killer was personally involved with the victim and emotionally attached to her. That was why he had destroyed her face, an attempt to disguise her identity so he would not get caught. But she did not think that was the case now. The facts were staring her in the face. The killer had mocked them by sending them a photograph of the victim before he had completely *altered* her.

'I don't think this is personal. And there are a couple of reasons why. Firstly, the condition of the victim prior to death was one of severe malnourishment. The only thing in her stomach was sulphuric acid. There was nothing in her smaller intestine or colon, which means she hadn't eaten for over forty-eight hours. The toxicology report found significant traces of benzodiazepine in her blood, a tranquilliser that can induce a sleep-like state and, in high enough doses, amnesia. They also found high plasma levels of fatty acids and ketone bodies which are present when the body is starved. Her bloods showed that she was deficient in vitamin D. The greyish pallor of her skin and the lack of this vitamin suggests that she had not seen daylight for some considerable time. Also we know from the needle mark and the bruising on her arm that the benzodiazepine was presumably administered intravenously, with saline to keep her hydrated. You can see in the photograph the killer sent that her arm is attached to an IV drip. She is just a body to him. One that he is keeping alive so he can physically change her. This is important to him. I believe he specifically selected her as his victim because she is clinically obese. It is the ultimate transformation to completely change her physically by starving her until she loses nearly half her body weight. He then cuts off some of her excess skin. Dyes her hair, eradicates her features with sulphuric acid and places green glass eyeballs in her sockets. This isn't personal to the victim. He is simply making her into a type. A type that is meaningful to him, and him alone. He takes one type, an overweight young woman with brown hair, and he transforms her into another type. The key fact to remember here is that he did not sexually assault the victim. He was only interested in altering her.'

The room was suddenly quiet. Harri reached over and picked up a drink. She needed one. She was worried that someone would make the connection between her own physical traits and the altered victim. She realised she was being paranoid. The link was too tenuous. *Or was it?*

'Why choose April Fools' Day to dump her body?' asked a young DC unknown to Harri.

Even though she had been expecting it, the question threw her. She was aware that Douglas was watching her – waiting for her reaction. She looked at the DC, and casually shrugged. 'I don't know why. Maybe he thought the joke was on the police? He sends us a photograph of the victim which arrived in the mail this morning. The killer is clearly playing with us, so what better day to begin than April Fools?'

'Wasn't the envelope addressed to you specifically, Sarge?'

Harri's face was emotionless. Professional. 'You're right. It was addressed to me. I wouldn't read too much into that though. The killer is clearly a misogynist. The evidence is lying in a morgue in the Royal Victoria Infirmary. Or, you can see for yourselves from these photos exactly how he treats women,' Harri suggested, gesturing towards the images. 'I'm the only woman in the Newcastle murder team. Do I think he was targeting me?'

No one said a word. The discomfort in the room was palpable. Harri could feel their eyes on her. Some trying, but failing, not to look at the brutal scar across her neck. Her long-sleeved T-shirt did not hide the disfigurement; it did not even come close.

'Yes. I do. The killer is a misogynist,' Harri explained. 'As the only female CID officer, I think he was trying to unhinge me. Scare me. Perhaps believing that sending it to me would get a greater reaction. But let me make it clear, this is not personally directed at me. Just the fact that I am a woman.' She left it at that and sat back down.

She looked over at Douglas to gauge his reaction. To see if he was buying what she was suggesting. She needed to distance any personal connection between the killer and herself. She had no choice if she wanted to remain on the investigation. She felt a surge of relief when he simply turned and addressed the room, now focused on the description they had of the killer and the urgency for the CCTV footage close to the crime scene to be analysed.

They still did not have a clear route for the transit van, either heading towards the crime scene, or exiting the area. The life of an unidentified woman was at risk if they did not track down his movements. It was a long, arduous job, sitting through countless hours of CCTV surveillance for that elusive shot of the van and the driver – that was if the witness's details were correct. So far, none of the residents had witnessed anything. So the only person they had to rely on was Samuel Riley, a University student walking home drunk from a party.

She looked past Douglas to the interactive board. Her eyes rested on the next potential murder victim; the young woman in the old-fashioned medical wheelchair. She currently had members of the team trying to find out the make of the chair and where they could be bought. The same with the IV stands and hospital beds. But Harri didn't hold out much hope. Anything could be bought on eBay, making it very difficult to trace. But the team were also scrutinising the website in case they came across a supplier with identical vintage wheelchairs or beds.

She couldn't understand the hatred. The resentment the killer felt towards the victim. Harri held her breath. *He resented her because she wasn't what he wanted. But it was all he had ... for now.*

Who do you want?

But she knew who he wanted. *He wanted her.*

Harri turned to the photographs of the murder victim – the before and after shots. He had destroyed the victim's identity and replaced it with a 'type'. They knew from the photograph that the killer had sent of the victim that she had dark brown hair and brown eyes. Yet, his type was blonde-haired and green-eyed – just like Harri.

She studied the damage caused to the victim's face from the acid the killer had thrown over her. The amount was substantial. He didn't want her to live. But even if she had lived through that sort of attack, Harri was aware that she would never have been able to talk, see or hear again due to the injuries she had sustained. On first appearances, the acid attack was indicative of someone out of control. Angry. Vengeful. But Harri was certain it had nothing to do with the actual victim. His vengefulness came from the fact that it hadn't worked. Altering her had not worked. Dying her hair, changing her eye colour. Cutting away the excess skin from her arms, then stitching the flesh back together. None of it had worked. So he decided to eradicate her features. To obliterate his failure. There were no vestiges of emotion here. No hatred – at least, not towards the victim. Because maybe it wasn't *her* that he specifically hated. Maybe he hated the fact that she wasn't who he wanted. Which meant she was expendable.

This scared Harri – a lot. It meant he would try again.

She stared at the enhanced image of the girl in the wheelchair, accidentally or otherwise captured in a reflection on the photograph the killer had sent them. She didn't think she could face dealing with another victim. She studied the enlarged pixelated face of the second woman; the one they all hoped was still alive. Despite the poor quality of the image, Harri could see that there was something about her. The way she stared directly into the camera; or straight at the killer. Despite her emaciated body, she didn't look like a victim to Harri – she looked like a survivor. Harri stared at her haunting face. Her eyes . . . There was something in those eyes that struck a chord. She was aware that the killer was playing with her – that this victim, just like the murdered one, was part of a game. *His game.* A game in which Harri was an integral part. Guilt consumed her as she realised with sickening clarity that she could be staring into the eyes of a dead girl – *all because of her . . .*

Chapter Fourteen

'Sarge?' shouted Robertson as he ran down the stairs to catch her.

Harri stopped. She had just left the briefing and was heading for some late lunch. It was now mid-to-late afternoon and she hadn't eaten since the morning.

'Here,' he said, out of breath as he handed over a missing person's report. 'Nineteen-year-old Tammy Summers. Local girl. Reported missing over four months ago.'

The photograph of the teenager instantly jarred. It was difficult to believe that this could potentially be their victim – 'Subject A'. *But not considering how the killer had altered her.*

Harri waited for the call from the lab. When it finally came, it was an answer she didn't want to hear. She hung up. There was no need for pleasantries. She didn't have time. She had a job to do: informing the victim's next of kin. She looked over at Robertson: 'Grab your coat.'

Harri looked at the victim's father. She knew to wait. To allow him to talk to her in his own time. He was in his early fifties but could have passed for seventy. The TV was on in the lounge but the sound had been muted. He watched, mesmerised as the news reporters discussed the young murder victim – *his daughter*. Hunched over. Tab smouldering in his hand. Milky eyes staring straight ahead. It was masochistic. But that was his prerogative. Harri had no right to tell him what to do in his own home. Or how to cope with the fact that it was his daughter's body that the news reporters were feasting on. She watched him, knowing that what she had told him had dramatically changed his life – for the worse.

The doorbell rang. Harri gestured at Robertson to get it. She watched the relief on his face as he headed off to the door. Any excuse to get away from the grief. Ordinarily, CID didn't touch this kind of situation. It would be left to uniform to deal with the crap hand that life sometimes dealt people. But when she had read this missing person's details she had a hunch that it was 'Subject A'; AKA Tammy Summers; nineteen years old and very dead. Someone had stripped her of her identity – so much so even her own father would not have recognised her. Harri had waited for the confirmation that the victim's DNA matched Tammy Summers. The missing teenager's DNA had been retrieved from an old toothbrush of hers, one her father had not been able to bin.

It meant the team could now personalise the disfigured body in the morgue. Her name, Tammy Summers. Her age, nineteen. Her favourite colour, orange. Her favourite food, Chinese. She lived – *had lived* – with her father, Trevor. Her mother, Sian had died from breast cancer when she was five. She was the youngest of four kids. When she hit ten, her father couldn't cope. Social services had been involved but were no help. She started running away from home around the age of twelve when her father tried to stop her seeing some local lad on the estate. Tammy Summers had a history of being rebellious and taking off. That was why when she was reported missing it wasn't taken seriously. No one took a DNA sample. They didn't think. She was a low-risk missing person.

She shook her head. 'I'm so sorry,' she said as he turned his attention back to her.

He wiped the saliva that had gathered at the corner of his downturned lips. 'No big deal, she said,' he mumbled, more to himself than Harri. 'No big deal . . .'

She let him ramble. It was better that way sometimes. Grief had a way of shutting people down, so Harri kept quiet and waited. She saw Robertson in the doorway of the lounge. She shook her head at him. Whatever it was could wait. This moment belonged to Trevor Summers.

He took a draw on the smouldering tab before stabbing it out in the overflowing ashtray. Harri cast her eyes around the room. The harsh bare bulb overhead spared nothing. She could see that in the last few months his despair had taken its toll. His three older kids had long gone. One in prison; drug-related crime, he had explained; not his fault – not really. One down south doing well for himself and the other struggling to bring up a family of his own. All lads. Then there was the 'bairn' as he called Tammy.

Harri watched as he fumbled with swollen, arthritic fingers for another tab. Wheezing, he lit it and inhaled. His watery eyes stared blankly at his trembling hands. She wished there was something she could do for him but there wasn't. A family liaison officer would be here shortly. Effectively to keep the press back. Once this became public, the rats would come, scurrying over one another to get an exclusive, regardless of the late hour.

'His name was John, she said. John? Could have easily been Tom, Dick or fucking Harry, eh? Like flies round shit they were around her. Beautiful lass, my bairn. Big and beautiful,' he said sadly. 'I didn't believe that was his name for a second. I could smell a bad'un from a mile off. Not that she listened. I was an old fart as far as she was concerned.' He took another drag as he dwelled on the past. 'But I knew . . . Knew he was a bad'un from the start.' He shakily inhaled again. Blew out smoke. 'I told you lot that she hadn't met him. Not in person like. That she only knew him through some dating thingy on her phone. An app I think she called it. They texted for a few days. Then he rang her and that was it. She packed a bag, borrowed money from me and went to London. Promised me she would keep in touch. And she did, kind of. She texted. She knew I hated texts. I got two texts when she got there and then nothing. I tried calling. But nothing. Told the police all that. Made no difference.' He took a deep drag and then stabbed it out. 'Last I heard from her was four months back.'

Harri resisted the compulsion to comfort him. What

could she say? Words from a stranger couldn't change what had happened.

'Never knew I had lung cancer, the bairn didn't. Kept it from her like,' he continued staring at his painfully misshapen fingers. They were still trembling. He never once raised his head to look at Harri. 'Thought, what with her mam dying when she had been so little like, better choose my moment. But that's gone now. Maybe if I'd told her she wouldn't have left.'

Harri didn't answer. She couldn't. Instead she watched him stab out his tab and helplessly grope for another one. He lit it, and sat for a while.

'Terminal now. Maybe better this way, eh?'

Again, Harri kept silent. It was enough. She was sitting with him. That was all he wanted. Someone to listen.

'Can I see her?' he eventually asked, raising his head and looking straight at Harri.

Harri gently shook her head. 'Best not, sir.'

Chapter Fifteen

'I need a word.'

Harri nodded distractedly. 'One minute.'

She was working through the information they had collated on the victim, Tammy Summers. She had members of the team looking at the victim's Facebook page and Instagram posts. Both accounts had been inactive for four months; the same day she left for London. The photograph the murder suspect used on the dating app was obviously not kosher. They had the image from Tammy's posts, sharing her 'virtual' boyfriend days before she disappeared. It hadn't taken Stuart, the forensic computer analyst, long to match the photograph of 'John', the man that Tammy Summers believed she was meeting, with an LA model.

Harri had asked for surveillance footage from King's Cross station on the off-chance that he – *her killer* – had met Tammy Summers off her train from Newcastle. But something told her that he would not have made it that easy for the police. As for her mobile phone, it had been switched off a few hours after she had arrived in London. Two texts had been sent, exactly as her father had said; then nothing.

'Now!' Douglas prompted.

Harri turned to him. The grim expression on his face told her it wasn't good. 'Sir?'

Douglas looked at the other ten or so members of the murder team. 'Not here. Outside.'

She followed him out of the Incident Room into the hallway.

'I would rather you heard this from me first. When the details the witness provided of Tammy Summers' killer was put into HOLMES 2 it came up with a match.'

Harri knew it was bad news – for her. HOLMES 2 was highly sophisticated software that connected the entire UK force.

'And?' But she already knew what was coming next. Had half-guessed this herself.

Douglas didn't say anything.

'My attack?'

Douglas cleared his throat before answering. 'Yes.'

'But it's not the same assailant. The MO is completely different.'

'We don't know that, Harri. Same build. Same clothes. Same accent.'

'It's just a coincidence, sir.' She could see from the concern in Douglas' eyes that he wasn't convinced. 'Seriously? This is ridiculous. How many assailants wear black ski masks to avoid identification?'

'Harri, both artists' sketches match.'

Harri looked at him, her face blank. 'That means nothing . . . Both suspects' faces were covered with a black ski mask.'

Douglas sighed. Frowning, he shook his head. 'If this is connected—'

'It's not!' Harri interrupted. She could not afford to be removed from the investigation. If Douglas thought there was the remotest chance that there was a connection between the killer and her rapist, then she would be assigned to a new case. Ultimately meaning that she would not be able to catch her rapist, now a killer.

'Is that all, sir?' But Harri could see that Douglas wasn't through with her. Not yet.

'Something about this doesn't feel right, Harri. The killer sends the photograph of the victim personally addressed to you. The victim, in case you had failed to notice, had her hair dyed to match your hair colour, her eyes replaced with green glass eyes. Again, your colour. Her height matches your height. And her weight . . .' Douglas paused as he looked at her. 'He had starved her so her build was closer in type to yours. You pointed out in the briefing earlier that this wasn't about an emotional attachment to the victim. It was about transforming her into a type. Physically petite, long blonde hair and green eyes. Just like you.'

She could feel the hairs on the back of her neck standing up. She was more than aware of that fact. But she would not allow Douglas to force her out. To make her move to another investigation because he thought there could be a link between Harri and the killer. She needed to remain on the job. *This job.* She had no other option. She needed to do everything in her power to get to him first, before he got to her. And she could only do that by being part of the murder team. But she could see that whatever DC Anna Jackson had said to Douglas earlier this morning had made him look at her differently. She wasn't imagining it. She could see it in his eyes – fear. Fear that something would happen to her while she was under his command. But she wasn't a victim; not any more. And she definitely wasn't his responsibility.

'You're playing right into the killer's hands. And you're allowing the knowledge of what happened to me a year ago to blur your judgement. The unknown suspect isn't after me. He's a misogynist. He hates women. I'm the only female on the team, so it's no surprise that he sends the photograph of the victim to me. It's about eliciting panic. Also ask yourself how many women are petite with blonde hair and green eyes? I'm not atypical, sir.'

Douglas didn't reply.

Harri knew that she was losing him. 'Tammy Summers' hair had been newly bleached?' It was a rhetorical question. 'Why? Because the killer is creating a "type". Altering her into his "perfect" woman. But that doesn't make her me.'

'Why eradicate any identifiable facial features?' Douglas asked. 'Think about it. Why make her face a blank canvas, apart from the glass eyes?'

Harri shook her head before he had a chance to articulate what he was thinking; *what she was thinking* – that the killer was altering the victim to look like her. 'It could simply be that he wanted to make it as difficult as possible for us to identify her.'

Harri could see that Douglas wasn't convinced, but he didn't bother arguing with her. There was a reason why. He was holding something back from her: 'Sir, what is it?'

'I had no choice but to leave a message for DI O'Connor.'

'What?' she demanded, shocked.

Douglas looked mildly surprised by her outburst. 'As the SIO in charge of your assault, one that is still unresolved, he would have automatically been informed. HOLMES 2 has found similarities between the assailant who attacked you and our killer. It is protocol. You should know that.'

'Since when did he become the SIO on my case?' This was news to her. After all, he had been her boss at the time and that had ruled him out from having anything to do with the case. *Not that it stopped him forcing his way into the crime scene and removing any suspicion about why his DNA was found in her bedroom.*

'I'm sorry, Harri, I thought someone would have informed you. He asked to take it over a few months back. Since he is no longer your boss, there was seen to be no conflict of interest.'

She disguised the shock she felt. But internally she was reeling. *What the fuck? Why would he want to take over the investigation?*

It took Harri a moment to absorb the implications of his move – for her. She realised it meant that as the acting SIO, he would never be caught. Nor would anyone suspect him of being her rapist.

But now he had taken two weeks off work. He had disappeared for a reason. Harri thought about the photograph and text she had received that morning. Then the murder victim, Tammy Summers, and the other unidentified victim in the wheelchair. She didn't believe in coincidences. Not where DI Mac O'Connor was concerned; for he had been savvy enough to force entry into her flat – a crime scene – ultimately eliminating any DNA evidence found at the scene. What else was he capable of doing?

'Do you need some time?' Douglas asked.

She looked up at him. Concern was etched into his brow. She resisted the urge to tell him the truth. That she did believe there could be a connection. If she did, then she was certain she would be removed from the investigation and assigned to another case. She had no choice but to keep it to herself. Not that anyone would believe her suspicions about DI Mac O'Connor anyway. Anna Jackson was testimony to that fact.

'I'm fine, sir,' she said. There was nothing else to say. She turned to head back into the Incident Room.

'Harri?'

She paused, hand on the handle, and waited.

'You would tell me if anything unusual happens? Anything that would suggest to you that your attacker was trying to get your attention?'

She kept her back to him. 'Why do you think he would want to get my attention?'

'Because in your victim statement, it says his last words to you were that he would come back to finish what he had started,' Douglas said quietly.

He was clearly uncomfortable admitting to her that he had read her victim statement. He had obviously gone through every detail of her ordeal to see if there was any other connection to their victim – 'Subject A'; Tammy Summers. Harri could not fault him. She would have done exactly the same in his situation.

'Of course I would tell you if I thought he was stalking me again, sir.' Harri made a point of turning round and looking Douglas straight in the eye. The last thing she wanted was any suggestion that she was telling him a blatant lie.

Douglas didn't say anything.

'You obviously know from my victim statement that he promised when he did come back, he would kill me,' Harri said.

He remained silent.

'Do you really believe if I thought Tammy Summers' killer was my rapist that I wouldn't be the first person to say it? I live every day with the knowledge that the man who raped me is still at large. That fact is with me every fucking hour of every fucking day, sir,' she said, ignoring Douglas' evident unease.

'Harri—' Douglas began. 'I'm sorry. I didn't mean to—'

'Is that all?' she interrupted. She didn't need his pity. That wasn't what this was about. She fought back the emotions she was feeling. She needed to be objective and stay in control. Ultimately, she needed to remain on the job at all costs. She had sworn that she would do whatever it took to apprehend her rapist and if that meant withholding information from Douglas, then so be it.

Douglas nodded.

She turned and went into the Incident Room. She didn't like withholding information from him, but she had no other alternative. Her only way to put an end to what had happened – and what could happen – was to get to her attacker before he got to her.

Whoever he was ... Mac? Wherever he was ...

Chapter Sixteen

She heard the subtle click, then the release of the lock before the front door was opened. It took her by surprise, despite the fact she had been fearfully anticipating it since 5:33 a.m. Terrified, she edged her way to the open bedroom door and listened. *It was him. Oh God ...* The fear of his sudden arrival shook her, making it difficult to breathe.

She waited. She could hear him mumbling. She strained to hear. He was on his mobile. She wondered whether he was on the phone to *her* – that woman. Holding her breath, she crept out the bedroom and stood as close as she dared to the stairs. But she couldn't make anything out.

She shivered. It was cold. The heating had been switched off for days. If he wasn't around then the central heating could not be turned on. He always took the control unit with him. He didn't like the idea of her wasting money. *His money.* She pulled the sleeves of her jumper down so they covered her trembling hands. Then she waited. It was late. Sometime after ten. She tried to hear what else he was saying. Then she heard him say another woman's name. She was certain of it. *The woman in the photograph. It had to be.* She stepped back, not liking the way he said it. She hated herself for letting it hurt her. And she hated him.

'Get down here!' he thundered.

She jumped back. Afraid. She could hear the edge to his voice. She wondered whether his plans had gone awry. Or perhaps the person he had been talking to had made him angry.

She crept out from the shadows and tiptoed towards the top of the stairs.

'I mean, NOW!'

She forced herself down the steps, gripping the banister with one hand to steady herself. Keeping her eyes down, she avoided his glare.

She reached the bottom step, then looked up and unintentionally caught his eye. The disgust cut straight through her. She recoiled.

'What the hell have you been doing all this time? I told you to clean up down here. Didn't I?' he demanded as he pointed down at the highly polished wooden floor. 'Well?'

She didn't answer. She couldn't see what he saw. Never did. But that didn't stop her spending hours on her knees polishing it over and over again.

'DIDN'T I?' he screamed. He grabbed a handful of her long hair, dragging her off the step and down the hallway. He shoved her onto her knees.

'No . . . Please . . . please . . . You're hurting me . . .' She winced, terrified that he would pull out the clump of hair he was twisting around his fist.

'Can you see it? Can you see that blood? I told you to clean it until not a trace was left. But you didn't, did you?

That's your fucking mess down there! Your blood contaminating my fucking floor!'

Tears flowed down her ashen face as he forced her head to the ground.

'I want this cleaned before I leave. Understand?'

She tried to nod. Couldn't.

'I can't fucking hear you!'

'Yes . . . yes . . .' she agreed. She would have agreed to anything to stop him hurting her.

Satisfied, he pulled her head back, twisting her hair even tighter.

Terrified, she waited. She could hear herself panting. Shallow gasps of breath.

He brought his face close to hers. 'I fucking hate you, you disgusting, ugly, fat bitch. It's no wonder that I can't stand coming back to this shithole and seeing your miserable cunt face.' He twisted the knot of hair in his fist tighter and tighter, until she screamed out in pain. Satisfied, he threw her to the floor.

She lay there, facedown, too scared to move. In front of her was a file. Three photographs had fallen out. She realised he must have dropped it when he had grabbed her. What fear she had dissipated, only to be replaced by a paralysing horror. She looked at the photograph closest to her. Her face . . . *Oh God, her face* . . . It had been so badly beaten. She looked at the next photograph. It was a brutal crisscross knife wound dug deep into the victim's chest. The third one was the worst: the victim's throat had been cut from side to side. She felt a wave of nausea, despite having dealt with equally gory traumas in

Accident and Emergency. But this was different. She recognised this woman. She was the one in the photograph that he carried around in his wallet. *It was her. The woman he obsessed about. The woman he wanted her to be ...*

But before she had time to fully process what she was looking at, an explosion of pain erupted in her lower back. It took her a second to make the connection that he had raised his foot and stamped on her spine.

She tried to breathe, but couldn't. The pain too crippling for her body to respond.

'Call yourself a wife? You're nothing but a lazy whore. I pay for everything around here while you fucking lie in bed doing nothing! DON'T I?'

She willed him to stop. But he didn't. She felt the next blow as he kicked her in the kidneys, the searing white pain so loud it drowned out his screams of contempt as he kicked her. Again, and again. Until she blacked out.

Chapter Seventeen

Harri had decided to call it quits and go home for a few hours' sleep. The rest of the team felt as enervated as she did. More officers had been called in to deal with the murder and to find the other unidentified victim, but at this precise moment they were no further forward. No closer to determining the identity of the killer. Even though they now had the identity of one of his victims; the one who was dead. As for the one who was alive, they had no idea yet who she was. *If she was still alive . . .*

Her phone rang. Harri checked who was calling her. It was the forensics laboratory. She had requested the photograph and the envelope sent by the killer be expedited. And if they found anything, to call her – immediately. It was late, but she expected no less given the seriousness of the situation; the other young woman in the wheelchair could potentially still be alive. *Unlike Tammy Summers.*

'Did you get anything?' Harri asked without waiting for an introduction.

'Yes. Two different sets of prints on the photograph,' a female voice answered.

Harri felt euphoric. She couldn't believe how lucky they had been. She had believed the killer would have worn gloves. It came as no surprise that there were two sets of prints; one of them would belong to her.

'What about the envelope?'

'Yes. Some partial prints, one of which matched a set found on the photograph. But the rest didn't match. Not surprising really considering the level of contamination it would have been subject to in the post.'

'Which prints matched with the photograph? Mine or the unknown suspect's?' Harri asked. She had warned the forensics lab that she had inadvertently handled the evidence and had submitted her own prints for cross-referencing.

'Yours. The other prints, which we have established as male, are only evident on the photograph. Even then I've only found partial prints so far. I'll keep at it, though. And if I do get a complete one, you'll be the first to hear.'

There had been exponential leaps in forensic science. One of them was a test that could determine whether fingerprints belonged to a man or a woman based on the amino acids left on them; the levels being twice as high in the sweat of women as in that of men.

Harri wondered why the killer would have handled the photograph without gloves on and yet place it in an envelope, stick an address label on it and post it with gloves on. It didn't make sense. Unless . . . *Unless someone was helping him? Was someone sending it from London for him to fool the police? To make the team think that their killer was based in the South, rather than here in the North?*

'Did you have time to examine the other photograph I sent?'

'I haven't had time yet.'

'Let me know when you get a chance. And thanks, I appreciate your help.' She cut the call.

Harri suddenly felt nauseous. She closed her eyes and waited for the feeling to pass. She hadn't expected there to be any prints or biological evidence left on the crime scene photograph of herself. He was too clever for that. After all, DI Mac O'Connor would be fully aware of the significance of forensic evidence.

She thought of the photograph of Tammy Summers. *Still alive . . . lying on that hospital bed.* Images of what the killer had done to her flooded her mind. She felt sickened at the unimaginable acts he had carried out. She was hopeful that they might be able to identify him with the prints forensics had found. Then they had a chance of saving the victim in the wheelchair. *Only if he is already in the system, though . . .*

Where are you, Mac? And why have you disappeared?

She stretched her bare legs out onto the wooden chest in front of the couch. She had forced herself to shower, and had changed into a T-shirt and pyjama shorts. Even though it was only the beginning of April, the night was milder than usual. She looked around the open-plan space. The lamp beside her threw out an eerie, shadowy light. She automatically checked each corner of the large room. Nothing.

It was just before midnight and she was more than tired, she was exhausted. But still, she couldn't settle. She took another drink. Noticed that half the bottle of wine was already gone. She glanced over at the deadbolted metal door. She had been facing it for the past hour, waiting. Just waiting for him to show himself. The baseball bat lay beside her on the couch.

She thought back to a year ago. To be precise, a year and a day. To when she had really believed she was going to die. During her attack she had clung onto life, promising herself that if she did live through it, she would eventually find him. Douglas wasn't the only one who was vigilant where her attacker was concerned. Not a day went by at work when she didn't check to see if anything had been entered into the database similar to what she had endured. Nothing had been reported to date. At least, until this morning's attack.

As for the text sent to her this morning, she had traced the mobile number to an unregistered phone. She took another drink of her wine as she thought about Douglas' concerns that the unidentified killer could be connected to her attack. The MO was different. *So why do* you *think it could be him?* She hadn't met him on some mobile phone dating app. Her attacker had stalked her. He had entered her ground floor flat with a set of keys that he had somehow managed to get. Had someone taken them from her locker at work and had a copy made? That was the only rational explanation that she could come up with. That was one of the reasons she had believed that it was someone at work; that one of her colleagues had held her at knife point, raped and assaulted her.

But who? DI Mac O'Connor? Why not? But then do you really think he could have killed Tammy Summers? If so why? To scare you?

Did she really believe Mac O'Connor could be Tammy Summers' killer? Maybe . . . But her rapist? *Yes.* His DNA had been recovered at the crime scene, as had the DNA of her close friends; including Anna Jackson and Harri's ex-boyfriend, both of whom had stayed overnight. But the recovery of Mac's DNA had been unexpected. After all, he had only been in her flat once, when he had walked her home two months before the attack. Harri had always questioned his motive for making his way to her flat and forcing himself into the crime scene. Especially after he had distanced himself from her following the night he had taken her home – the night he had crossed a line. Angry that she had rejected him, he had made it clear that he had wanted her off his team. Now that he was the SIO of her ongoing rape and assault case, it would be virtually impossible to prove he was her rapist. He had shrewdly put himself in a position where he would never be suspected.

She sighed. Rubbed her face. She was tired. She had gone over and over the reasons why Mac had forced entry into her flat – into what had become a crime scene. But to her there was only one answer – *he* was the rapist. She thought back to the night she had invited him in. They had had another drink together.

And then they had . . . Harri wasn't sure. Her memory was vague. She had been too drunk to remember the exact events. But she remembered that they had been close together on the couch, laughing about something ridiculous at work. Then the next moment, they had started to kiss. It had been gentle, explorative at first but had soon become filled with passion. Somehow they had ended up in her bedroom and that was when . . . She stared at the now-empty glass of wine she was holding. Her hand was trembling slightly. She forced herself to remember exactly what had happened after that. But all she could recollect was struggling with him and shouting for him to stop. To get out. Which he had done. Eventually. But she knew he had only pulled back out of fear that the neighbour above her would hear her screams. It was no surprise he would have covered himself. That he would have made an appearance as her concerned boss at the crime scene, to eliminate suspicion if DNA evidence was recovered in the room.

She put her glass down on the chest, deciding against another drink. She had had enough. And she had also had enough of rethinking the night she was raped. But it was easier said than done. Her mind would not let it go. *Why? What did you miss? Evidence? Something that would tell you the identity of your attacker?*

She thought of Mac; again. Couldn't help herself. When his DNA sample had been recovered at the crime scene – her bedroom – he had never explained that he had visited her flat before the investigation.

Harri understood perfectly why he had withheld that piece of intelligence – self-preservation. After all, it would make him a key suspect, regardless of his professional standing. But Mac had kept silent. He had instead allowed others to accept that his DNA was present from forcing his way into her bedroom only after it became a crime scene. She understood his silence and why he wanted her off the team – at whatever price. Since the rape, she had repeatedly questioned her decision to keep quiet about the night Mac had come back to her flat. It was simple: she had been crippled with fear that she would not be believed. There had been no witnesses, so it would have been her word against his; a DI, highly respected by both his colleagues and superiors alike. If she was honest, DC Anna Jackson's reaction when Harri had confided that she believed Mac was her rapist, had been enough to silence her. Enough to convince her that no one – not even a close colleague and friend – would believe her against him.

Harri thought back to that night when he had come back to her flat after the pub. He had forced himself on her, despite her resistance. What had really frightened her was the fact that the more she struggled, the more he persisted – the more he enjoyed it. His sexual aggression had terrified her. When he finally stopped, he had been furious with her. Blaming her for starting something that she had no right to end. She had often questioned whether her rape had simply been him finishing off what he had started that night.

She shuddered as a cold chill suddenly enveloped her body. Her mind turned to the photograph and text sent to her that morning. Could it have been Mac? For all she knew, he could be here somewhere, watching . . . stalking her. Or was it just coincidental that he had taken leave the day before; giving him the opportunity to come to Newcastle and hand-deliver the photograph taken of her after her assault? Now he was acting SIO of her case, he would have access to all the evidence – including the crime scene photographs.

She sighed. She could drive herself insane thinking about it. She then thought of the murder victim. She had been murdered by a sadistic misogynist who had tortured, physically altered and then murdered Tammy Summers. Could Mac be capable of such a horrific crime? *Maybe . . .*

He had effectively disappeared, giving him the opportunity to murder and dump the body. But Tammy Summers had vanished four months earlier; her killer had held her captive. He had not only imprisoned her, he had starved her to the extent that she had lost nearly half her body weight. That took time and planning. Could Mac have carried that out and continued his job as normal? *Maybe . . . Anything was possible. Especially considering the victim had been heavily sedated. Had the killer kept her in such a condition? If she had been drugged the killer could leave the victim for hours or days at a time.*

Harri shuddered at the thought. She noticed the barely touched chicken salad sandwich that she had thrown together. She had no appetite, which wasn't surprising. Stretching over to pick up the plate, she took a bite of the wholemeal bread. Forced herself to chew it. Winced at how dry it felt in her mouth. Then swallowed. She repeated this action until she had eaten half of it. She was acutely aware that she had the choice to eat – unlike the victims. Someone had taken that right away. The question plaguing her was, *who?*

Suddenly she heard a creak. It had come from the other side of the metal door. She listened, holding her breath as her heart notched up a few beats. Nothing. *Shit!* It was an old building. It creaked now and again. Wood expanded and contracted. Then she heard it again. It was coming from the floor below.

She reached for the baseball bat. All the floors were empty, apart from hers. Occasionally she would hear something. A noise. Indiscernible. It came with the territory when you lived in an old warehouse. Usually she would have music playing to make her feel more at ease. But not tonight. Instead she was shrouded in silence. The fact that the envelope had been hand-delivered had unnerved her. It meant that *he* knew where she lived. It wouldn't take much to realise that she was the only inhabitant in the building. *Stop it . . .*

Harri leaned her head right back against the brick wall behind her and thought about the victim. *Which one? Tammy Summers or the other woman in the photograph?* But it was the girl in the wheelchair who haunted her.

Her eyes had seemed to stare at Harri, beseeching her to help. *To save her from him . . .*

She looked down at the blurred black-and-white CCTV still of the Ford transit van in the open file spread across her knees. They had managed to find another shot of the van but they still couldn't make out the registration details. Nor did they have a clear image of the driver's face. However, they knew it was the right van as the driver was wearing a black ski mask, exactly as described by the witness.

It was now a waiting game. Other CCTV footage was still being scrutinised throughout the area. It would take them days to analyse all the surveillance footage. What struck her as odd was that the unknown suspect had appeared to have avoided the main roads. Not only that, it was as if he had known where the surveillance cameras were positioned throughout the city. Somehow, he had circumvented them. Did he have knowledge of their whereabouts? But how would he have access to this sort of intelligence?

She looked at the artist's sketch of the unknown suspect based on Samuel Riley's witness account. It made her skin crawl. A face in a black ski mask with slits for his eyes. It looked identical to the man who had attacked her. She remembered how he had whispered that he had fantasised about raping her. About holding her by her long blonde hair and staring into her green eyes as he raped her. Again. And again.

It's just a black ski mask . . . But you don't believe in coincidences, Harri.

Fuck . . . fuck.

She scrambled for her mobile. Picked it up. Found the number. Pressed dial before she could change her mind. Then waited as the phone connected. She listened as it rang and rang and rang. It cut to voicemail. *Where are you, Mac?*

DAY TWO
SATURDAY: 2ND APRIL

Chapter Eighteen

When she finally went to bed, it was after 2:00 a.m. She had been distracted by the commotion on the Tyne Bridge shortly after midnight. Furious sirens and flashing lights suggested someone had jumped into the unforgiving, black waters below. It wasn't an uncommon occurrence. It didn't take her long to fall into a restless sleep with the baseball bat held securely to her body. *Just in case.*

Harri woke up startled. She was drenched in sweat. Again. She had had the same recurring nightmare. It was always about that night, waking up to the feeling that someone was in her bedroom. Watching . . . waiting.

She glanced at the radio alarm clock. 6:01 a.m. *Shit!*

She had forgotten to set her alarm. She was late. She threw her quilt back and jumped up. She rushed over to the sink and turned on the cold tap. Let it run before throwing water over her face. The shock of the icy water hitting her skin startled her, forcing the night-mare into the dark recesses of her mind. She looked up at her face in the mirror above the sink, making a point of not letting her eyes drop to her neck. Or down to the angry crisscross scar above her left breast. She watched as water dripped down her pale cheeks. A few hours' sleep had done her some good. She didn't look as crap as she did yesterday, as she had done after countless disturbed nights. Typically she would wake up from the nightmare around four. Then she would lie awake, rigid with terror, feeling as if it had just happened all over again. She would wait for the alarm to go off at 5 a.m. and would go for a six-mile run before getting ready for work. But not this morning. For some inexplicable reason she had slept straight through until 6 a.m. That was unheard of.

She turned to the window. A messy, blood red dawn was emerging over the black river. She walked over and looked out at the arc of the Tyne Bridge. It was already swamped by burnished headlights as cars either headed into the city, or left, driving south. For a moment she wondered if she would ever return to London.

Maybe. Maybe the day Mac O'Connor leaves the Met.

When she had left the North East at the age of eighteen, she had never intended to return. And yet, here she was on a Saturday morning, getting ready to go into work in an apartment she had bought overlooking Newcastle's Quayside. She had committed herself to a place that she had run as far away from as possible twelve years ago. Why had she come back here? Because it was the only place that made her feel safe. But she was acutely aware that childhood memories couldn't protect her. No one could – apart from herself. Maybe she had made a mistake in coming back? After all, she had no family here. No friends. Just ghosts.

She thought of her father; DSI George Jacobs. He had died in the line of duty. *He didn't just die* . . . She bit down on her lip, hard. It still felt too raw. Too painful to remember. She had been a daddy's girl; an only child. Her father had meant everything to her – and vice versa. Her adoration of him had influenced her choice of profession. More so after his death. Her mother had never quite managed to be a part of their relationship. She had always been on the periphery, watching them; jealously watching them. Her exclusion was not intentional on either Harri or her father's part, she just hadn't fitted in. She had been too different from them: cold, uncommunicative, sad. *Or was that after he had died?*

Harri couldn't remember. She couldn't remember her mother before her father's death. Whatever memories she had of her childhood centred on him. They were happy, joyous memories filled with laughter and unconditional love, but the absence of her mother was significant.

She let her eyes drift away from the warm glow of the moving lights across the bridge to the oily deep river below. She shivered as she remembered her mother. She wished she hadn't.

She went over to the kitchen space. She needed a coffee. Then a shower. Then she would head into work, deciding that she didn't have time to run now. She switched the kettle on. Looked around the empty apartment. She liked the space. The solitude. It was starting to feel like home. She was beginning to feel safe here. While the kettle boiled she walked over to her vinyl collection. Decided to blast out some music while she still could without annoying any neighbours. She bent down and fingered through the LPs. She surprised herself as she was reminded of what she had collected over the years. At least half of them had belonged to her father. She decided on Lou Reed's *Transformer*. She placed the needle at the beginning of the third track – 'Perfect Day'. She stood still for a moment, waiting with anticipation as the needle flitted over the scratches, giving out a husky crackling through the amps. Then she smiled as she heard Lou Reed's hoarse voice begin to sing. In that moment she felt more alive than she had done in a long time. She had survived. *He* hadn't come back as he had promised. 1st April had ended. Nothing had happened – at least not to her.

Her smile faded when she heard the final lyrics of the song. The words stung her. *Was she going to reap what she had sowed?*

Chapter Nineteen

She bent over the toilet bowl and vomited. She watched as blood trickled down the pristine white porcelain. The pain of throwing up had exhausted her. The searing explosion in her side every time she breathed suggested that he had broken her ribs.

She lay down on her side, resting her head on a towel she had placed on the tiled floor. Spit mingled with blood dribbled out the corner of her mouth. She left it there, feeling too faint to wipe it away. She closed her eyes and willed herself unconscious. Anything to take away the constant pain. The last thing she remembered was him stamping on her back. Then nothing.

When she had come to, she had still been lying in the hallway, in her own blood and a pool of cold piss. She had gingerly touched her face and felt several gashes across her forehead, a deep cut above her eye and one across the bridge of her nose. She could only assume that he had raised her head back to see if she was conscious and then smashed her face off the floor in an attempt to wake her. It hadn't worked.

She had somehow managed to crawl to the downstairs bathroom, which was where she now lay. The light coming through the window suggested that it was morning. She knew she had to force herself to get up and assess the damage to her face, to her body. And then clean up the mess on the floor – her mess. That was what he called it when she bled, or vomited because he had punched her too hard. She had only once peed herself, and that had been in absolute terror when he woke her in the middle of the night, blinding her with a torch as he poured a two-litre bottle of water over her face, forcing it up her nostrils and down the back of her throat. Waterboarding was a technique used as an act of torture; one that he had had no qualms inflicting upon her. She was well aware of the parallels between torture and hostage victims and ones of domestic violence – the only difference being that prisoners had the hope of being freed.

She could feel the tears threatening again. But she wouldn't let herself cry. Not this time. This time she refused to feel sorry for herself. To waste away in her own pity. She realised no one was going to help her now. She was on her own, and from the beating he had meted out, she knew she didn't have long before he crossed the line – before he actually beat her to death. She hated him more than life itself. And that was what she had to focus on. She had to stay strong if she was going to survive.

But how?

She wasn't stupid – despite what he called her. She knew the statistics regarding domestic violence. She had been prepped to look out for the signs when she had trained as a nurse. Then when she had started work in

Accident and Emergency, she had seen first-hand the effects of domestic violence, never once believing that she herself would become a victim. In England and Wales two women were killed each week as a result of domestic violence. The last thing she wanted was to become part of that statistic. She was also aware that on average a woman would be assaulted thirty-five times before making her first call to the police. She had endured well over that figure and still she hadn't contacted anyone. She couldn't; he kept her locked inside the house with no access to a phone. His reason – he didn't trust her.

But this wasn't about her any more . . .

This was about the victim she had seen in the photos on the floor. The blonde-haired, green-eyed woman whose photograph he kept in his wallet. She had heard him on his mobile as she had started to come round. Realising that he was sitting on the stairs talking, she had remained on the floor feigning unconsciousness. He was getting ready to leave. He had a holdall and some other things that she couldn't make out. But she had distinctly heard him say that he had been preparing for this moment for a long time. She had tried not to react as she heard him say that he would make her relive the night she had been raped and had her throat slit. That he would finish what he had started.

Panicking, she tried to remember his conversation on the phone when he came in, before he had lost his temper. He had mentioned the murdered girl on the news.

The file he had dropped on the floor. The photographs.

You're being ridiculous ...

She blocked out the words she had heard. *Or thought she had heard.* For he had said he was going to kill the woman in the photograph. *The woman he was obsessed with ... the woman he had tried to change her into.*

Chapter Twenty

Harri came out of Douglas' office. She had just had the unpleasant job of updating him. The lab had called back to say they had found a complete print on the photograph of Tammy Summers. A print and a DNA sample was more than the team had hoped to find, but that was where it ended. Neither matched anything held on the database. The killer had never been detained by the police. So they still had nothing. On either the murder suspect, or the other victim. Harri felt somehow that she had failed to deliver. But it was not for want of trying. Everyone was busting a gut trying to find something; anything, regardless of how tenuous. Police officers were out in force knocking on doors in the streets surrounding Jesmond Metro and the crime scene. But so far, no one had seen anything. Their only witness was James Riley. All the information they had regarding the killer's appearance had been sourced from him and the size-eleven footprints that Munroe had found at the crime scene.

The postmark on the envelope was London. Whether that was where the killer resided was questionable. If he did, then why travel north to Newcastle to dump the victim? It didn't make sense. Unless it was personal. Did that mean he had a connection to the city?

Harri had been relieved that Douglas had mentioned nothing more about a connection between her attack and Tammy Summers' murder. It meant that she could keep her head down and continue working on the murder investigation. She needed to track down the girl in the photograph before it was too late. There was something about her face, the way her eyes had stared at the camera – the killer – defiantly, that had touched a nerve. Harri had felt an inexplicable connection with her. She wanted to make sure that she found her – alive.

Harri walked down the corridor, heading for the large open-plan office. She had some leads she wanted to follow up herself before taking a late lunch. She had come into work at 7:00 a.m. and despite not stopping, she felt as if she hadn't achieved anything. Also the station had been more chaotic than usual. On top of the expected Friday night crimes, two suicides had been reported. Both had happened in public, before midnight. One suicide victim had jumped in front of a train at Newcastle Central Station, and another had jumped off the Tyne Bridge. That was why she had heard such a commotion down on the Quayside just after midnight. But it was the suicide victim's jump off the Tyne Bridge that had caught everyone's imagination; he had doused himself in petrol and set himself alight before climbing up onto the edge of the bridge and then plummeting to the black waters below. Footage of the man consumed in a ball of flame falling to his death had been uploaded onto YouTube by one of the multiple witnesses who had filmed the suicide on their phones. Harri was relieved that she wasn't dealing with it. She couldn't begin to imagine how his family would be coping with the knowledge that his horrific death had gone viral. Human nature never failed to surprise her. She thought of the depravities that Tammy Summers must have been subject to for the past four months of her life. In particular, the last few hours before her death.

Harri reached the open doorway of the office. She could hear the murmur of voices filtering out into the hallway. Some relaxed, others more formal, as if on the phone. She walked in. It seemed as if everyone stopped talking as she did so as if they had made the connection between her own assault and the murder victim, but she knew that was not the case. It just felt like it. Then she noticed a brown envelope identical to the one delivered yesterday. The one from the killer. It was sitting on her desk. A cold chill trickled down her back to the base of her spine. She forced herself to act normal and walk over to her desk. She looked at the printed address label on the envelope. It was identical to yesterday's. Same postmark: London. It suggested he had an accomplice. Unless he had returned to London after dumping the body early the previous morning. It was possible. *Anything is possible right now.*

Harri dragged her chair out and sat down behind her desk. She pulled open her drawer and took out a pair of latex gloves from a box. She put them on. Slowly. Carefully. Willing her hands not to shake, she picked up the envelope. It was addressed directly to her, again. She opened it. Put her hand inside, readied herself. She pulled out the contents. Again, one photograph. She looked at it. It was of an emaciated girl wearing a hospital gown in an old-fashioned wheelchair. An IV was inserted in her arm and the portable IV stand was positioned to the side.

It's her ... The girl in the photograph sent yesterday. Shit ... SHIT.

Harri didn't want to think about what this meant, but she had no choice. She had been expecting this. This meant the girl was dead. Or, that she would be soon. But yesterday she had received the photograph *after* Tammy Summers' body had been discovered. *Has he changed the rules?* She felt physically sick. *Her eyes ... Blank. Lifeless. As if she had given up. As if she knew what was coming next ... The defiance, the fight had gone.*

A feeling of desperation consumed her. She had wanted to find her. To save her. She knew what it felt like to be held captive and subject to someone else's perversities, not knowing whether you would survive. Not knowing what he would do to you next.

Harri recalled the night of her attack. She could feel it. Breathe it. Touch it; it felt so real.

He had twisted her arms behind her back and hand-cuffed her. As if expecting to still see the marks, she looked at her wrists. There was nothing there – not any more. She rubbed her right wrist, remembering how badly bruised and cut it had been. For she had struggled. *Fuck, how she had struggled.* She reminded herself that this was not about her. This was about some sick bastard who had some young woman held captive. Who had already murdered once. And who was now blatantly goading the police – goading *her*?

Harri had to force herself to face the question; was what was happening connected to her? *Is it, Harri? Is he torturing them and killing them because of you? Because he can't get you?*

She looked back at the photograph. Her eyes rested on the identity tag held in the victim's bony hand. It read 'Subject B. T.O.D.: 2 April C.O.D.: Starvation'.

Fuck . . . FUCK!

She was still holding her breath as she stared at the girl's face, realising that she was more than likely dead; they just hadn't found her yet. Or if she wasn't dead, chances were she would be by the end of the day, because they had nothing on the killer. Nothing that could tell the police where to even start searching.

She finally exhaled. Tried to think about it objectively. She couldn't get emotional. If the girl was dead, then she would have to deal with it. It didn't detract from the fact she had a job to do; to catch the sick son of a bitch. But one question kept plaguing Harri: *Why you? Why is he sending* you *the photographs?* But she knew the answer. It was her rapist. He had returned to kill her. But first, he was having some fun with her – *at the victims' expense.*

She knew that Douglas would be asking the same question – *why you?* She needed a plausible answer. One that would prevent her from being removed from the investigation. For if she was seen as a target, she would be immediately suspended. She remembered the text she had been sent yesterday, and the photograph of herself. She was being targeted, but she had no choice but to deal with it. Instead of being the hunted, she needed to remain the hunter.

Harri carefully held the photo in her gloved hand and pushed her chair back. She needed to take this to Douglas. It changed everything. *She had a really bad feeling that the girl in the photograph would be found before the day was over . . . Dead.*

'Talk to me,' Douglas instructed.

The station was on high alert. The murder team had been briefed, as had uniform. It was now a waiting game. All leave had been suspended and every available officer was on duty. They had extra uniform out on the city streets looking for anything unusual. But nothing. *So far.*

Harri sighed, shook her head. 'What do you want me to say?'

She was sitting in Douglas' office. On his desk lay the most recent photograph.

No call had come in – yet. So they were hopeful that the young woman was still alive. But with each minute that passed, that hope was fading. The photograph was a threat. One that Douglas was taking seriously – very seriously.

'Can you think of any reason why the victim was dumped on the pathway off Eslington Road?'

'Maybe because he knew that the path is well used by commuters? It leads straight to Jesmond Metro, which means the body would definitely be found.'

Douglas frowned. 'It's a risky strategy, don't you think? He was running the risk of being spotted. Which he was, by a student cutting through on his way home.'

'But the killer wasn't bothered, sir. He talked to the witness. He didn't know whether or not the witness would be able to recall what he said.'

'What does that tell you?' asked Douglas.

'That he was confident he could handle himself against the witness. Also he's arrogant. He's playing with us. He wanted a witness to see him. To pass his description on to the police. Also I imagine whatever he said to James Riley would have been of some significance.'

Douglas considered what she said.

'He thinks he has outwitted us, sir,' Harri continued. 'That we won't be able to apprehend him. After all, what do we have? A description of a tall, athletic male dressed in black, wearing new trainers and a black ski mask. He was even confident enough to not wear gloves when he handled the photographs, aware that he has never been arrested before and, I suspect, arrogant enough to believe that he will never be caught.'

'The question is, why? Why is he so cocky?'

Harri shrugged. 'Because he really believes he will not get caught. He had the knowledge to circumvent the surveillance cameras throughout the city. He completely eluded us. So far we have only a couple of images from one security camera but there is not enough detail in the shot for us to get a registration number or a clear image of his face. I think this was planned. The route towards and away from Jesmond Metro was executed with precision.'

'I'm not so sure . . . Maybe he was lucky?'

'I disagree. The only footage we have of the van is on Eslington Road. Why not leave the van parked in the back lane between Eslington Road and Eslington Terrace so it would be hidden? Why park it on Eslington Road directly in front of the building next to Castle High School where it would be recorded?'

'Because he did not expect anyone there, Harri. It's a non-residential area. A lot of those buildings are business premises. At one end of it you have Jesmond Parish Church and Church House School and at the other end Castle High School before the road leads onto Eslington Terrace. He dumped the body in the early hours of the morning. The metro line had been closed for hours. I am sure that the student took him by surprise. But I agree with you that his reaction was not one of fear, but of arrogance. Of wanting to be seen.'

'He's playing with us. He wants us to see him. But he was wearing a black ski mask so his face could not be seen.' Harri thought about the significance of the mask. She was starting to feel a sliver of unease at the thought he was out there; waiting for her. The image of the victim in the wheelchair haunted her.

'Harri?'

She realised that she must have looked as sickened as she felt. She had to shake the unease off. The last thing she wanted to do was to alert Douglas' suspicions. 'I'm fine, just need to eat something, that's all. As for the suspect, he wanted the witness to see him, but he didn't want his movements noted and he managed it, even though there are over 900 council CCTV cameras in the city, from public buildings to car parks. Then we have private businesses with security cameras too. I just don't understand how he managed to avoid detection.'

'You think there is a chance he is a council employee? Someone with access to this intelligence?'

'I don't know,' Harri answered. It was an honest reply, because she had no idea how he had effectively disappeared without trace. The only camera footage they had of the white transit van was from a private security camera positioned at the entrance of the large building next to the school. It had been converted into apartments and was one of the few residential buildings on that street, but unfortunately none of the occupants had witnessed anything. The image was also blurred and of poor quality. The camera's function was to film whoever approached the entrance, not the road or the path directly opposite.

'At this point we're looking into all possibilities, as you know.'

She nodded. She was not the only one who had found it odd that in a city with 900 CCTV cameras, the unknown suspect had been able to disappear. Douglas had ordered details on anyone within the council who could have access to CCTV camera locations. But Harri had a gut feeling he was wasting resources. She couldn't shake the thought that the killer was much closer to home than either of them realised.

'You used to live around that area, didn't you?' Douglas asked.

Harri tried to gauge why exactly he was asking before answering. She nodded, without giving him a direct response.

'Your father mentioned he lived in Jesmond once, that's all,' Douglas explained.

Harri didn't quite believe him. 'There's no connection, sir.'

'I wasn't implying that. It was just a detail I recalled.'

Harri looked him straight in the eye. 'I left the area shortly after my father died.'

Douglas nodded sympathetically.

Not that Harri wanted his sympathy. All she wanted was for him to stop trying to make a connection between the killer and her. 'I don't see the relevance between where I lived as a child and where the killer left the victim. And just for the record, I lived a fifteen-minute walk from Jesmond Metro station.' She had not been to the house since the day she left for University. That was twelve years ago. And even after so many years, the idea of returning still filled her with dread. It was something she never intended to do – ever.

'And there is nothing about the area where the killer dumped the body that strikes a chord with you?'

Again Harri could feel herself bristling at the question. 'No, sir.'

'Fine. I was just hoping that if this young woman has been . . .' Douglas faltered as he considered what could have already happened to the girl in the wheelchair. '. . . been left somewhere, you might have an idea where?'

Harri was surprised, but forced herself not to react. In truth she did not have a clue about where the killer would dump his next victim. 'I have no suggestions, sir.'

Douglas nodded as if he had expected that response.

'I know the killer is addressing the envelopes to me, but that is as far as it goes. Like you, I have no clue who he is. Nor do I understand why he is sending me photographs,' Harri lied. 'No one wants to catch this bastard more than me. Especially before he lays a hand on another . . . on her.' She was about to say 'young woman', but the body was so atrophied that it looked more like that of a young, starving girl.

Harri stared at the photograph. The desperately sad image filled her with a paralysing helplessness; a foreboding that it was already too late for her – *for them*.

Douglas sat back in his seat. 'Tammy Summers went to London. We assume she met the killer. That suggests he brought her up from London.' His eyes glanced down at the London postmark on the envelope. 'Either he has an accomplice who is posting these for him, or after he dumped her body he drove back down to post this new photograph.'

'Either one is a possibility. We're still running checks against white transit vans registered in this area and London. But . . .' Harri shrugged. 'It will take some time to compile a list and then we need something more than we have to narrow it down.'

Douglas sighed. Harri looked at him. He didn't seem to have slept.

'Is everything OK?' Harri asked. Before Douglas could reply she added, 'And I don't mean with the job, I mean personally?'

Douglas couldn't hide his weariness as he met Harri's concerned gaze. 'I'm fine. I've just got a lot on at the moment. We've got one murder victim and the threat of a second one at the hands of a sadistic killer we have no leads on. A killer who is intent on proving he can outwit us. Which is exactly what he is doing.'

Harri didn't say anything. There was nothing she could add.

'No matches back on the missing person's reports?'

'Not yet, sir.' Harri felt his desperation. The whole team did. She had set Robertson and Michaels the task of searching through all missing person's reports over the past year, trying to match the pixelated image of the victim's face. Harri had instructed them to narrow the search down by looking for larger women aged sixteen to twenty-four, but she had been surprised by how many fell into this category. She had read a study recently that stated that more than two-thirds of men and almost six in ten women in the UK were either overweight or obese. All they had to go on was a pixelated image of the victim and the photograph they had just been sent. She had scrutinised the photograph of the victim to see if she could see any loose skin, which would indicate extreme weight loss. It had proven too difficult to make out. But Harri had a hunch that the killer had a 'type' and that the first victim, Tammy Summers, fitted exactly what he wanted – a clinically obese young woman whose body he could radically change. This was about completely altering the victim. Recreating her so to speak. It would be too easy to target a physically petite victim. Harri was certain that the killer got immense pleasure out of starving his victims. For he was in control of every aspect of their bodies. It was part of the game for him. Taking someone and completely changing them into . . . *Who, Harri? You?*

She thought about Tammy Summers and how different she had looked in her missing person's photograph to the image the killer had sent of her lying immobile on a hospital bed with an intravenous drip in her arm. So much so her own father would never have recognised her. She was half her previous weight. Her large voluptuous body had disappeared, replaced by sagging folds of loose skin that hung from her emaciated frame.

Douglas gave Harri a resigned look. 'Here's hoping we have more to go on at the briefing later.'

Harri took that as permission to leave, so she stood up.

'One last thing, if anything suspicious happens you'll let me know immediately?'

'Of course, sir,' she answered.

Douglas narrowed his eyes. 'I don't think it is a fluke that the killer is sending the photographs to you, Harri. He's chosen you for a reason.'

She suddenly felt sick. She waited for Douglas to say that he had no choice but to remove her from the investigation.

Instead, he shook his head, clearly not comfortable with the situation. 'Just make sure you tell me if anything happens, no matter how ridiculous, let me know. Any time of the day or night, you can call me. OK?'

Harri nodded at Douglas, her countenance impassive despite the tumult of emotions she was feeling. She left the room feeling like crap. She had withheld information. But until she had conclusive evidence that Tammy Summers' killer was indeed the same person who had raped and threatened to kill her, then she had no choice but to keep quiet. It was simply self-preservation. She needed to be on the job – the hunter, not the hunted.

Harri closed the door behind her. She heard Douglas' phone ring, then his assertive voice answering it. Then she felt her own phone vibrate. Pulled it out from her jeans pocket. Checked it. It was a text from the same unknown mobile number. She clicked it open:

Do you know who I am yet, Harri? I'm closer than you realise.

She stared at it, forcing herself not to react as two of the team walked past chatting. She looked at them. Wondered whether it was them. But she knew it couldn't be.

Shit ... Shit ...

She had hoped it had gone away – that he had gone. But *it* hadn't. *He* hadn't.

She looked again at the words: *I'm closer than you realise ...*

Chapter Twenty-One

She sat perfectly still and waited. There was no one left to keep her company. He had taken her away – the one he had called 'Subject B'. The other one didn't count. Not any more. She looked down at the skeletal body lying, twisted, on the floor. Her sick-smelling skin, now the colour of parchment, clung desperately to her brittle bones. She envied her oblivion. She might as well be dead. Her body had fallen to the floor, slipping through his hands as he had attempted to transfer her from her bed to the wheelchair.

She squeezed her eyes shut against the noise. Every so often it played on a loop in her head. A disturbance that she couldn't drown out. The snapping of bones against the hard, wooden floorboards. Then the screaming. High-pitched and animal-like; so far removed from any human sound that she had not realised it was coming from the other girl's crumpled, pitiful body.

The noise had abated – for now. Relieved, she opened her eyes again. Willed her to wake up. *Wake up or die . . .* But she did neither. She just lay there on the floor, eyes open, broken. She knew what was going to happen to this girl. What he would do to her. *For she was useless now . . .*

The tears continued to slide down her sunken cheeks as she waited. For him.

Because he's coming back for her. I can feel it . . .

She had been in the wheelchair facing the unresponsive girl for hours now. *Or was it weeks . . . months?* Time made no sense to her. Not any more.

Days blurred into nights in the blink of an eye.

Her chest felt damp. Cold. Uncomfortable. She couldn't move her hand to wipe away the tears. So they continued to fall onto her hospital gown, soaking through to her slack skin.

Her eyes shifted from the floor to one of the beds – 'Subject B's'. It had been stripped bare. *When had she gone? She tried to remember. Then it came back. The unimaginable acts. The sound of the scalpel scraping against the metal table as it cut through her flesh. Then the toxic smell, followed by choking. Her gasps for air. Her struggle to live. Then . . . nothing.*

Now there was just her and the one who was already dead on the inside. The one who lay oddly twisted on the floor. She was neither living nor dead and knew nothing of what was to come.

She thought of the countless graves outside the sanatorium. *So many . . . So many of them.*

The screech of a needle being dragged across an old LP brought her back. Crackling and static filled the ward as the antiquated gramophone began playing the melancholic piano score composed by Debussy in 1890. It was a magical piece with a dreamlike quality that should have instilled a sense of serenity, but instead all she felt was terror as the needle dragged itself over the vinyl.

He was back. A faint smile crossed her lips. She knew he would return. He always did.

She couldn't see him. She was positioned with her back to the double wooden doors. But she felt the rush of cold ward as he threw the windows open wide to cleanse the ward. The smell had become putrid. She breathed in. Savoured the freshness. She opened her mouth to taste the cold, sweet air.

Suddenly she felt him behind her. Then the tape pressed hard against her cracked and bleeding lips. The shock resonated through her. She knew why. She knew what was coming next. He wanted to make sure she couldn't scream. For he was going to make her watch him altering one of them – again. She was confused. It didn't make any sense.

There was only her and the patient lying on the floor with the broken body left.

She tried to lick at the duct tape, to push it back with her tongue. But her tongue was too swollen and cleaved to the parched roof of her mouth. She watched, helpless, as he lifted the broken one up from the floor. She heard a loud snap of bone as he forced the body upright in the wooden wheelchair. He pushed her head back to stop it lolling forward; her neck was broken.

She watched as he stood back and took a photograph. Just as he had with the other two. But unlike the others, her unblinking eyes were glazed and unfocused. Her neck twisted at an odd, eerie angle. It would look as if she was already dead. But she knew that the girl with the broken body wasn't that fortunate.

Oh God, for her sake, please let her not feel anything ...

Then he left her sitting contorted in the wheelchair facing the open windows. He walked over, stood behind her own chair. He spun her around and started wheeling her towards the double doors. Panic overwhelmed her.

Take her ... Take her! Not me! She won't feel anything ... PLEASE! NOT ME!

But he didn't hear her. The black duct tape kept her screams repressed.

The gramophone continued to play its scratchy, haunting melody as he wheeled her out the doors and down the ramp to the ground floor. He then turned the wheelchair and pushed her along the hallway heading towards the stairs leading down to the basement.

NO! NOT ME! Please ... not me.

Tears rolled down her terrified face. She knew what was waiting down there – *the cutting slab.*

Chapter Twenty-Two

'It's not her!'

Robertson and Michaels both turned from their computer screens as she burst into the CID computer room.

'Sarge?' asked Robertson.

Harri handed them each an enlarged image of the girl in the wheelchair's face. 'This is from the photograph sent this morning, right?'

'That's who we have been searching for in the missing person's files. But it's difficult as she would have looked very different then,' Robertson answered.

'That's if she was even reported missing,' Michaels pointed out.

'No. Listen to me. The picture is different from the one yesterday.'

'I know, the image yesterday was really poor quality,' Robertson said.

'You're not listening to me. Look closely at this image,' Harri instructed as she handed Robertson the photo from the previous day. 'Can you see that her face is different?'

Robertson frowned. 'Not seeing it, Sarge.'

'Look. See? The shape of the nose is different.'

'I dunno, it's really difficult to tell. Maybe ... maybe not.'

'Let me have a look,' Michaels said. He studied both images, then shook his head. 'Fifty-fifty if I'm honest. I would get someone to scan them in and see if they match.'

'Stuart in computer forensics has already done that. Despite the poor resolution of the reflection of the victim in the mirror, they are definitely not the same person.'

'Shit!' muttered Robertson. He looked first at Michaels and then at Harri. 'So you're saying he has two unidentified victims, not one?'

The look on her face was enough. To distract herself from the text she had spent some time scrutinising the photographs in case she could glean some information about their location. It was then that she had realised there was a slight discrepancy between the victim's face – or *faces*. She had taken the images to Stuart and then spent the last ten minutes updating Douglas, who hadn't taken it well. She had been instructed to find something tangible on the victims' identities, which meant looking through lists and lists of missing person data. Understanding why the killer chose a victim involved knowing the victim's backstory. In other words, victimology; the more you understood what made someone a target, the closer you came to finding your killer.

'Fuck!' muttered Michaels.

'Now tell me you've found something close to a match?'

'We've got about a hundred maybes and that's what we're working through now, Sarge,' answered Robertson, stretching his arms out and yawning.

'OK. Let me see what you've got,' Harri said as she pulled over a chair.

Robertson clicked from one missing person's photograph to another. She scrutinised each one and before she realised it twenty or so faces had disappeared in front of her, replaced by countless more.

'Stop. Go back,' Harri instructed.

Robertson did so.

'Yes. Her.' Harri looked at the photograph of the missing female. Robertson and Michaels had been right when they had said that it was difficult to match the severely emaciated faces in the two photographs with the missing persons on file.

He had completely altered them ... starved them beyond recognition.

'Let me read her details,' Harri said.

'Sure,' answered Robertson as he brought them up. 'What exactly are you looking for, Sarge?'

'For someone that reminds me of Tammy Summers.'

Michaels shot her a puzzled look. 'Why?'

'Because there was something about Tammy Summers that made her get on a train and go to another city to be with a man she knew nothing about.'

Robertson laughed. 'You're just out of touch, Sarge. Happens all the time. People hook up for a night, or even just a couple of hours for sex with complete strangers. Most times they don't use their real names. Sometimes they don't even exchange names. There's loads of dating apps for that kind of thing.'

'You'd know about that, wouldn't you?' scoffed Michaels.

'What? Don't act all innocent with me. I've seen your profile on loads of dating websites mate! Reckon you need to rethink your profile photo of you with your mam, like!' Robertson laughed as he chucked an empty polystyrene cup at Michael's head. 'You bloody loser!'

Harri suddenly saw the connection. 'Can you increase the size,' she said.

Robertson and Michaels continued messing around.

Harri turned to them. 'Stop fucking around! I'm trying to work here!'

'Yes, Sarge,' answered Robertson, trying to hold in his amusement.

'Louisa McPherson . . . *Where did you disappear to?*' asked Harri as she stared at the young, pretty face.

'What makes you think she could be one of the victims?' Robertson asked, frowning as he enlarged the image of twenty-year-old Louisa McPherson. 'She's a nice-looking lass. Not the usual mingers that we get on here.'

Harri shot him a look.

'Sorry, like. But you know what I mean? She looks normal. As if she's not been in trouble or anything.'

Harri knew perfectly well what Robertson was referring to – it was fair to say that most young missing persons came from a challenging background; they might have grown up in council care, had an abusive parent, step-parent or an alcoholic or drug-addicted parent. Most cases, they had something to run away from – not to.

'Because it says here that she had an all-right life. She wasn't running from anything; or at least anything obvious. She was a second-year psychology student in London. Her sister reported her missing two months ago. Louisa McPherson is originally from Newcastle . . .' Harri faltered as she read the next-of-kin details.

'Robertson, grab your coat. You're coming with me.'

'Fucking loser!' he mouthed at Michaels as he jumped up.

'Michaels, you're looking for someone who is atypical for a missing person. Stable family life. Job or college even. Tammy Summers had no reason to leave home. She was adored by her father and, I assume, her brothers. The key here is that she was seen as a low-risk missing person because she had run off with boyfriends in the past. What was it about her that made her go?'

Michaels shrugged.

'Because she met someone on a dating app who said all the right words. That's what. She trusted him. Why wouldn't she? Nothing bad had ever happened to her. And that will be exactly the same with the two other victims. I guarantee it.'

'I don't follow. You're saying that they're desperate to get a bloke to love them?' Robertson asked.

'No. That's not what I'm saying. But this exceptionally hot-looking guy hits on her. Says all the right things. I mean, for all we know he has done his research and checked out her social media profiles. He knows what to say to make her feel comfortable with him. To make her trust him. For her to believe that he could be the one because he seems to know her. He'd fake a unique connection between them, one he built by using the stuff she has posted. Think about it. Tammy's mum died from cancer when she was five. I bet he said his mum had died when he was young too. He will have used whatever he could to get into her head and for her to trust him. Ultimately, with her life.'

'How do you know all that?' Robertson asked, frowning.

'Because he thinks he's a clever bastard and every part of this has been a game to him. I bet he is good-looking in the flesh and really charismatic. It would have been too easy for him so he's made the game more challenging. I would suggest he's been used to having women throw themselves at him—'

'Sure it's not Robertson that you're talking about, Sarge?' laughed Michaels.

'Fuck you!' Robertson replied.

'For God's sake, will the two of you shut the fuck up?'

They both looked at her. 'Right. You,' Harri said to Michaels, 'better have something for me when I get back. So pull your finger out your arse and start looking for our other victim.'

'Yes Sarge,' Michaels answered. 'Which one?' he asked, confused, looking between the two photographs.

'I won't know until I get Stuart to run these two images

and compare them to Louisa McPherson. So for now we're still looking for two missing persons.'

Michaels nodded and turned back to his computer screen.

'Right, let's leave Michaels to get some work done. You, with me,' Harri instructed Robertson.

She was sitting in Abbi McPherson's Victorian terraced flat in Jesmond. It was now midday. It was a decent-sized property with panoramic views over Jesmond Dene. She took a sip of the freshly ground Italian coffee that Louisa McPherson's older sister had made them. Robertson stood looking out the window. He had his hands behind his back as he scrutinised the CID pool car parked below.

'It's a really safe neighbourhood, Detective,' Abbi McPherson told Robertson. 'Your only worry is the old lady downstairs who isn't that good at parking. My car takes a few knocks every time she attempts to reverse in.'

Harri looked around the flat. Photographs of the two sisters dominated the room. What was also obvious was that Louisa McPherson fitted the suspect's type: a pretty girl with long dark-brown hair, brown eyes, five foot three and physically large – very large, unlike her sister. Harri couldn't help but notice the uncanny resemblance between Louisa McPherson and Tammy Summers before both young women had disappeared.

'Your parents?' Harri asked.

'They're dead. Car accident abroad. Work-related trip and . . .' She shrugged it off.

Harri could see that years of repeating the same line to people had taken the edge off. Or at least, that was how Abbi McPherson wanted it to appear. She had built such an impenetrable wall that the fact her sister was missing did not seem to even cause a ripple of emotion.

But Harri knew that underneath that thick layer of resilient armour was a young woman screaming in agony. For she recognised the signs. The blank, glazed look as she repeated a personal tragedy as if it was too trivial to really mention.

'Is this you and your sister?' Robertson asked as he picked up a photograph off the windowsill.

She turned and looked over. Nodded. 'Louisa must have been six then and I was ten, nearly eleven. We had just moved from London to Northumberland to live with our grandmother. She did everything she could for us. Bought us ponies. She had the land for stables and grazing. She spoilt us really,' Abbi recalled, smiling.

Harri could see the first crack of emotion in her smile. Robertson nodded.

'You reported Louisa missing, when?' Harri asked now the civilities were over.

'Nearly eight weeks ago now.'

'Do you have any idea where she would have gone?'

'She told me two days before she disappeared that she had met this guy on some dating app and that they had just "clicked" and he was "the one". Her words, not mine. I wasn't convinced.'

'Why not?' asked Harri.

'He seemed too good to be true. When she sent me a picture I really started to question his motive.'

'Do you have the photo?'

She nodded. Stretched over and picked up her mobile up from the table where she had also placed the cafetière and plate of untouched biscuits.

She offered the phone to Harri. 'See? Too good to be true. But Louisa wouldn't listen to me. She thought I was insinuating that because she was so fat . . .' She paused, as if surprised she had actually articulated those words, 'I mean big, that someone as good-looking as him wouldn't be interested in her. But that wasn't what I meant. It was a whole combination of things that made me sceptical. Anyway, we had a huge argument and I haven't heard from her since.'

'So you reported her missing?'

'Yes, but it wasn't taken seriously once the police had talked to her Uni tutor. He said that a few days before I reported her missing she had requested a year's leave to go backpacking around the world. They accepted that.'

'You didn't?'

'Of course not. I expressly stated to the police that Louisa and I had had a huge argument which was unheard of for us, and that I was concerned about a new boyfriend of hers. But my concerns weren't taken seriously. I even contacted her tutor to see if he could persuade Louisa to postpone her travelling plans until she had finished her degree.'

'How did the tutor respond?'

'He was sympathetic of course. But he, like the police, expressed no concerns over Louisa's refusal to answer my calls or texts, or the fact that her Facebook page had not been updated for a few days. He said that Louisa had come to see him about taking a year's break. She wanted to travel and she had the opportunity to go with a friend. Allegedly she was very persuasive. It seemed Louisa had played on the fact that we had lost our parents at a young age. So he granted her the time out even though she was already halfway through her second year. Suggested quite pointedly that maybe it was healthy for Louisa to distance herself from her past.'

It was hard not to note that Abbi McPherson seemed to have separated herself from her sister's childhood trauma – the one they had shared equally.

'I take it that story meant she was deemed a low-risk missing person then?'

Abbi nodded. 'Yes. Despite my attempts to get someone to listen to me.'

'Tell me Ms McPherson, what exactly was it about this boyfriend that made you suspicious?'

'Firstly, he wasn't her boyfriend as she had never actually met him. Then there was the fact that he liked everything she did. He had studied psychology, but at Newcastle. He wanted to backpack around the world too.'

'That's not that unusual amongst students though, is it?' Harri pointed out. She wanted Abbi McPherson to be clearer about what had suggested to her there was something wrong.

'No . . . but it was odd. It was just too full-on, too sudden. He seemed to have too much in common with Louisa. Loved the same films and music, yet Louisa had eclectic tastes. He had read exactly the same books. I mean stuff like *Beloved* by Toni Morrison and Abraham Lincoln's *Gettysburg Address*. How random is that?'

Robertson caught Harri's eye. It seemed that the killer was exactly as she had suggested earlier; stalking his victims' social media profiles and gleaning as much information as he could to gain their trust. After all, if the victims had signed up to a dating app to meet 'the one' and that 'one' presented himself as charismatic, with identical tastes and life experiences, then they might have felt they already knew him; a kinship of sorts. She felt sickened by the predatory cunning exhibited by this unknown suspect. The same person behind the fake LA model's photograph had also ensnared Tammy Summers; a victim from a completely different cultural background and yet, he had also spoken her language. Convinced her that he was 'the one' so well that she left Newcastle, never to return – alive.

Harri handed the phone back. It was the same man whose image Tammy Summers had posted on Instagram and Facebook. The forensic computer analysts had trawled dating apps looking for this fake profile, but it had clearly been removed. This hadn't surprised Harri. After all, he had what he wanted. *Them*. Three in total – or at least, three that they knew about.

'Don't you need it?'

'We'll get it later,' Harri said. She didn't want to tell Abbi McPherson her sister had been abducted by a man who had met another young woman on a dating app – and murdered her.

'Something else struck me as odd. He claimed his parents had died when he was a teenager. He said it was a yachting accident. They both drowned. Odd, don't you think? That he lost his parents as well?'

Harri refrained from commenting. 'Is this a recent one of your sister?' she asked, pointing to the photograph on the table near her.

'Taken in Thailand. We spent Christmas just gone there. Our grandmother passed two years back and so . . .' She gave a half-hearted shrug.

Harri stared at the missing woman's face. Stuart had confirmed that the skeletal girl in the wheelchair was definitely not Louisa McPherson. But he had also said that the face in the first photo in all probability belonged to Louisa, as it had come back as a ninety per cent match. It was enough for Harri.

'May I?' Harri asked, picking up the silver-framed photograph.

'It was taken on New Year's Day. We had such a great time that Louisa made me promise that we would return for this New Year's Eve . . .' she faltered, realising the significance of what had just been said.

Harri put the photograph back down on the table, ignoring the sudden coolness in the room. Abbi McPherson was no fool. It was clear that there had been an update on her sister. Otherwise, why were they there?

Her missing person's report had been filed as low-risk. No one had taken her fears seriously – until now.

Harri discreetly shot a look Robertson's way to say that he was needed. This was why she had brought him. It was easier to deliver bad news with two of them.

Abbi McPherson watched as DC Robertson came over and sat down. The solemn expression on his face was enough. 'Is she dead? Did he kill her? This John?'

Harri felt Robertson stiffen at the question. It was direct and devoid of any emotion.

'No,' Harri began. 'We believe there is a chance that your sister is still alive.'

For now.

Chapter Twenty-Three

The call they had been dreading came in: a suspicious death had been reported; a young female – badly disfigured.

The team had been in a briefing when the news had hit. They had been discussing the two missing victims; one unknown, one identified as Louisa McPherson. Now they only had one victim alive. There was no question in anyone's mind that this suspicious death was connected to their killer.

Harri shivered as the cold, damp air clung to her. She and Douglas had headed immediately to the crime scene. She had now been waiting around for over ten minutes to see the body. The reflection of the girl in a wheelchair staring at the camera was imprinted on her mind. It was Louisa McPherson's eyes that haunted Harri. She stood steeling herself, silently hoping that this wouldn't be her body. That she would still, some-how, be able to find her before it was too late. But she had to accept that it was already too late for at least one of the victims.

Douglas was still busy talking to the Crime Scene

Manager, James Munroe. Whatever they were discussing was serious; a conversation that Douglas had made clear she wasn't invited to. Not once had Harri witnessed the good-humoured banter that was the norm between them. Instead, Munroe had stopped Douglas as soon as they had turned up at the crime scene. He had approached the car before Douglas had even got out. Munroe's usual light-hearted demeanour was gone. He wore an unfamiliar, harried expression. Whatever he had wanted to talk about was serious.

As if reading her mind, Douglas turned and looked over. His expression unnerved her. He looked concerned. Worse, he looked worried. *For who? Her?* He turned back to Munroe, who agitatedly pulled the hood down on his Tyvek suit. He ran a latex-gloved hand through his hair as he considered what Douglas was saying. They were both standing by the entrance to the forensics tent that covered the body and the crime scene. Not that Harri had seen the victim. For some reason, Douglas and Munroe were keeping her at arm's length.

She looked around the dark alleyway; shivered. It was 2:03 p.m. Rain had settled, bringing with it black, sullen clouds that blighted the sky. It only added to the overall mood of despair. She stared across the stone wall at the cemetery beyond. She could make out St Andrew's Church set back in the gloomy grounds. She felt uneasy, despite the police presence. As if someone was watching her. She turned to the Victorian terraced houses behind her, whose neat and ordered yards backed onto the alley. It was a good neighbourhood – *she should know.* One that would reel from the news that a young woman had been murdered and dumped while they had gone about their day. *Or had they?* For everyone was a suspect. No one had reported anything suspicious to the police. Not until a dog walker had found the victim's body shortly before 1:00 p.m. The dog had picked up a scent and caused enough commotion for the owner to investigate its find. Uniform were already collecting statements so they could correlate information and cross-reference it. But from what she had gathered, no one had seen the killer. Cemeteries and overgrown allotments merging into one another tended to be avoided – more so on a dark morning. It was gloomy in the alleyway. Even more so in the graveyard and church in front of her. She glanced over at the crime scene. The body had been dumped in an allotment. Until its – her – discovery, the body had been blanketed in a shadowy shroud; the overgrown trees and hedges blocked out any natural daylight. Nor were there any streetlights down that stretch. Ordinarily, there would be no need for them.

The arrogance of the killer worried her; even assuming he had dumped the body early in the morning, the glow of lights from the houses behind was evidence that this was a residential area. Someone could have seen him. Identified him. This told Harri that the area was significant. Connected to her. Choosing to dump the victim here was a risky strategy, a change from the previous day. He had left Tammy Summers' body by a busy Metro station and the school Harri had attended as a child, but in the early hours of the morning. She looked over again at the church, which dated as far back as the twelfth century. Its denomination was Church of England; she should know; as a child her mother had religiously brought her, every Sunday. She remembered the too-tight clasp of her mother's pale hand during those services and the nip those nimble fingers would mete out if she dared fidget.

She shivered as the hair on the back of her neck stood up. She despised being here. Hated the feel of the place. She wished that Douglas would hurry up. He had his back to her now but was still talking to Munroe. *Come on, sir. Hurry up!*

She stamped her feet in an attempt to force the blood to them. She felt irritated. Uncomfortable in her own skin. Harri willed herself to block out the disquiet she felt. But she couldn't – which made her even more agitated.

She felt her phone vibrate. She fumbled under her Tyvek suit to reach it. Took it out. It was a text from the same unknown number. She clicked on it. Stared.

Do you know who I am yet, Harri? I can nearly touch you.

She felt her stomach lurch as a wave of nausea hit.

Then a second text appeared:

Is your skin crawling now?

Whatever unease she had been feeling was replaced by a cold sliver of fear that slid under her skin and spread out. *Shit!*

She had underestimated him. He had stalked her before; had learned everything there was to know about her. So why not again? If this really was him. W*ho? Mac? For he had effectively disappeared. For all she knew he was close by, watching her every move.*

Whoever he was, he was out there somewhere, watching her, waiting. She wondered whether he was watching her now. The scene had been sealed off. Both ends of the back lane were inaccessible. A perimeter had been set up that limited who was allowed in or out of the area – which even included Fairfield Road and the allotments further down. Only police and SOCOs were allowed anywhere near the crime scene, and even then they needed to be signed in. It would be impossible for whoever was texting to be watching her. *Unless it was another officer.*

She shook the idea off. It was crazy. This was connected to her past. It couldn't possibly be a colleague from the Northumbrian force. Her attacker was London based – his accent had given him away. The murderer was also from London. But whoever had sent the text knew that she was at the crime scene of another murder victim. She put her phone on silent and hid it in the inside pocket of her jacket, decided to deal with it later. What could he do to her here surrounded by police? *Nothing. Even if her rapist and the murderer were the same person. And even if he was close by, watching her.*

'Harri?'

It was Douglas. 'Let's go,' he called.

She joined him and Munroe.

The Crime Scene Manager's concerned expression was enough to know that it was bad.

'Ready?' Douglas asked.

She nodded at him and walked on the platforms towards the forensics tent. The killer had taken the body onto one of the allotments that ran parallel to the cemetery. The double wooden gates locking the premises had been forced open.

As she started to follow Douglas, Munroe stopped her: 'Harri . . . wait.'

She looked at him, unsure of what was wrong.

'You don't need to see this. Trust me.'

'Thanks for the heads up, but I'll cope,' Harri assured him, puzzled by his sudden concern.

Something in Munroe's eyes told her she had made the wrong call.

She shook it off as she followed Douglas' retreating figure.

The first thing that hit her was the smell. Rotting flesh. Cloying and sickly sweet, it hung heavy in the claustrophobic air. The putrid smell was more typical of a body that had been festering for days.

She couldn't bring herself to look at the victim. It was a defence mechanism to stop herself from throwing up – because right now that was all she wanted to do.

'Do you want some air?'

Harri shook her head. 'I'm fine.'

She didn't have time to feel sick. Time was against them now. The killer had murdered a second victim – that left one still alive. *Maybe ...*

'You sure you're all right?' asked Douglas.

'Fine, sir,' replied Harri, even though the opposite was true. She was on the job. Before she willed herself to look at the body one thought went through her mind: *Don't let this be her ... Louisa McPherson. Please ...*

She swallowed down bile. Forced it back as it fought its way up again.

Harri made herself look at the victim. She willed herself not to react. *Not here.* She forced herself to be objective. This was a body. A gruesomely altered body. But it was a body she needed to look at. A body and a crime scene that she had to appraise; for the sake of the surviving victim.

There was no doubting that it was the work of the person responsible for Tammy Summers' death. Both victims were virtually identical, apart from one distinction: the killer had dressed this body in a hospital gown. Like the first victim – Tammy Summers, or 'Subject A' – this body was severely malnourished. Her features had also been eradicated by sulphuric acid and prominent green glass eyes had been positioned in the partially destroyed eye sockets. Harri noted the long, recently bleached blonde hair. Finally, her eyes rested on the identity tag, which named her as 'Subject B'.

She bent down to get a closer look. The D.O.D. was the 2nd April – that day. 'The same tag the victim was holding in the photograph,' Harri said as she turned and looked up at Douglas.

He simply nodded.

She looked back at the body. It was intact. Apart from where the victim's excess skin had been stitched back together with thick, ugly nylon. Black sutures held the skin together on the inner arms. Infection spread out from between the excess folds of skin on the victim's thighs. The area was a disquieting purplish black, suggestive of necrotising fasciitis, more commonly known as the 'flesh eating disease'; a condition that killed two out of every five people infected. It was rare in the UK. Tammy Summers had blood poisoning – from the infected skin that had been cut and stitched back together. She found it hard to stomach what he was doing; effectively butchering them with no regard for sterile equipment or anaesthetic. *Why would he care? He kills them anyway . . .*

She was acutely aware that the killer was playing a game with them; but she had no idea of the rules of the game or why it had started in the first place. She knew that nothing was accidental – including the location where the victim had been dumped. For Harri was certain that the victim had not died here. Exactly the same as the first victim. But where? They were clutching at straws when it came to the killer's location; even whether it was in London or Newcastle. Theories were being put together and empty buildings had been searched, but nothing. The white transit van still hadn't been found. Surveillance footage at the Tyne Tunnel had been studied on the off-chance that the killer had driven to and from London that way. Seemingly not. He was outwitting them at every juncture, every corner; he wasn't just one step ahead, he was a hundred miles.

'This location must mean something,' Harri suggested. 'It has to, or why leave her here? It's too out of the way. You would have to know this existed to bring the body here.' Their killer had to know this city. His accent suggested he was from London, but it was clear that he knew Newcastle; that he had a connection to it.

Douglas didn't answer. She looked at him. Something was wrong. 'Sir?'

He ignored her as he crouched down next to what was left of the victim's face. Sulphuric acid had been thrown over her head, face and neck, causing the flesh to bubble and melt as the liquid had burned its way through to the bone. The acid had completely eradicated one side of her head, dissolving the dyed blonde hair, penetrating through the skull to the brain tissue below. It was an utterly execrable act.

Fuck . . . fuck . . .

She made herself block the horror. Forced herself to be analytical. She wondered why the victims were named as 'subjects', but she still didn't have an answer; other than the obvious that it was some form of experiment. She had also looked up the meaning of the noun: '*A person or thing that is being discussed, described, or dealt with.*' She knew when it came to a premeditated murder that there were no coincidences; every detail was planned, every act deliberated over. It was no accident that the killer was describing his victims this way – they had become 'subjects' that were being 'discussed', 'described' and 'dealt with' by the police.

'Harri ...' Douglas said. His voice was low. Tense. *Ominous.*

She shifted her attention to him, realising he had lifted the hospital gown back, exposing the body. 'Dr Blake noted it earlier when she called time of death. She mentioned it to Munroe because of the significance,' Douglas said.

Harri stared at the black, ugly stitches around the now flat breasts and the taut lower abdomen where it was brutally evident that the killer had cut away the excess skin from the skeletal body. He had altered her even more than the last victim.

Douglas looked up at her, waiting for her reaction.

Her stomach twisted when she realised what was wrong. Douglas wasn't referring to the horrific, crude surgery. *No ... NO.*

She willed her eyes to look above the victim's now exposed left breast. But she knew. Recognised immediately the mark the killer had left. A crisscross wound inches from her heart. Identical to the one her attacker had stabbed into her own left breast.

He's turning them into you, Harri. Oh God ...

Even though she knew that the killer had altered Tammy Summers to look like her, this was something she had not expected. The reality was too overwhelming. She thought she was going to throw up. Could feel the saliva pooling in her mouth. Her body felt hot. Her face suddenly flushed; burning. She turned away from the horror of what the killer had done. The knowledge of what the next stage of alteration would involve. She stumbled out into the stinging cold air; into an afternoon that had suddenly got much darker.

She heard Douglas' voice calling her. She ignored him.

'Harri!'

She continued walking. He caught up with her and grabbed her arm.

She shook him off. Angry, defiant. 'What do you want me to say?'

'This is personal. The wound on the victim's chest is identical to your own.'

She refused to answer him. Refused to accept what it would mean for her.

He shook his head at her reluctance to accept what he was saying. 'The choice of location wasn't random and you know it, Harri.'

'Do I?' she threw back. But she knew this was personal. And she didn't need Douglas telling her that.

'You grew up in one of the houses that back onto this alleyway. I think that's bloody relevant, don't you?' Douglas demanded.

She narrowed her eyes. 'What? So you're checking up on me now? Reading the report about what happened to me a year back not enough for you? You need to go delving into my past? MY past! It belongs to me and if I don't want to disclose something I don't think is significant then that is my right!'

She saw the wounded reaction at her accusatory words.

'Right now, you're his target,' Douglas stated. 'So anything that is connected to you concerns me. I have a killer trying to alter his victims so they look like you. One victim now stands between you and the sick bastard that butchered that poor young woman back there!'

Chapter Twenty-Four

Harri looked at the whiteboard. Her eyes rested on the victim's crisscross wound. She couldn't deny it; the similarity was startling. Right now she was struggling to come up with an answer that would appease Douglas. He would want to remove her from the investigation – the killer had made it obvious now that he knew her – *intimately.*

The text she had been sent yesterday came to mind, the first one: '*Do you know who I am, Harri? For I know you – intimately'.*

She breathed out slowly. Shakily.

But it was always personal, Harri. You knew that from day one when he hand-delivered the evidence photograph of you. Then the text. Followed by the photograph of his first victim, Tammy Summers, addressed to you. So why are you so surprised that he marked her chest identically to yours? What didn't you fucking get? Did you really think you could contain this?

She had to focus. She didn't have long to figure out what she was going to say to prove that she wasn't a liability to the investigation; that she was indispensable. That he needed her. It was the last thing she wanted; to be taken off the case while there was still a victim out there. The team were under no illusions as to the fate of Louisa McPherson if they didn't find her. The unknown killer had already warned them with the first murder victim, Tammy Summers. Now they had a second body. And an ID: Shannon O'Brien. They had been lucky – the victim's DNA had been in the system due to an attending officer having the foresight to request her toothbrush when she had been reported as a missing person.

'He's one fucking sick bastard all right!'

Harri turned as Robertson walked into the room. She nodded. She wasn't much in the mood for talking.

'Why do you think he's done that?' Robertson asked, pulling up a chair beside her.

'Which bit?' Harri asked. She watched him frown as he studied the images on the whiteboard. The tension between them had lessened considerably, enough for her to believe that they had put their differences behind them. Harri put it down in part to the meeting with the missing victim's sister, Abbi McPherson. Robertson hated emotional scenes as much as Harri, but they had dealt with it – together. It was on the drive back to the station that Harri had noticed a change in Robertson's attitude; it was subtle, but enough.

'The crisscross stabbing. Doesn't seem to fit.'

'I don't know.' No one on the team, aside from Douglas, knew the connection between the wound on the victim's chest and the scar hidden beneath Harri's long-sleeved white top. It was only yesterday Douglas had checked the details of her assault, which now seemed like an eternity; in that time two bodies had been found, and it had been established that a third missing person had also been abducted by the same killer.

A year ago her rapist had promised to return. And he had – the photograph and the texts proved that. She had tried to get a trace on the phone, but it was only switched on briefly when a text was sent. However, she had used her role as deputy SIO to get location data on another mobile phone: DI Mac O'Connor's. He had been in Newcastle the same day she received the photograph of herself. Currently, his phone was switched off, but she was sure he had remained in Newcastle. She had no choice but to try to stay on the investigation, to keep her access to resources otherwise unattainable. If she was temporarily suspended or forced to take leave then she would have no way to keep track of Mac's whereabouts. And the last thing she could share with Douglas was her fear – belief – that Mac was her rapist, and perhaps their killer. Nobody would believe her. She had no choice but to prove it.

'You OK, Sarge?' Robertson asked.

'I just want something so we can nail the bastard,' Harri replied. She looked at the crisscross wound on Shannon O'Brien's left breast. She was acutely aware that even though her assault had made national news, details of the crisscross wound had never made it to the public. It confirmed in her mind that her rapist was the killer. For *he* was the one who had marked her – just as he had identically scarred Shannon O'Brien. She automatically thought of DI Mac O'Connor. She had tried his mobile again but it had cut straight to voicemail. He had effectively disappeared. However, he had been savvy enough to request two weeks leave to avoid any suspicion. He had time on his hands – *enough time to play games with her. Enough time to kill* ... Harri tried to rein in her thoughts. All she had was circumstantial evidence. But then there was his DNA recovered by forensics in her bedroom.

'We all do. Sick son of a bitch!' Robertson agreed, interrupting her thoughts.

They all wanted to get the killer; but she had her own reasons for wanting it more.

'Why do we do this?' he said, gesturing towards the crime scene photos.

Harri frowned at him. 'It's not like you to get philosophical, Robertson. You feeling all right?'

'Seriously. Look at what he's done to them.'

'We do it because it's our job. Sometimes it feels like we're making a difference when we take some little scrote off the streets. Others, like this case, are the shit ones. You take the good with the bad, Robertson and just pray to God that you can still sleep at night.'

'I imagine her parents won't be doing much of that tonight,' Robertson said.

Harri looked at the 'before' shot of Shannon O'Brien – her missing person's photo. She fitted his type; young, pretty, very voluptuous, long brown hair and brown eyes. She breathed in. Held it for a moment. She had to, otherwise she might have lost it.

'What did they say when they were informed?'

'Same deal. She met someone called "John" on a dating app. He'd used the same photo of that LA model. Only difference is she lived in Bristol. Same result though. She told her parents that she was going to London. She never returned. A couple of texts were sent from her phone to appease them. Then nothing,' she replied, not adding 'until now.'

'How come her DNA was in the system?'

'Someone had been extra zealous when taking a statement and had requested her toothbrush for DNA. Simple. Not that she was listed as a high-risk missing person or anything. She had had an argument with her parents when she left and texted saying she was staying in London. But same story, all her social media accounts had not been touched. Same deal with her bank account. Four months her parents have lived not knowing, and now they do.' She looked at what was left of their daughter. Not that they would ever recognise her.

'Pleased I didn't have to make that call. I've had my stomach's worth after today and yesterday. Can't stand all that shit.'

'What? Grief?'

'Yeah. I never know what to say or do. You know? You're trying to get a statement from someone who's just been told that their daughter or sister has been murdered and you're using them, like. Trying to find out shit so you can get on with the job and all they want is to be left alone to deal with it . . .' Robertson shrugged off whatever else he had wanted to vent.

'Like I said, you take the bad with the good.' She looked across at Louisa McPherson's gaunt face, enlarged by their computer analyst, Stuart. Her eyes seemed to stare straight at Harri. Defiant, strong – a survivor. *But for how long? How long do we have before he alters you too?*

She touched the scar across her throat. *How long before he turns you into me? Or are we already too late?*

'You know this is personal! For fuck's sake, Harri!'

Douglas rarely swore. She held her tongue.

'I have the autopsy report here for God's sake! It was expedited by Blake, given the seriousness of the situation.' He slammed the file on his desk. 'Christ! I've just spent two bloody hours watching it!' He leaned over the desk towards Harri. 'The knife used was different but aside from that, what the killer did to her was virtually identical to your—'

'Wound,' she interrupted. 'A Masakage knife was used on me, sir. My attacker used one of my own knives. Ironic, don't you think?' Harri asked. She had often wondered why her rapist had not brought a weapon. Also how he knew where to find the Japanese knife. It wasn't in plain view. It had been stored in a box in a drawer in the kitchen. It had been a gift from her ex – it had meant something to her. Her rapist had taken the knife when he left. She had often wondered whether he had kept it as a trophy. 'You know the knife was never recovered? If it's him, why wouldn't he use it again?'

Douglas didn't reply. Instead he ran a hand over his cropped hair.

They now had the cause of death: cardiac arrest; similar to the first victim. Her bloods had also shown signs of starvation and septicaemia. However, this time the killer had marked the victim with a crisscross wound. Douglas had attended the autopsy without Harri, instructing her to remain behind. Not that she was bothered. It was a scene that she did not necessarily want to witness. Nor did she want anyone's pity – especially not Eleanor Blake's. She knew the pathologist would have had to compare the stabbing against Harri's own injury. She had no choice. The similarities between Harri's attack and the murders were too apparent. She was part of the investigation now.

'This whole time he has been sending you correspondence and you've batted it off.'

'As we all did.'

Douglas shook his head. 'You really expect me to let you continue working on this investigation?'

'Yes, sir.'

He looked at her as if she had lost her mind. 'I don't think I can stand back and watch you become another victim.'

Harri couldn't help but think 'again'.

'Can't you see he is playing with you? He marked Shannon O'Brien in an identical manner to the way you were . . .' Douglas' voice trailed off, unable to say it to her face.

'The way I was attacked?'

He nodded.

'The only correlation is that he has by chance stabbed her in a similar manner—'

Douglas didn't give her a chance to finish. He picked up the autopsy file and threw it at her. 'Take a good look and then tell me that this is coincidence!'

She took it. Stared at the first photograph. Then looked at the one underneath. One was a close-up of the victim's body and the other was of her; taken after her attack. There was an uncanny similarity between the knife wound inflicted upon her body and the victim's. The only difference was that the victim's chest was also blighted by thick, black sutures.

She could feel Douglas' eyes on her, waiting for an acknowledgement that he was correct. That the unknown killer was playing her; playing them.

She replaced the photographs and put the file down. 'I agree they are similar, sir.'

'It's more than that, and you know it.'

'All we know is that it appears as if he is copying injuries that I sustained.'

'Injuries you were subjected to during an assault, Harri. It didn't happen by chance. Tell me how exactly he knows the unusual wound on your chest? How he was able to replicate it so accurately?'

Harri broke away from his gaze. She was at a loss as to how to answer. Shannon O'Brien had not been stabbed with the Masakage knife that her rapist had used. If the killer was the man who had raped her, then why had he not used the same knife? It didn't make sense. Unless he had disposed of it? The only fact Harri was certain about was that Tammy Summers and Shannon O'Brien's killer was obsessed with her and what had happened to her a year ago.

'Do you think that this murderer is the same person who attacked you?' Douglas asked, acutely aware she had not answered him the first time.

She had repeatedly asked herself the same question. She realised she was an anomaly; both detective and victim. *But which one are you now, Harri? Has he targeted you because you were a victim? Does that make you more vulnerable, susceptible to his games? To his desire to terrorise you?* She may have had her suspicions that Mac was behind her rape, but she couldn't be certain he was a murderer. *Or maybe he could be?*

She forced herself to silence the thoughts racing through her mind. She could not articulate them, otherwise she would be signing her own suspension. She had to lie. 'The MO is completely different. It's the signature that is similar and he could have copied that. The other injuries could not be further removed from my attack. If they were the same person, I would have expected him to use the same knife.'

Douglas still didn't look convinced. She couldn't blame him. But she had to try to persuade him that the killer and her rapist were not one and the same; otherwise, she would be removed from the investigation, and she had too much to lose. She needed to be in a position to catch *him* before he caught her.

She cleared her throat before continuing: 'I was stalked first, for about a month, and then attacked in my own home. He had keys to my flat. It was personal. That's the difference. The MO here is the antithesis of my attacker's. As far as we can establish, the young women he selected aren't known to him. He has not had sexual contact with either of the victims. They are, as he calls them, "subjects". By blighting them with sulphuric acid he dehumanises them.' She stopped for a moment as she thought about the way he was physically changing their bodies. 'He held Tammy Summers hostage for four months so he could starve her. Then he cut off the excess skin on her arms. Next is Shannon O'Brien, but he takes it to a new level. Not only does he physically alter her hair, eyes, face and even her body shape, he marks her with a crisscross wound on her breast. Then he leaves the murdered body for us to find.' Harri stopped for a moment. She looked at Douglas. 'The difference is, I was left alive.'

'In your victim statement you said he told you he would come back to kill you,' Douglas pointed out. 'Also the killer is altering his victims to look like you, Harri. Doesn't this suggest to you that your rapist and this killer are linked? That they could be the same person?'

Harri did her utmost to remain impassive. She didn't want to give Douglas any hint that she was acutely aware of the connection. That she believed her rapist and the killer were the same man. 'Maybe he got a kick out of leaving me with the fear that one day he might come back? But he hasn't, sir. And I don't believe he will,' she said as she unflinchingly held Douglas' sceptical gaze.

The last thing she was about to tell him was that her rapist had made contact. That he was back. And he was watching her. That her darkest fear had become a reality. Worse, that he was taunting her by torturing women and altering them to look like her.

She had only shared her deepest fear, that her attacker would actually come back to finish what he had started, with Dr Michael Adams. She had spent countless sessions with her counsellor talking about this fear. Michael had challenged her; had made her feel uncomfortable; had forced her to look into the abyss and beyond. Crucially, he had shown her how to save herself. How to face this debilitating terror. It was something only she could do for herself. Not the police. Not her boss. Her.

Douglas wearily sat down. He rubbed the stubble on his chin as he considered what she had just said. Harri could see his refusal to accept that the killer and her rapist were two different suspects. Not that she could blame him – it was exactly what she believed. But she needed to convince him somehow that her attacker was not the murderer.

'And the killer's signature?' Douglas asked. 'What do you make of it?'

She shook her head. 'I'm not entirely clear on his needs here. I would say that he is driven by sadism, misogyny, anger and above all, a need to be in control.'

Just like the assailant who raped you …

She silenced the intrusive thought. 'But why he stabbed Shannon O'Brien the way he did, I can't say.' She already knew the answer, but as soon as it was acknowledged there would be no discussion about whether she should be removed from the investigation; it would be a given. The text she had received on 1st April taunted her. The first of three that she had not disclosed to Douglas: *'Do you know who I am, Harri? For I know you – intimately'.*

Only her rapist and the team dealing with her attack knew the details of her injuries. If the killer had replicated her slit throat only, then she would not necessarily have considered that he and her rapist were the same person. After all, she refused to be shamed by the scar or keep it covered up, despite people's discomfort at seeing it. Whereas the crisscross wound was intimate – a scar that was permanently hidden from view.

'Anger, hatred. Both emotions that fit in with his signature aspect. His motivational drive. You see, they don't have your face. So he destroys their features. A reminder that they are not you.'

Harri didn't respond. She was more than aware that they were dancing around the fact that Douglas was building up to taking her off the investigation. The third text she had received this afternoon at the crime scene came to mind. The words he had texted suggestive that he was the killer: *Do you know who I am yet, Harri? I can nearly touch you.* Followed by: *Is your skin crawling now?*

'Why dye their hair blonde, like yours?' Douglas continued. 'Eradicate their facial features? Place green glass eyes in their eye sockets, the colour identical to yours. Why alter their bodies so they look like you? Both victims were significantly overweight when he abducted them. He chose them so he could starve them so their physique would be in keeping with yours, Harri. He then surgically altered them, cutting away their excessive skin. It's a small mercy that both victims' toxicology reports found high traces of the sedative benzodiazepine in their blood.' He shook his head as he stared at her.

Harri waited.

'He wants them to be *you*, Harri,' Douglas said.

Harri could not ignore the concern in his eyes.

'I don't know him. So why would he copy what my attacker did to me?'

'Are you so sure it isn't the same person?' Douglas asked. 'Physically they match. Height, build, even the accent. The fact that they both wore a black ski mask and black clothes.'

Harri searched for a reason why they couldn't be the same man. She needed a plausible one to appease Douglas. 'The black ski mask is what differentiates them, sir.'

Douglas raised a questioning eyebrow. 'How?'

'The intention behind it is not the same as my rapist's reason for wearing it. The black ski mask that my attacker wore was part of his signature: covering his face enhanced the sexual pleasure he derived from raping me. He had been building up to that moment; before that night all his messages revolved around one theme: raping me while he wore a mask. He said that it had been a fantasy he wanted to act upon when he found the right person.' Harri stopped for a moment. She could hear his voice – still. He had distorted it, giving it a sinister, eerie sound. She had deleted the messages and texts, not realising the extent of her stalker's obsession.

She forced herself to continue: 'The ski mask was part of my attacker's MO, as it hid his identity, but also it was part of his rape fantasy. The killer we're dealing with used a black ski mask, not for sexual gratification but to hide his face so he would remain unknown. That was all it was to him; something that gave him the anonymity to elude us. The black ski mask was more than that for my assailant. Much more. They might not be the same person.'

Douglas didn't argue with her. But then this wasn't some abstract crime they could theorise or speculate about – this had happened to *her*. She knew she hadn't convinced him. She had failed to convince herself.

Harri waited for Douglas to speak. To inform her of his decision. The crisscross stabbing on Shannon O'Brien's chest was a direct reference to her. The killer had altered the victims – to look like her.

'You know I have to report these findings.'

She could hear the regret in his voice. It was clearly a difficult decision for him.

But she had already accepted that Douglas would have to do it. After all, it was only natural. If someone was copying what her attacker had done to her that night, the first person that they would need to eliminate from the investigation was her unidentified assailant. *Still out there ... somewhere*. She nodded at her boss. 'I understand.'

'I'm sorry, Harri, I really am.'

She could see from his expression that his sentiment was genuine. But what scared her in that moment was *why* he was sorry. Was it because he genuinely believed that her assailant had killed these two young women to scare her? To let her know he had not finished with her? Or . . . was it because he was about to transfer her to another case?

'If you don't believe the killer is your assailant, why do you think he is targeting you?'

Harri looked at Douglas and shook her head. She felt numb. 'I don't know the answer to that, sir.'

Douglas sighed as he leaned back in his chair. He glanced down at the photographs lying in the open file on his desk and shook his head, unable to hide the sadness he felt at the decision he had to make. 'I have no choice given the circumstances but to remove you from this investigation.'

'Sir—'

'I wish I didn't have to do this, Harri. But I would rather it came from me personally than from one of my superiors. It's protocol. You could jeopardise the investigation,' Douglas replied.

'How?' asked Harri, trying to keep the desperation she felt out of her voice. She needed to be part of the investigation. If she didn't, then she would not be able to keep looking for anything that could possibly be linked to her attacker.

'If the killer's main focus is you, then the obvious strategy is to remove you from the case. So that it isn't about you any more.'

Harri shook her head. 'It isn't about me. It's about him. If you take me off the investigation, don't you see that he's winning? That this might be exactly what he wants? To see me removed from the team. Suspended or forced to take leave. And then what? What happens to me then?'

Douglas took a moment to consider what she had just said. 'I am sorry, I have to stand by my decision. If I don't, my hand will be forced.'

'But only you and I know about this,' Harri insisted. She knew it was a long shot.

Douglas looked at her. She could see the resignation etched on his heavily-lined face before he spoke. 'I can't allow you to remain on the investigation. And I have to consider the possibility that your life is in danger.'

Harri stared at him.

'He knows where you work. He knows about your attack, the scar on your chest.'

She couldn't argue; he was right.

'Do you think he knows where you live?'

She hesitated before answering. Her mind threw her back to the envelope containing the photograph of her mutilated body. She was acutely aware that if she answered 'yes', she would not be allowed to return to her apartment. Or to return to work. And she would be seen as having withheld evidence.

'No. No one knows where I live. Apart from you, sir.'

Douglas would be considering all options. One of which would be to move her to a secure place. Somewhere that the killer could not get near her. But she didn't want that. She wanted to remain in control of her life. She had already lost control once before and she would be damned if she let it happen again.

'The building is unoccupied, apart from my floor. The main entrance is bolted, as is my apartment. No one could get in. I have made certain of that.'

She could see that he wasn't convinced. 'You definitely don't have any idea who this man could be?'

'No.'

Douglas weighed it up for a moment. 'All right, I need a list of everyone you have been in contact with since your attack, including anyone you have been intimate with . . . I mean physically.'

She refrained from informing Douglas that she had not had sex with anyone since before she had been raped. He would figure that out from the list; it would be short, with no surprises; the only people she had been in contact with since the attack were her colleagues. She had no friends outside the job; nor did she have any friends on the job. Not any more.

'What are you thinking?' Douglas asked her.

She realised there was no point in hiding it. 'That the only people I know are on the job. I haven't seen anyone from the Met since the attack and then . . .' She faltered as she recalled the months she had spent trying to put her life together. Trying to live with the physical scars he had left. Then there were the mental scars. She looked at Douglas, met his inquisitive gaze. She could see pity in his eyes – for her. She felt a surge of anger. Defiance. She didn't need his pity. She had coped – *was* coping. She had put her past firmly behind her. *Have you? Then why is someone trying to make you face it – again?*

245

She realised that Douglas was waiting for her to finish. 'I know no one. No one outside the job here.'

Douglas nodded. 'Harri, there are only two possible scenarios. Either the killer is your rapist. Or, the killer is someone connected to the police. Someone who has accessed your victim statement and reports. If this is the case, the question is, why?'

Harri thought of the photographs taken of the graphic injuries she had sustained. Then of the photograph delivered to her apartment building. *Mac? Let it go, Harri ...*

'Are you telling me everything?'

She met his concerned gaze. 'What else would there be to tell?'

'You tell me.'

Harri shook her head. 'No. There's nothing else to tell you.'

Douglas nodded.

'So what do I do now?' Harri asked.

'Compile that list for me while I look into assigning you to another investigation.'

'You really think this will end by taking me off the case?'

'No,' answered Douglas. Simple and straight to the point. 'But I have no choice.'

'You do know there are no signs of a white transit van on any of the CCTV footage near the crime scene by St Andrew's Cemetery or the route leading into or away from the city?'

'I am aware of that,' answered Douglas.

'It means either he knows the exact locations of the city's surveillance cameras or he used a different vehicle.'

Harri had spent that morning getting as many of the team as possible studying CCTV footage. But they had found nothing. They had narrowed down registered owners of white Ford transit vans in London and Newcastle to under three hundred. It was now a case of cross-referencing the owners' details against the information they had on the killer – which wasn't a great deal.

'It's no longer your concern, Harri. You've got thirty minutes to compile that list. Then we'll talk about where I'm going to reassign you.'

She nodded. 'What happens next? I mean, with the killer?'

Douglas shrugged. 'I wait for his next move.'

Harri resisted the urge to challenge this decision. It made her uncomfortable. Out of control. If the serial killer was her rapist, which she suspected despite what she had said to Douglas, then she needed to be part of the investigation at all costs – her life could depend on it. Maybe this was what the killer wanted all along? For her to be removed from the murder team, isolated and vulnerable.

Suddenly Harri felt like her world had ended. Now he was the hunter and she was the hunted.

Chapter Twenty-Five

He raised his glass of scotch: *To you, Harri and to the end of Day Two.*

He took a swig. Held it in his mouth, appreciating the warmth and subtlety of the single malt. He swivelled his chair around to regard the glistening city below.

He switched the large flat screen TV off. He felt an unbearable ennui when it came to the news. It was either filled with political tittle tattle or speculative dribble touted as current affairs. Not that he needed a news update. He already knew what was about to unfold. *Unlike Harri Jacobs.* But this was what she had wanted. 'Closure' was what Harri had requested. He felt nothing but antipathy for the psychobabble word 'closure', but as her doctor he had honoured his patient's request – to give her the 'closure' she had so desired.

He took another drink as he shifted his attention to the computer screen. He studied the live stream footage from the maximum-security psychiatric hospital. There were seven patients currently incarcerated. Females; all highly dangerous and volatile; all under twenty-four-seven surveillance and his professional authority.

He clicked on room two. The occupant had caught

his attention. There was something about her that he didn't quite trust. He was concerned for the safety of the other patients and staff in her company. He needed her to become integrated and over time, he hoped she would come to accept her new environment – and him. The others had reacted well to their therapy, but she was the anomaly. He just didn't seem to be able to get through. No amount of counselling, repeat evaluation or different meds seemed to work. She seemed to be impervious to any kind of psychological help. Part of the problem was that she was in denial and that this prevented her from ever being able to make a full recovery. He had already tried ECT – electroconvulsive therapy – which had failed. It had involved sending an electric current through her brain to trigger an epileptic seizure to relieve her of some of her more extreme mental health symptoms but despite countless attempts, the treatment had been unsuccessful.

He decided he might have to take a different approach. Disappointed, he watched her lift her T-shirt up and start poking around under her bra. He knew that she wasn't rearranging her bosom. No. She was removing something from her special hiding place – the red-raw and infected open flesh under her heavy breasts. He waited as she poked through the wound that she had dug out with her own fingers, producing a piece of broken glass.

Disinterested, he swilled the malt around in the glass. Then took a drink. He knew what she intended to do with the broken glass. That was one of the many reasons she had been sectioned.

She started to distractedly pick at the raw scars on her left arm. Over time, she had filled the arm with paperclips. Some buried so deep she couldn't reach them. Others close enough to the surface for her to bring them out. When she did succeed in excavating one, she would simply rebury it. It appeared a harmless occupation. But he knew why she had been committed. Her obsessive compulsive self-harming had extended beyond her own body. It was the first case of its kind. She was now one of his case studies, known as 'Angel'; which was rather ironic, considering why she had been incarcerated. She intrigued him, but not in the same way as Harri Jacobs.

He had already decided that if his male client was unsuccessful, he had countless other means at his disposal. Other ways of cleansing Harri Jacobs of her inner demons. He stared at the live surveillance footage into, it seemed, her dark eyes. She was now intently watching the camera. If all else failed, this one would have her uses. He thought of Harri and wondered what she would make of her – his 'Angel'. *Would she remind you of your mother, Harri? Would she? For that is one demonic creature we never had the chance to exorcise*. He took another mouthful as he considered the possibility. But first, he had to see whether she survived the third day.

He clicked off the live stream surveillance footage and searched through the hundreds of sessions he had recorded with 'John'. Found the one he wanted. The recording that he had made shortly after the last counselling session with Harri Jacobs. Her epiphany had been to accept that she needed to come face-to-face with her darkest, deepest fear – 'John'. Ironically, it was only because of his sessions with 'John' that Harri Jacobs had ended up being referred to him. What had happened to Harri had been the result of years of counselling 'John'. Not that Harri knew that. Nor ever would. She knew nothing about 'John'; aside from what he had done to her.

No, she would never be aware how he'd pushed 'John' to face his demons – her. All his documented case studies were encrypted; not for patient confidentiality, but to protect him from the savage minds that would not understand his progressive practices. However unconventional, they worked. He had the other case studies to prove it.

He swivelled the chair back to stare out at the dark skies, waiting for the recording to begin. He listened as 'John' sighed. It was filled with exasperation. He recalled how he had waited for him to talk.

Thirty seconds passed. The silence awkward. Pulsating.

'I know now.'

Silence.

'What I need to do.'

He remembered how he had slightly raised an eyebrow at this statement. It had taken 'John' some two years to get to this realisation.

Silence.

'Aren't you going to ask me?'

He had shaken his head at this challenge. These sessions were not about him – they were about 'John' and his obsession with Harri Jacobs. He was merely the facilitator. His job was to listen. Not judge. Not advise. Not question. His patients had to find their own way towards release. Of course, he would make subtle nods in the right direction. He had to, otherwise they would obviously fail.

Again, silence.

He knew that 'John' was disappointed, even if his expression was typically blank. He had wanted his psychologist to metaphorically clap his hands at this statement. Not that he needed to ask his client what he planned to do. He had adroitly seeded the thought again, and again.

'It wasn't enough,' he said.

Dr Adams studied the contents of his glass as he absorbed this statement. It still intrigued him. *Even now.*

'Raping her and slitting her throat was not enough for you?' The voice low, gentle, inviting.

A wave of irritation hit Dr Adams as he listened to his own inane question. It was a one-off aberration. But still, it pricked at his intellectual pride.

Silence.

He visualised 'John' looking at him with a flicker of distrust.

'No. The other thing.'

'The promise you made to return to kill her after you left her barely alive seven months ago?'

'Yes.'

'I see.'

He took another mouthful of scotch as he listened. He had understood perfectly well why the threat had not been enough. After all, it was not the denouement he had subtly imparted to him countless sessions earlier.

'I want to kill her.'

He could see himself nodding at this statement. It was understandable considering what had happened because of her. They had history. But it was his story that had caught Dr Adams' imagination.

'But first, I want to . . .'

'Make her fully appreciate your obsession with her?'

Dr Adams listened to the words he had spoken five months ago. He cast his mind to what was happening now. To how those words had come to fruition.

'Yes.'

'And how will you do that?'

It was a rhetorical question. He had guided him ever so subtly to this point.

'I will alter others and give them to her. Then she will see.'

'And if she doesn't? If she doesn't understand why you have altered these women? If she doesn't realise who you are?'

He listened to the stillness. Remembered how he had studied his client's face for some kind of emotional response. A glimmer of humanity. But there was nothing. Whether Harri Jacobs had been the cause of this lack, or it had never actually existed, he could not tell.

He had waited for a reply. And when it came, it failed to surprise him.

'I will end my obsession.'

Silence.

'You know what I plan to do to her?'

Silence.

Dr Adams saw himself nodding in response. 'John' had repeatedly shared his murderous fantasies during their earlier sessions. He knew down to the most miniscule detail exactly what 'John' had in store for her. He also knew he was more than capable of carrying out such unimaginable acts of inhumanity.

He waited until the recording ended. He finished his scotch as he deliberated. He still couldn't say what the outcome would be for either 'John' or Harri Jacobs. He was merely the facilitator. His job was to simply record the results of these two case studies.

Chapter Twenty-Six

'I understand this must be really difficult for you,' Harri said.

She was alone in the CID computer room. The remaining team members were in the Murder Room, which was kitted out with multiple computers and phones, so she would not run into anyone from the investigation in here. She didn't have much time left. Douglas had asked to see her. She had been assigned to a new case. He had repeated that it was beyond his control. She was now seen as compromising the multiple murder investigation. He had offered her the chance to go home early and start the new assignment in the morning, but she had refused. She needed to remain at work.

She would never ordinarily have broken the rules, but she had decided she had nothing to lose. She had cleared her call with one of the Avon and Somerset Constabulary liaison officers assigned to the latest victim's parents first. At this stage, no one knew she had been removed from the investigation.

Mr O'Brien was asleep after taking a knock-out dose of eszopiclone. So she was left with Mrs O'Brien, who was still struggling to come to terms with her daughter's murder.

'He still had a job to do. See? Couldn't stop going in could he, because Shannon had gone. Anxiety and stress the doctor had called it. So given the personal circumstances, what with our Shannon, she gave him sleeping tablets,' she said, sighing. 'Been on them for four months. Can't sleep now without them.'

Harri waited. It wasn't her place to interrupt. Not yet at least. She knew that Penny O'Brien was just thinking out loud, but that was fine by her. Everyone dealt with trauma differently. She looked at the time. 5:19 p.m. She was acutely conscious that she shouldn't be questioning the murder victim's next of kin after she had been removed from the investigation, but she wanted to do everything she could to help track down the killer before it became known that she no longer had authorisation. Harri wasn't one for accepting second-hand information, and she was acutely aware that time was running out for her – and Louisa McPherson.

'Pleased he can't hear this anyway,' Penny O'Brien continued. 'I couldn't say anything in front of him. He didn't know, see? And I only kept quiet about it at the time because I knew he would go mad. He still sees her as his little girl . . .' She paused.

Harri heard her sniff a couple of times and then the ruffled noise of a tissue close to the receiver.

'And I can't tell him now . . . not after what's happened. When Shannon started chatting to this John on this dating app something about it didn't feel right. So when she was going to London, I demanded an address.'

Harri could hear a drawer being opened and the

contents being pushed around as she searched for something.

'No . . . I can't find it. I'm sorry. I'm sure I put it in a drawer. Or maybe I hid it somewhere so Will didn't find it. I wrote it down when she rang me from London. This John had said that once she was at King's Cross station he would text her where to meet.'

Harri breathed out. She told herself that the address would have been fake anyway; same as the photograph he used for his profile.

'It was thirty something, Islington. But for the life of me I can't remember the street.'

'Don't worry. It might turn up later,' Harri reassured her.

'He was married though . . . That's what our Shannon had said. They had been chatting for some time and she wanted to meet up and he kept putting her off. Said he was busy with work. She kept insisting. That was my Shannon. When she wanted something she went all out to get it. Then he told her he was married. That he wanted a divorce, which is what they all say. He said that his wife was going away for a few days so she could come down. But he had to be careful nobody saw them together. She had to make her way to his place by herself. When she arrived he texted her the address to his place in Islington. She rang me when she was outside. Said it looked posh with a high gated entrance. That she had to be buzzed in.'

Harri absorbed what she was being told.

'I know it was somewhere in Islington though.'

Harri's flat had been in Islington. She didn't want to

say that finding it would be impossible without the street name. 'Shannon definitely rang you from the property?'

'Yes. We're very close, Shannon and I, she tells me everything. I told the officer who dealt with the missing person report that she wouldn't not keep in touch with me.'

Harri kept quiet, it wasn't her job to point out to Penny O'Brien that she was discussing her daughter in the present tense. Her heavy silence told Harri she had realised her mistake.

'Your statement said that you had a big argument with Shannon. Was that why she was evaluated as a low-risk missing person?' Harri finally asked.

'Her dad and Shannon had a blazing row. He didn't want her going off and meeting some bloke in London that she didn't know properly. He said some things he shouldn't have done, like the bloke was no doubt using her. He didn't believe anything that he told our Shannon and said if this photograph of him was real why was he interested in her? Shannon took it bad. Thought her dad was referring to the fact she was big. She left the next day without even saying goodbye to him. Then the last I heard from her was that phone call, and a couple of texts the same night saying she was really happy and wasn't coming home because of what her dad said. Broke his heart it did. And now . . .' She faltered, sniffed.

'I'm really sorry,' Harri replied. She waited a moment before asking the question she had bided her time to ask.

'What was it about this John that made your daughter want to have a relationship with him despite the fact he was married?'

Silence. Harri realised that she was crying. She looked at the time. Wondered how long she had left before Douglas would come looking for her. She was already five minutes late.

'He told her the marriage was over. That they lived separate lives and he was just waiting for the paperwork. She wanted a lot out of the divorce. More than he felt she was entitled to. You see, he had money. At least that's what he told Shannon. And from what she said about the gated house it sounds like it, doesn't it?'

'It does,' agreed Harri. 'Did he ever tell Shannon what he did for a living?' She thought of the fake photograph the killer had used.

Penny O'Brien sighed heavily. 'That was the thing, see? The reason Shannon didn't want to let him slip through her fingers was because he said he was a model who had a chance to break into acting. He had just landed a big part in some film that was going to be shot in LA. Shannon was obsessed with celebrities. Followed a lot of them on Twitter and Instagram. As soon as he offered to take her with him to LA . . . well, there was no changing her mind after that.'

Harri thanked Mrs O'Brien and hung up. She mulled over what she had been told. Whether or not it held any weight she couldn't say. Had he treated Shannon differently? Was this his way of getting her to trust him? Just as he had done with the other two victims. All she knew was that it was a different tactic but the same result. She would have to go into the Murder Room and add this new piece of information to the profile. It seemed that their killer might have a property in Islington. This would explain the London postmarks.

Harri considered whether he had murdered the victims at this unknown property in Islington and then driven the bodies up to Newcastle. Both murder victims had been dead for between eight and twelve hours, which gave the killer enough time to murder them in London and then drive up to dump them.

She thought of what they knew about the killer: he drove a white transit van and he knew details about Harri that had never been publicly released. She started searching, knowing that she was running out of time. Frustrated, she looked at the names and addresses of white van owners on the computer. Scrolled down. She was looking for something, anything that would stand out – *to her*. If this was about her, then there was no one better equipped to see a connection. She had already checked to see if any of the registered owners worked within the Met or the Northumbrian police force. The result had come back negative. Not that it surprised her. She printed off the list of names and addresses to look at later. She thought about the significance of Shannon O'Brien being given an address in Islington. Did he actually live there or was he trying to fool the police? Mac O'Connor lived in Islington . . .

Did that make Mac their killer? Her rapist?

She was hungry, tired and still in shock. The killer was

playing a game with them – with *her*. What troubled her was that the key to his identity could be down to Harri. *Was he the same man who had attacked and raped her?* She knew the answer. She could feel it. They were the same person. The question she couldn't answer was why he was doing it. For these were not simple murders; they were brutal, sadistic killings using a scalpel, a needle, black nylon and sulphuric acid. The question she kept asking herself was whether DI Mac O'Connor could possibly be behind these horrific mutilations.

'Sarge?'

Harri spun round. DC Michaels was standing awkwardly in the doorway.

She hurriedly started gathering up the printed paper. One thing Douglas could not abide was tardiness. He already had enough reasons to suspend her completely, without adding to it.

'You need to get someone to talk to Shannon O'Brien's mother. ASAP. She has just disclosed some new information,' Harri said, as she turned to leave.

'What?' asked Michaels, confused.

'Just do it,' Harri ordered.

'Yes, Sarge.'

'Why are you still standing there?'

'The witness, James Riley, just called.'

Harri frowned, irritated at his obtuseness. 'And?'

'He's finally remembered what the killer said to him.'

Harri knew that his reluctance had nothing to do with the fact that she had been removed from the investigation. No one knew – yet. Which meant that whatever the witness had heard could only be bad news for them. *Or her.*

'I haven't got all bloody night, Michaels!'

Crimson blotches spread across Michaels' cheeks. 'He said: "Tell Harri this proves how much I love her."'

She recoiled on hearing those words. *Sick and twisted.* 'Have you told the DI?'

Michaels shook his head. 'Not yet, Sarge. I thought you would want to hear it first.'

Harri nodded. She watched as Michaels quickly retreated.

Her skin was crawling . . .

The crisscross stab wound on the second victim's chest: the green glass eyes, the dyed blonde hair, the facelessness? Their bodies physically altered . . . He is turning them into you, Harri . . . 'This proves how much I love her.' He is turning his victims into you to prove how much he loves you. Oh God . . . What is he planning on doing to you, Louisa?

Chapter Twenty-Seven

'Shit!' Harri cursed as she reread the first report. She had just finished the second report. She had two seemingly unrelated victims. Time of death less than an hour apart. Choice of death – suicide.

She resisted the urge to kick the wall. Anything to get rid of the pissed-off feeling that was eating her up inside. She was stuck in here – Douglas' office – while the team were in the Murder Room being briefed on the latest developments. That would include the killer's message that the witness had finally recalled. She shuddered at the meaning of those words: *Tell Harri this proves how much I love her.*

Douglas had given her some time to herself, worried that she might feel uncomfortable at her own desk in the open-plan room shared with other colleagues.

There was a knock at the door.

'Come in.'

'Hey, Sarge. Brought you a coffee and a chicken and mayo sandwich,' Robertson offered. 'The DI thought you might need it.'

She sat back and watched him place the coffee and sandwich on Douglas' desk. She realised she hadn't eaten. Not that she had the appetite to stomach anything after being removed from the investigation. She had never felt so powerless.

'See you've been promoted eh? Got an office all to yourself,' Robertson commented.

'Yeah. You can get an upgrade as well if you want. All you have to do is become some psychopathic killer's obsession. No big deal, really,' Harri replied, unable to help herself, even though she knew that Robertson was only trying to make light of it.

'Look . . . Sarge . . .' Robertson shrugged awkwardly. 'It's a shit situation. All the team want to do is nail this fucker before—' He abruptly stopped.

'Before what?'

Robertson looked even more awkward.

'He kills me?' Harri shrugged in turn, then reached over and picked up the coffee. 'Thanks, Robertson, I appreciate this,' she said. 'And you're right, it's a shit situation. But I'm counting on you lot to get him . . . And you will.'

Robertson gave a nod of acknowledgement. He didn't seem that convinced, which told her the investigative team were still no further forward.

'Sit down for a minute.'

He looked as if it was the last thing he wanted to do. But he did.

'Do you have any possible leads on the van yet?'

Robertson reluctantly shook his head. 'I know I shouldn't be discussing anything with you, Sarge. But if I was in your situation, I would want to know every miniscule detail.'

'Thanks.' Harri replied. She was warming to Robertson. There was more to him than met the eye.

'How about the third victim? Any news?'

'Nothing.'

Harri turned her attention back to the computer screen.

'Is that the guy who jumped off the Tyne Bridge last night?'

Harri nodded. 'Believe me, it's not that exciting. Bloody stupid is what it was.'

'Yeah, but it's been posted all over social media.'

She was aware of that; it was why she was so pissed off. It had been her job to trawl through endless mobile phone footage of the bloke jumping.

'There's something about this suicide which is suspicious though,' Harri mused.

'Like what? Guy doused himself in petrol, set himself on fire while he was in the car. Then like a nutter he got out and jumped into the Tyne.'

Harri was aware of the details; she had watched it – repeatedly. It was a horrific spectacle. A blazing man jumping to his death; a ball of fire plummeting into the dark unwelcoming waters below. His body had been recovered and an autopsy was currently being performed. She was waiting to hear the outcome. She expected it to be straightforward. Why not? But something told her she would regret accepting the case.

'Robertson, help me out will you? I just want to make sure I'm not imagining this,' Harri asked as she found the recording that had so troubled her. She turned the laptop screen to face him.

'Look at the car the victim gets out of. It's quite blurred and the camera phone is understandably focused on him because he's set himself on fire. But look. See here.' Harri pointed to the corner of the screen. 'You see him?'

'Shit!' muttered Robertson. 'That looks like someone getting out the back of his car.'

Harri nodded. 'Look at this film here. Different angle. Can you see him watching the suicide victim? Waiting until he jumps and then disappearing into the chaos.'

'Do you think he was set on fire by someone else?'

'I can't say yet. I would need Munroe and his team to examine the vehicle. But there's something not quite right about this. I'm not sure whether the victim intended to jump to his death, or if he was jumping to try and save himself . . .'

It didn't take Harri long to establish that it was suspicious – in both cases. There were too many things that linked the two suicides. She had studied endless footage of the minutes leading up to his spectacular jump from the bridge and she was certain that another man had been present in the car. Then this unidentified man – over six foot, dressed in a long, black coat and a baseball cap that obscured his features – disappeared after the victim had jumped.

The force's resources were stretched to capacity with

the murder case, so the only help she had been given was Robertson and a handful of officers. Not that she was complaining – unlike him. He had taken it hard that he had been removed from the multiple murder case. But not quite as hard or as personally as Harri had taken her own suspension.

'See?' Harri pointed to the blurred grainy CCTV Nexus had provided of the Central Metro station. It was a five-minute walk to the Quayside from Central station and the Tyne Bridge.

Robertson nodded. 'It looks like he's reaching out to stop him from jumping.'

Harri shook her head. 'Watch again. This time look at the unknown suspect's other arm. It's hidden from view but there is a second where I swear it makes contact with the victim's back, unbalancing him as the Metro approaches. I reckon he knew exactly where the surveillance cameras were and he's positioned himself so only this side of him is on view. The side that shows him reaching out, but failing to grab the victim, while simultaneously the obscured hand pushes him. I've watched the footage leading up to it and it seems as if they were having an argument. The victim walks away up to the end of the platform and the suspect follows him. Then it looks as if the victim jumps and our suspect is trying to save him. I've managed to track him on some CCTV footage immediately after but then there's nothing until we find what appears to be the same suspect on the Tyne Bridge watching as another man jumps to his death. I didn't spot him at first. It was only when Stuart enlarged this image for me that I noticed a figure in the crowd wearing a baseball cap and coat similar to the suspect on the Metro platform. I then got Stuart to run a match of images taken from both suicides and it's the same man.'

'Shit, Sarge,' Robertson muttered.

'We need to know what connects two local thirty-year-old Caucasian males, both in full-time employment, financially solvent and low-risk victims, with this unidentified male,' Harri instructed as she looked at the grainy frozen footage of the man. It was impossible to make out any identifiable traits. Even the image they had taken of him from Nexus was poor quality. To add to their frustration the baseball cap was pulled down low over his face, preventing them from seeing his features.

She couldn't ignore the disquiet she felt about the witness – *suspect* – who had been present at both suspicious deaths. Two men, Elijah Hofmann and Anthony Johnson, had died in Newcastle on the same night, less than hour apart, witnessed by the same man. Harri didn't believe in coincidences.

'We need to interview their next of kin,' Harri said.

'Come on, Sarge. You know I hate that shit. And they've already given statements which we've read. Repeatedly. There was nothing in there. They didn't know each other.'

'Something connects these two suspicious deaths and it's our job to find out what.'

'But it's late.'

It was just after 9:00 p.m.

'You're right,' Harri agreed.

Robertson couldn't hide his relief.

'Which means that they'll be home,' Harri continued, ignoring Robertson's crestfallen expression.

Chapter Twenty-Eight

She heard him breathe out. Heavily. Harri was aware that Robertson was having a tough time. He couldn't stand grief. This was bad; enough for Harri to feel uncomfortable.

She looked at Anthony Johnson's heavily pregnant wife. She refused to sit down and instead, kept pacing backwards and forwards, despite her parents' pleas.

Harri ignored the scathing looks from them. Both sat on the opposite sofa, grim-faced, tight-lipped and furious at Harri and Robertson's unwelcome intrusion.

Chantelle Johnson abruptly stopped pacing and spun round, her pale, hollow-eyed face etched with unimaginable pain.

Harri's update that her husband's suicide was now being treated as a suspicious death had only added to her stress levels, just as her parents had predicted.

When they had knocked, Chantelle Johnson had already gone to bed. So Harri had taken the opportunity to glean as much as she could from the parents about their son-in-law. She had found out nothing more than what was in their statements.

Then Chantelle had heard their voices and understandably come downstairs. She and Robertson were now sitting like hostages waiting to be released. She was still trying to negotiate the terms with the victim's highly volatile, heavily pregnant wife. Harri could only wait it out. The last thing she wanted to do was make matters worse. *If that was possible.*

She waited as Chantelle Johnson stood facing them – *her* – with her hand placed protectively over her swollen belly. Tears were flowing down her face. The anger had seemingly dissipated – for now. As had the screaming. When she had overheard that her husband's suicide was now a suspicious death, she had become hysterical – just as her parents had predicted. After all, on being informed of her husband's suicide that morning, Chantelle had to be administered with a mild sedative by an emergency GP.

But now, Harri had moved the goalposts, Chantelle was being forced to relive the fact that her husband was dead. Worse, that someone might have poured petrol over him, set him on fire and then watched as the victim, consumed in a ball of flames, jumped to his death.

'Who would do that to Anthony?'

'I can't answer that question. But that's the reason we're here. To try to figure it out,' answered Harri.

She watched as Chantelle Johnson shook her head, still not believing what had happened to her world. 'He was loved by everyone. No one had a bad word to say about him. No one . . .' She looked at her parents, who both nodded in agreement. 'I have no idea who could do this . . . Who would want . . .' She faltered.

Harri gave her a moment before continuing. 'You said in your statement that you went to bed at 9:30 p.m. last night because you were tired and you left him watching a film on the TV. That was definitely the last time you either saw or had any contact with him?' Harri asked. She didn't like doing it, but she had no choice.

'I've already said all that!' she spat back.

Harri nodded. 'I just want to make sure I haven't missed anything . . . And you have no idea why he would have left the house and driven to the Tyne Bridge?'

'No!'

Harri steeled herself. 'The name Elijah Hofmann, does that mean anything to you?'

She had caught Chantelle off guard. Her anger, gone. Confused, she shook her head.

'Had you ever heard your husband mention his name?'

'No . . . why?' she asked.

'I was just wondering if they were friends. That's all.'

'Is he responsible?' she asked as she looked at her parents, then back at Harri.

'No. I was just eliminating his name,' she replied.

'Maybe he knew him from school? I don't know,' Chantelle said, shaking her head. 'But I don't recall his name.'

'Did you both go to the same school?'

She shook her head as she sat down with her parents. 'No . . . different schools. He went to Church House School in Jesmond and I went to a school in Durham. We went to his old school for an open day a month back to register the baby and Anthony pointed out a framed photo in the hallway taken of his year. I asked who was who in the photo and he had named all of his classmates, but he never mentioned that name. I'm sure of it. You see, we're obsessed about names, we can't agree—' She stopped short, suddenly realising.

Harri nodded, not showing her surprise that Anthony Johnson had gone to the same school she had attended. She looked at Chantelle's distraught eyes. She forced herself to compartmentalise and move on.

'Have you found his mobile by any chance?' Harri asked. She watched as the father took hold of his daughter's trembling hand.

'No,' he answered.

Harri nodded. Anthony Johnson's phone had not been found either in the car or on his body. There was a chance that if he was carrying it, it had fallen to the bottom of the Tyne river. But Harri had a feeling that wasn't the case. She was certain that his phone was relevant. Elijah Hofmann's mobile was also missing.

'Seriously, I'm fine sir,' repeated Harri. Her eyes were focused on her laptop as she talked to Douglas. She had been back at the station for over an hour working on what information they now had on the two suspicious suicides.

'You sure you don't want to call it quits for the night?' Douglas double checked. 'I can drop you off on the way.'

'Not yet. And don't worry about me, Robertson has already said he'd give me a lift home.'

'Make sure he does.'

Harri heard the line click dead. She picked up the bottle of water by her side and took a swig.

No witnesses on the platform at Central station had noticed the man with the baseball cap. Too busy on their phones or chatting to friends. She had watched the CCTV footage of the other passengers, which backed that up. No one saw what happened to Elijah Hofmann until it was too late and he had jumped – or was pushed – in front of the oncoming train.

The same was true with the other suspicious suicide. No one had noticed the suspect.

She looked at the clock: 11:49 p.m. She decided maybe it was time to call it a night. Nothing connected the two victims. *At least not that she could see.* She had already checked out Anthony Johnson's Facebook page and there were no messages there to suggest that he had arranged a clandestine meeting with someone late on Friday night. She had also run a check on his phone. He'd made no calls or sent any texts that evening; the only call received came from a number that wasn't in his contacts.

The number matched Elijah Hofmann's missing phone. The call had been made around the time he had jumped – fallen – under the train. Elijah Hofmann calling a stranger just before he killed himself – or was murdered – didn't make any sense. *Why? What are you not seeing, Harri?*

DAY THREE
SUNDAY: 3rd APRIL

Chapter Twenty-Nine

She deadbolted the door behind her and then flicked the lamps on. She felt agitated. Suddenly she had no control over her life. *Again.* She had an uneasy feeling that they – the police, Douglas, Harri – were playing right into the killer's hands. That this was what he ultimately wanted – Harri ostracised from the team. Alone. Vulnerable.

Douglas was holding a briefing at 8:00 a.m. to officially inform the rest of the team that she had been removed from the investigation. She assumed that the details of her assault would be picked over and analysed as the team tried to establish the connection. Douglas wanted to see whether word got back to the killer. And if it did, then he would know for definite that it was someone on the inside. Harri hadn't argued. There was no point. She understood his rationale, but didn't accept it. He had agreed that she could work on another case. However there was a caveat; he would be sending a car to collect and drop her off before and after work. Harri had asked him how long he intended on having her chaperoned. He had replied: 'For as long as it takes.'

She took out a bottle of beer from the fridge, carried it back over to the couch and sat down. She was too wired to sleep, even though it was after 1:30 a.m. She needed time to think. Not about the suicide investigation but about the one she was no longer involved in; one that she was integral to – as the killer's obsession. She thought of the evidence photograph, hand-delivered on the first anniversary of her attack. Then the four texts she had received; all from the same unknown number.

It doesn't make sense. Could your attacker really be this killer? Yes. But why the other victims? The MOs didn't match. What was she missing?

The two texts she had received yesterday at the crime scene came back to her. She scrolled up to the first one: *Do you know who I am yet, Harri? I can nearly touch you.* And then the second: *Is your skin crawling now?*

The texts were sent while she was at the alley where the second murder victim had been dumped. Coincidence? She doubted it. But did it make the person behind the texts her rapist or the killer responsible for two incomprehensible murders – or were they the same person?

If so what connected her to the murders? What connected her to him? The fact he had raped her?

She thought about both crime scenes. Both personal to her. The first had been a few minutes' walk from Church House School – her old school. The second crime scene near St Andrew's Church had filled her with unease because her bedroom had once faced out onto that graveyard – onto that alleyway. The allotment where

Shannon O'Brien's body had been found was further down from her childhood home, but it was close enough for her to know this was personal. The question that Harri was struggling with was how the killer knew all this about her.

The answer lay in whatever connection there was between her and the killer. She was acutely aware that he was trying to provoke a response. *He was killing for her ... and he was enjoying it.*

She knew that the texts and the crime scene photograph were connected to the sick and depraved game being played on the police – *on her* – by the unidentified serial killer. She took a slug of cold beer. Swilled it around in her mouth as she realised that she had no idea at all about the killer. None. Unless her suspicions about Mac were correct. That he was her rapist. But did that make him a sadistic killer?

What have you done, Harri, that would cause someone to kill for you? To try to turn his victims into you ...?

She lay in her bed with her eyes open. She couldn't sleep. She had tried for the past hour. She turned over, sighed, then kicked her left leg out from under the quilt. She was too overtired and too damned hot to get comfortable; yet as soon as she kicked the throw off her, she was too bloody cold. She lay there, listening to the stillness. Even that was irritating her.

Then she heard something. She was sure of it. The creaking of a door opening downstairs perhaps. Or closing? She jumped upright. Waited, feeling the adrenaline course through her body. Her sixth sense was screaming that something was wrong. That someone was in the building. It wasn't her imagination. *He was in the building. He had come back – as promised.*

She had spent a year waiting for this moment. She crept out of bed and quickly pulled on some jeans, a T-shirt and her boots. She grabbed her phone and stuffed it in her pocket. She then crouched down behind the door, and waited, baseball bat ready.

Then she heard it. A noise that made the hairs on the back of her neck stand up – a heavy whirring, grinding sound that reverberated around the old building as the 1930s elevator stirred to life.

FUCK!

Clunk … clunk … CLUNK …

She could feel her heart thundering in her chest. *Shit!* She felt paralysed as she listened to the lift as the groaning mechanical wheels and pulleys dragged it further and further towards the fifth floor. For a brief moment she thought about ringing Douglas. Then discounted it. What would she say? That the lift had started to move? If it was nothing more than an electrical fault she would look ridiculous – worse, scared.

What the fuck are you going to do, Harri?

She gripped the baseball bat tightly as the wailing screech of the lift got closer … And closer. She knew what she was going to do. And she knew that she wouldn't hesitate.

The first time he had attacked her, she hadn't been expecting it; even though he had stalked her, she had not imagined that he would have the keys to her flat. She wondered whether that had happened here; had he also managed to get keys to the building; to her apartment?

No . . . It isn't possible. But if not, who's out there?

She felt icy fingers trail down her back as the lift clunked to a halt. It had stopped – on her floor. An eerie quiet descended upon the building. It was waiting for her to react. To do something other than remain behind a metal door clutching a baseball bat. She held her breath and waited. Nothing. For a split second she looked at the alarm clock: 4:09 a.m.

Shit . . . shit . . . shit . . .

She didn't know what to do. Whether to call Douglas or not. One second she had decided to call him, the next second she had talked herself out of it. *Come on Harri, think!*

She couldn't. She was paralysed. *What if he is out there . . . waiting for you?*

But she knew that the lift doors hadn't opened yet.

Why is he waiting? Why doesn't he just come out?

She steadied herself, waiting for him to make a move; to open the doors. Nothing. It felt like hours as she remained silent, barely allowing herself to breathe, ignoring the deafening pounding of her heart as fear adrenalised every particle of her body. Sweat edged its way down her back.

She shot a furtive glance back over at the alarm clock: 4:12 a.m.

What the fuck is he doing? Come on, you fucker!

She leaned against the door; holding her breath, she listened for the slightest noise. Nothing. *Shit ...*

She didn't know what to do. But she knew that she couldn't remain hiding behind a locked door for the rest of her life.

Come on Harri, fucking do something!

She released the deadbolt and opened the door slightly. Enough to make out whether anyone was on the dark landing. She raised the baseball bat as she pushed the door further open. She couldn't see anyone. She checked the door that led to the stairs. Nothing. She then looked at the lift. Its doors were closed. But she knew someone was inside. *Him? Mac?*

The twisted knot of fear in her stomach tightened its hold. She contemplated approaching the lift doors and opening them; confronting whatever was behind.

Fuck ... fuck ... Come on, Harri ... Make a decision.

If it was him, then maybe it was time to face him. To balance the ledger. She was damned if she was going to let him touch her again. *Ever.*

She knew this wasn't an electrical aberration. It had never happened before. Someone was in the building – with her. That someone had pressed the button for the fifth floor, sending the lift up here. Whatever or whoever was behind the doors was intended for her. She could hear her heart beating faster and faster as she got closer. And closer.

Keep focused. Arm raised, baseball bat ready.

She willed herself to be calm. She had made a decision. One that she was prepared to live with for the rest of her life. Rather that, than live in fear every second of every day until he finally killed her.

Standing to the side of the doors, she used her elbow to press the open button. Then held the baseball bat back, ready, with both hands.

Fuck . . . fuck . . . MAC?

Chapter Thirty

She couldn't feel her body any more; the damp had seeped under her skin and into her bones. The cold numbness had even spread to her mind, dulling her thoughts. She was beyond tired. Whatever fight she had come in with had receded into the beckoning shadows. She felt a connection with the others, now that she understood the futility of it all. She wasn't getting out. She would remain forever seated in this old-fashioned wheelchair wired up to an IV drip. She willed herself to open her eyes. To look. For self-pity was not an emotion she allowed herself. *Not yet, at least.* But when she did, there was nothing but blackness surrounding her.

She strained to hear him below. She needed to know that she wasn't here on her own. But she was the last one. All the others had gone – with him.

She was sitting facing the window. It had been left wide open. The wetness of the night air caressed her skin. Not that she could feel it any longer. If she looked down she would see that her hospital gown clung to her like a second skin. Hanging limp, like her own flesh. But she couldn't look down. She could only look straight ahead. Out at the graves. The blackness had swallowed them.

But she knew where they were, she had memorised every one of them. She was sure he had buried *her* out there, alone, in the cold ground; the one with the broken bones – the broken *neck*.

Suddenly the gramophone scratched into life. The melodic notes stung at her senses, causing her hair to rise. She sat motionless in the dark and waited. Then she felt him behind her. Not that she could see a reflection in the window panes, for the entire sanatorium was shrouded in darkness.

He pulled the wheelchair back, away from the window, then spun it around and pushed her out of the ward into the hallway. She could see light spilling out from under the door ahead. He opened it and wheeled her in, blinding her as the bright lights stung her eyes. Then she grew accustomed and realised she was in an old bathroom with floor-to-ceiling tiled green and white walls. A rust-stained claw-foot bath stood in the centre. Empty. Against one wall stood an original Victorian toilet and free-standing wash basin.

She felt him start to brush her hair. Slowly. Delicately. An icy chill crept through her body. She knew now – *it was her turn*.

Fuck ... fuck ... no ... Not yet.

Terrified, she looked at the open medicine cabinet on the wall by the toilet. She could just make out the label on the vintage brown bottle: *Craig's Solution Hydrogen Peroxide*. She knew what was coming next. She watched, mute, as he took the lid off the bottle. The sharp, toxic smell filled the bathroom. He wheeled her over to the shower area, then pulled her head back and started to pour the solution over her hair.

She tried not to panic. To slow her erratic breathing down. But this was just the beginning of the process – the first step of his alteration. She tried to move her head. To object. But it was restrained by a leather strap; as were her wrists, torso and legs. She attempted to speak but nothing came out, for he had stuffed her mouth full of cloth and sealed it tight with duct tape. *Again.*

She thought of the others as the peroxide slid lazily down her taut neck. Of what she had witnessed him doing. For some reason, she had refused to believe it would happen to her. After all, she had been the privileged one. The one he had allowed to watch as the others died. For some reason she had taken this as a sign that he would keep her alive. Forever.

She closed her eyes against the burning chemical and waited. Finally he released her head so she could look straight ahead. Her hair, slick with hydrogen peroxide, hung in dripping clumps down her gaunt chest and bony back, burning her skin.

She stared into the blackness of the hallway opposite. Stared and stared, until she saw something in the shadows. She willed the light from the bathroom to push the darkness further and further back. Just enough for her to see – *them.* Three old wooden wheelchairs lined up against the wall. Debussy's third movement from the *Suite Bergamasque* scratchily continued on and on.

*My name is Louisa McPherson. My name is Louisa …
Louisa … Louisa McPherson …*

She repeated this mantra over and over, trying to erase
from her mind what he had just called her.

Subject C.

Chapter Thirty-One

Harri was sitting in Douglas' office. It was 9:10 a.m. The station was reeling from the news about DI Mac O'Connor.

She had been brought back here after Mac's badly beaten body had been rushed to the Royal Victoria Infirmary. The latest update from theatre wasn't good. His heart had stopped twice during emergency surgery to reduce the swelling to his brain. They had resuscitated him twice. The second time it had taken longer to shock his heart into beating again. It took less than five minutes for a patient to die after a cardiac arrest. It had taken the surgical team four minutes to revive him. Whether he would have brain damage was yet to be seen; repeated blows to his skull had caused internal haemorrhaging.

She exhaled. Slowly. Blocked the images of his unconscious, bloodied body lying there. She thought it would feel good. It didn't. It sickened her to her core.

She now had conclusive evidence that her rapist and the serial killer were the same person. The forensics lab had called her at 7:10 a.m. She had forgotten about the photograph of her that she had handed in. The technician's findings had put an end to any sliver of doubt that her rapist and the serial murderer were unconnected. Not that she had doubted it. A fingerprint and DNA had been recovered from the photograph; it was identical to the print and DNA evidence found on the photograph of 'Subject A' – the first victim, Tammy Summers. It all had been part of his game – his fun at her expense. He had left the evidence for her to find; eventually.

She had a lot of answering to do and right now she wasn't so sure of the consequences. She couldn't stop herself from trembling. It wasn't the black coffee she had drunk – it was the brown envelope addressed to 'DS Harriet Jacobs' on Douglas' desk. It had just been delivered. The postmark, identical to the other two envelopes – London.

She hadn't been allowed to open it. Douglas had dealt with that. But she had been granted the right to see the contents. The serial killer had not sent a photograph of Louisa McPherson as they had anticipated; instead, this image was of her.

It was a picture of her running along the Quayside. She recognised it. It had been taken in the early hours of Friday morning – 1st April; the first day of the murder investigation, the day when Tammy Summers' disfigured body had been reported. The photograph was a close-up of her sweating face. Her New England Patriots baseball cap was pulled down low; but not too far down to obscure her bright green eyes. That was all that was visible – her green eyes. The killer had scratched out every other facial feature, so it eerily resembled a feature-less mask.

Across the bottom of the photograph he had typed: *Now you are perfect.*

She thought back to that run. To the unease she had felt. Then to the photograph she had found afterwards. The stark image of the injuries to her face and the brutal wound across her neck. *That was personal.* It had thrown her back to when it had happened. It had brought back all the emotions associated with that night: fear, shame and above all, terror. She thought of the texts she'd been sent. The repeated question: *Do you know who I am?*

She bit her lip as DI Mac O'Connor's virtually unrec-ognisable face came to mind, his skull so shattered that part of it had collapsed. She had been so certain that he was her rapist.

How could you have got it so wrong, Harri? How?

But she knew how. She had been played. *He* had played her. She had only realised that Mac could not be her rapist after she had called the emergency services. *But by then it was too late ...* It was only then that she read the text sent at the exact moment she opened the lift doors.

You were always too perfect for him. Do you know who I am yet, Harri?

She had stared at Mac's lifeless body as the paramed-ics had attended to him. If he had not been wearing his legendary leather jacket she would not have recognised him. She had walked straight into the killer, her rapist's, trap. She now had Mac's blood – his life – on her hands. Her silence regarding the photograph and texts had potentially killed him. If she had shared the information with the team, with Douglas, then perhaps she wouldn't be here in the midst of all this chaos. And Mac's life wouldn't be in jeopardy. The text confirmed he had left Mac's body for her. The forensic evidence recovered from Mac's clothes matched the DNA on both photographs sent by the killer on the first day of the investigation; one to her home, the other to her workplace.

How did he get to you Mac? And why ... Why the fuck did he want to kill you?

She realised that only Mac would be able to tell them that. That is, if he lived, never mind regained consciousness.

A sliver of unease snaked its way down her back. She had wanted Mac O'Connor hurt – *dead, even?* She had been so sure that he had raped her. Now she was at a loss as to who the real attacker and killer was. But time was running out. It was a very clear message – he had turned his attention fully onto her.

She looked at the other item sent with the photograph that morning. It was an identity tag, identical to the ones that the victims had been holding. It had her name on – DS Harriet Jacobs: Subject D. The D.O.D. – *the date of her death* – tomorrow. 4th April. The cause of death was blank. Her throat felt too tight.

Harri shook her head, not quite accepting what she was seeing. She could feel Douglas' eyes on her. She readied herself for the onslaught. She had had no choice but to tell him about the texts; texts she now believed were from the unidentified serial killer; the man who had clearly set out his intentions to kill her.

She raised her head to meet his gaze. Douglas' expression was dispassionate; controlled. Too controlled. But his eyes belied his face. They burned at her with such intensity that she was forced to drop her gaze.

'When the hell were you thinking of telling me about these texts?'

'I thought it was a prank ... That someone at the station was playing a sick April Fools' joke. What happened to me isn't a secret so I assumed it was a colleague. It seemed the most rational explanation.' She felt awkward – she had been caught lying. She tried to convince herself that she had just been selective with the truth.

'And the photo of you after your attack?'

'Same. I just thought someone at work had accessed the evidence and took a copy of the photograph, sir.'

Douglas didn't look convinced. In fact, he was furious with her. She had crossed a line. She had withheld evidence, unwilling to accept that it could be from a killer who had sadistically murdered two young women and was no doubt preparing to kill his third victim, Louisa McPherson – *if he hadn't already*. A killer who had made it clear to Harri that the fourth victim would be her.

'It wasn't your decision whether or not to take these texts or the photograph seriously, it was mine. You completely ignored the chain of command and took matters into your own hands.'

'I waited until I was certain it was him—'

'That's my point,' Douglas interjected. 'You waited! What if he had abducted you this morning? It could have been you lying in theatre right now. Or on an autopsy table. You don't get to decide what is and isn't significant, DS Jacobs. That's my job!'

'I did inform you sir. Now,' Harri tried. She could see from the flash of anger in his eyes that he wasn't impressed.

'That's because you had no other choice.' He clenched and unclenched his right hand as he looked down at the evidence on the table. He studied the photograph of Harri's face and the identification card, identical to the ones tied to the murdered victims' toes.

'For fuck's sake, Harri! You even had the photograph he delivered to your apartment sent to the lab without my permission! You explicitly told me he did not know where you lived! Who knows how long he's been stalking you!'

She didn't say anything. Douglas was right. She had withheld information, bypassed his authority and lied. All so she could catch the man who promised to return to kill her. It had all blown up in her face. DI Mac O'Connor's life was currently in the hands of the surgeons. Louisa McPherson was still missing and two young women had been murdered – all because of the killer's obsession with her. He had specifically chosen very large women who he had drugged and slowly starved so they lost nearly half their body weight and then he had physically altered them, cutting away layers and layers of excess skin and stitching the flesh together. He had removed all identifiable traits – their facial features melted away, their eyes and hair colour changed to match Harri's.

The phone rang.

Harri remained perfectly still despite the sudden adrenalin surge. She assumed it was news about the white transit van. The names and addresses of registered owners of vehicles that matched the van had been scrutinised. Not one name was connected to either the Met or the Northumbrian force. Or to Harri.

'DI Douglas,' he answered.

She watched his expression, trying to gauge what he was being told. If they had found something tangible that could lead them to the serial killer.

'Fine,' concluded Douglas.

He hung up and wearily rubbed a hand over his face.

'Sir . . .'

He sighed. She realised that he wasn't going to share whatever he had heard. 'Question is, what do I do with you?'

'You let me do my job. I'm getting somewhere with the suicide case, sir. You haven't got the resources to assign it to someone else.'

He shook his head. 'Too dangerous. I've already said that until we catch this bastard you are staying right where I can see you. You've refused to be taken to a safe house, so you stay put.'

Harri had been forced to pack clothes for the next few days; or until they found the killer. After all, she was now the primary target. Since she had refused the safe house or a hotel room with an armed officer stationed outside, Douglas had offered to let her sleep in his spare room when he quit for the day – which might not happen for some time, given the seriousness of the investigation – rather than have her staying at the station. He was intent on monitoring her every move. Not that she could blame him, considering.

Her phone rang. She pulled it out and put it on silent.

'Sorry, sir. It's Munroe. I asked him to examine something connected to one of the suicides and he said he'd call if he found something suspicious.'

Douglas sighed again. 'All right. You can continue working on the two suicides. But I need to know your exact whereabouts. You need a piss, you ask me first. Understand?'

'Sir.'

'And if you dare disregard that order, then believe me, I will have no choice but to suspend you and put you under twenty-four-hour protection.'

Harri nodded. She didn't care what caveats Douglas put in place, as long as she could stay on the job. She needed something to focus on, to take her mind off the fact that she was the primary target of a psychopathic serial killer. She was being hunted. She thought of DI Mac O'Connor, fighting for his life. She had been so focused on him, the real rapist had completely eluded her. It was obvious that it had to be someone connected to the police, but the searing question was, *who*?

Chapter Thirty-Two

Her phone vibrated again: James Munroe. She had been meaning to call him back. She still felt nauseous. She knew it had nothing to do with lack of sleep, or food. It was the fact that she had fucked up, big style. And Mac O'Connor had ended up a casualty. The Met had been in touch with Douglas. Questions were being asked on both sides. However, Mac was the only one who could fully answer them. A police officer would be positioned at all times outside his hospital room. That was, if he made it through surgery. His wife had been informed and was making the journey up from London.

She tried to steady herself. She had to let it go. For now. She needed to prove to Douglas that he needed her and that he could trust her to do her job. She looked at her vibrating phone and clicked *answer*.

'What did you find?' She had asked Munroe to examine Johnson's car. The fact he was calling told her he had found something.

'The driver could not have poured the flammable liquid over himself. The direction of spray is indicative of someone behind the driver throwing it over him.'

Harri had already come to this conclusion, but it was good to hear it vindicated.

'Thanks, Munroe. I owe you one for putting in the time for this. I know you're stretched.'

'Not too stretched to help you out. You OK? Just . . . I heard . . .'

Harri nodded. To herself, for no one could see. 'Yeah . . . I'm coping.'

'That's all I need to hear. But if you want something . . . anything, you've got my number. Yeah? No matter what time it is, you ring me.'

Harri had to hold her breath to keep in the tumult of emotions she was feeling. 'I will,' she mumbled.

'Promise me?'

'I promise . . .' Harri answered, trying her damnedest to hold herself together. Munroe had often worked with her father, and she knew he was assuming responsibility for her in his absence.

It was early Sunday afternoon and she had spent the past few hours trying to find a connection between the victims. Something that tied the unidentified man to them; for she was certain that these men had not chosen to die. Munroe's findings had also corroborated her suspicion.

Medical information from their GP practices had confirmed that neither victim had been suicidal. Autopsies had now been carried out, given the suspicious circumstances. The findings were no surprise; both men had died from the injuries they had sustained. There was nothing unusual in the toxicology reports. The first victim, Elijah Hofmann, had had a high concentration level of alcohol present, which was to be expected; he had spent the night, as he did every Friday evening, with friends in The Forth Hotel on Pink Lane, only a two-minute walk from Central station. His three friends had been questioned and Harri had read through their statements. Nothing out of the ordinary had happened and Elijah Hofmann had been in typically good spirits.

Both men's apparent suicides had been completely unexpected to their families and friends. But it was the second suicide that had received most media attention; the spectacular and gruesome death had been filmed by other drivers on the bridge and shared via social media, where the footage had received countless hits. It was like a virus spreading from one host to the next. The police had no chance of trying to contain it, let alone remove it. It was at times like this that Harri questioned the contemporary world and its macabre fascination with footage of horrific events. Her mind turned to Jason Tanner's friends, who had filmed him murdering a homeless man so it could be shared on social media.

Troubled, she stared at the suspect's obscured face. It was impossible to identify him. What connected these two suicide victims? Something did: the man in the baseball cap and long, black coat.

She steeled herself as she waited for the phone to be answered. It was 5:52 p.m. in Dubai.

'Yes? Hofmann residence?'

'Detective Sergeant Jacobs, can I talk to either Mr or Mrs Hofmann? They're expecting my call.'

Harri waited as the line temporarily went dead.

'Detective Jacobs?'

'Mr Hofmann. I am deeply sorry for your loss.'

'I am sure you are. Why did you want to talk to me? My wife and I both gave a statement yesterday regarding our son's . . .' He let the word hang. Not quite able to say it.

The silence was awkward.

'I'm ringing because I believe his death to be suspicious.'

'Meaning what, exactly?'

'I can't say for definite, but I believe someone wanted to hurt your son and stage it as suicide.'

She heard a sharp intake of breath and the muffling of the mouthpiece as he hissed something to his wife. Then: 'I said as much to Eva! I said to her, "why the hell would Elijah take his own life?" He had too much to live for. You know he had just been made a partner in his law firm? Only happened a week ago. And he had just bought plane tickets to come over here next month.'

'I need to ask if you know anyone who might have wanted to hurt him.'

'You mean, murder him?' he asked, unable to hide his incredulity.

Harri had not been expecting such a direct question.

'Yes, Mr Hofmann.'

'No! Of course not. Elijah got on with everyone. No one had a bad word to say about him.'

Again, Harri had read as much in his friends' statements.

'Did he have a girlfriend?'

Harri knew the answer, but she wanted to double check. She heard him sigh. He covered the mouthpiece again and said something to his wife.

She waited.

'No. Split up with Rebecca two years ago. Been single since.'

'One last question, what school did Elijah attend?'

'What significance does that have?' he demanded.

'I need to know as much about your son's background as possible.'

'He went to school in England. Church House School in Jesmond. He was there from five to eighteen. Does that help?'

'I am sure it will.' That was the connection between the two suicides; both Elijah Hofmann and Anthony Johnson went to the same school and would have been in the same year. Both men were thirty years old; the same age as Harri. Both pupils at Church House School; the same as Harri. She had not recognised either of them as adults but accepted that the last time she would have seen them would have been when they were twelve. Nor had she recognized their full names. Not at first, as she had only ever known them by their nicknames. 'Did he ever mention another pupil called Anthony Johnson?'

She waited. 'Yes. My wife is saying that Anthony was one of his closest friends at school. Why? Don't tell me you think he's connected to Elijah's . . . death?'

'I'm not sure yet, Mr Hofmann. You see, Anthony died on the same night as your son. It happened less than an hour later. At a different location.' Harri thought back to her conversation with Chantelle Johnson late last night. She had been adamant that she had not recognised the name, and that her husband had never mentioned it.

'How did he die?'

'He jumped from the Tyne Bridge.' Harri decided it was best to leave out the fact that he had plummeted to his death, consumed in a ball of fire. She was sure he would find out soon enough.

'Coincidence?' he asked.

Harri could hear the scepticism in his voice. 'I can't say at this stage.'

'You've got no idea who would do this? Who would want to make people believe he had taken his own life? It's . . . It's beyond anything I can comprehend!'

'We're doing our utmost, Mr Hofmann, to find out exactly what happened to Elijah, and why.'

'We're on a flight to the UK later this evening. I hope by tomorrow afternoon you have more information for us.'

She could have waited until they had arrived in Newcastle the next day. But she needed to find out as soon as she could whether there was anything that connected the two murdered men. And now she had.

'Do you know if Anthony and Elijah were still friends?' She knew it was a long shot, as they did not follow each other on social media. In fact, Elijah's friends had never heard of Anthony Johnson. Nor had Johnson's wife heard Elijah's name mentioned. She found this odd, but not unusual. She herself, like many people who went off to University, had no contact with friends from her school days. She had moved on – literally. And she assumed that was the case with both Elijah and Anthony. But they must be connected by something from their past – *a past that had caught up with them.*

'Not as far as we were aware.'

'I appreciate your help, Mr Hofmann and again, you have my sincerest sympathies,' Harri said.

'If you'd known my boy, Detective Jacobs, you would have realised that he wouldn't hurt anyone. He was a good man. A son any father would be proud to have raised . . . Why would someone want to hurt him?'

Harri didn't answer him. She couldn't. She listened as the line finally went dead.

She sighed. Took a drink of coffee as she mulled over what they had so far. She picked out a chocolate biscuit from the packet Robertson had left.

As she ate it, she thought about the date they had both died – 1st April. She knew it wasn't a coincidence. Nor was the fact that they had both attended Church House School in Jesmond – the same school as her.

She didn't believe in coincidences.

Chapter Thirty-Three

'Thank you for returning my call,' Harri said.

'I'm sorry that you've had to wait so long. Right, I've had a look through the school records and there is nothing here.'

'Are you certain?' Harri frowned at the newspaper article she had managed to find. It had taken her hours of searching for anything, regardless of how tenuous, that tied the school to the date: 1st April. Finally she had found something; whether it was of any significance remained to be seen. She had been hoping that Mrs Donaldson, the current headmistress of Church House School, would be able to enlighten her. It seemed not.

'Absolutely. I checked and none of our pupils have been involved in any such accident. Obviously, it would have made my job easier if you could have given me the pupil's name and age.'

'I'm sorry. I knew it was asking a lot of you.'

Harri's eyes scanned the local newspaper article in case she had missed something. She could feel Mrs Donaldson bristling at being summoned to her office on a Sunday for nothing more than a suspicion.

'You said it involved a student from CHS. Otherwise I would not have wasted my time. You do know there are two other schools in Jesmond?'

'I made a mistake, I apologise. The article said the pupil was from CHS,' lied Harri. She knew that if she had told the headmistress that the article described the victim as a boy from Jesmond, she would have found herself waiting until tomorrow.

Harri reread the article – again. It had been published eighteen years ago on 2nd April. It had reported that the evening before, a school boy from Jesmond had been seriously burnt. He had been throwing siphoned petrol over a pile of leaves and twigs in Jesmond Dene; a narrow wooded valley that stretched for nearly two miles along the River Ouseburn between South Gosforth and Jesmond. It was an inner city haven for dog walkers, naturalists and kids.

Not realising that some of the liquid had splashed onto his clothes, he had struck a match to light the bonfire and ignited. It had been a small item of news, one that had not appeared anywhere else. The victim's name and age had been omitted. The article had gone on to state that there had been no suspicious circumstances and the police had dismissed it as an accident, explaining why there were no records of the incident within the police database.

Harri had also checked the Freeman Hospital and the Royal Victoria Infirmary, but neither one had admitted a male of school age suffering from serious burns on the night of the accident. It was an enigma.

Whether it was connected to the two murders, she couldn't say.

'I suggest you talk to the other local schools in the area. Now, if that's all?'

'Did you notice anything unusual in either Elijah Hofmann or Anthony Johnson's records? Anything that would connect them?' Harri asked, ignoring the fact that the headmistress had clearly had enough of having her time wasted.

She heard Mrs Donaldson tap a pen on her desk repeatedly before answering: 'No, Detective Sergeant. Nothing. If I had, I would have told you.'

'Did they get into trouble for anything connected with another pupil?'

'They both had exemplary records. Academically, socially and on the field. I'm afraid I can't tell you any more. But I became head teacher here ten years ago. Both these pupils had left by then.'

'One last question, did anyone drop out of their school year?' Harri asked. She thought that maybe Elijah Hofmann and Anthony Johnson had bullied someone. It was the only answer she could find that might connect them to their killer.

She heard the headmistress sigh. She had clearly had enough of Harri's demands.

'Look . . . I'm not intending to be uncooperative, but that would take time.'

'I can come to the school now, and wait. Or you can call me back?' Harri suggested. This was no longer two unconnected suicides, or even suspicious deaths.

These were two linked murders, staged to look like suicides. But why? Who wanted both these men dead? She was certain the key was buried somewhere in their past.

The constant pen tapping ended. Abruptly. 'I'll call you back.'

Satisfied, Harri sat back and looked across at the whiteboard. It hit her hard again; the grainy image of a man plummeting from the Tyne Bridge, his body devoured by flames. It was inconceivable. But it had happened. The image was right in front of her.

The victim's wife had said in her statement that her husband had everything to live for; the same was true of Elijah Hofmann. Both men were well-liked, respected and had no enemies to speak of. But the evidence on the whiteboard told her the opposite was true. However, neither had any priors, nor had either one been subject to harassment or threats of any kind. At least, any that had been reported to either the police, or family and friends.

She considered the significance of the date when they had died; Friday, 1st April. Elijah Hofman had been pushed in front of an oncoming train at exactly 11:01 p.m. Then at 11:06 p.m. a call was made using his phone to the next victim, who then must have met the murder suspect, considering the footage of him getting out of the victim's car to watch Anthony Johnson's burning figure run to the bridge's edge, climb over and then jump without a second's hesitation. That had happened just before midnight.

The man wearing the baseball cap must be connected somehow to both men. She had had two of the officers assigned to her piece together CCTV footage from Central station. The man could be seen following Elijah Hofmann through the busy station and then underground to the Metro platform. The attack was not random – the second murder proved that – so Harri assumed that the killer must have known that Elijah drank in The Forth Hotel on a Friday night and that he always left around eleven-ish to catch the train back to his flat. The killer must have known Anthony Johnson's mobile number to make the call from Elijah Hofmann's phone.

The connection she had was that both had attended the same school. *But was that enough?*

She turned as Robertson walked into the room.

'What did you get me?'

'Tuna melt, just like you asked,' he answered, throwing her the package.

Harri caught it in mid-air. 'Cheers.'

'Did anything come from that head teacher?'

Harri shook her head. 'Waiting for her to call back.'

Robertson placed a black coffee on the desk next to her and then pulled up a chair.

'You heard if they've got any further in finding Louisa McPherson?' she asked him. She had heard that the other murder team were getting closer and that the Islington location Shannon O'Brien had mentioned to her mother was key, but that was all she knew.

'Nothing,' he mumbled, chewing. He wiped his mouth

before adding, 'Too busy working to get a chance to talk to anyone.'

Harri accepted what he said, even though she had seen him chatting in the corridor to DC Michaels, who was still assigned to the original investigation. Douglas would have briefed everyone, Robertson included, not to share any new developments for fear of compromising the investigation, or more likely, herself. Douglas was no fool; he was acutely aware that she had withheld information in the vain hope that she would be able to get to her rapist before he got to her. Now she had no chance.

'Did you get any further with the *Evening Chronicle*?' Harri asked. They had tried to contact the journalist who had written the article but had hit a dead end, literally; the journalist had died in a car crash five years back.

Robertson shook his head. 'Nope. They have no idea who the kid could be. Like they said, it happened years ago.'

'What about Robert Fraser's personal things?' Harri asked. The journalist had had no immediate family or friends, and had lived anonymously in a cheap hotel room in the city centre. It seemed that no one knew very much about him. Or cared, for that matter.

Robertson shrugged as he attempted to chew through an inordinately large chunk of steak and cheese baguette. 'Cleared out when he died. No one had an address for his next of kin, or even any mates. Chances are it was binned.'

Her phone rang. She wiped her hands on a paper napkin before answering.

'Thanks for getting back to me so quickly.'

'It was easier than I thought it would be. There was only one student in Hofmann and Johnson's year who left during their time here.'

'What year were they in at the time?'

'Year Seven, so that would have made them twelve.'

'What was his name?'

'Marcus Fletcher.'

'Are you sure?' Harri asked.

'Absolutely. Attended our school from the age of nine to twelve.'

'When did he leave?'

'His fees were fully paid up until the end of the year, but it appears he never returned to school after the Easter holidays.'

'Why?'

'Well, that's the odd thing. There's no reason given.'

'Why does it strike you as odd?'

'Simply because we are an outstanding school. We do a good job at keeping our students and parents happy. We have to, there is stiff competition out there. If a student feels unhappy, we do everything in our power to fix it. If they still insist on leaving us, we make a point of understanding why, so we can prevent it from happening again. So Marcus Fletcher leaving with no intervention on the school's part, or explanation, is highly irregular.'

'Would your predecessor know why he left?' Harri asked.

'I would expect so.'

'Thank you. I appreciate your help.'

'Don't you need his name?' she asked.

But Harri had already hung up.

Chapter Thirty-Four

She knocked on the door again. No response. She looked at Robertson. 'You did call ahead?'

'Yes, Sarge. He said he would be waiting for us.'

'I hope so considering the crap I went through to convince the DI of the importance of me coming here.'

It had taken some doing, but she had managed to persuade Douglas to let her leave the station, on the condition she was accompanied by DC Robertson. She was in no mood for returning empty-handed. Irritated, she banged her fist. 'Police!'

The door was thrown open by a tall, white-haired gentleman. 'What?'

Harri was momentarily caught off guard by the authoritative figure of Tobias Patterson. He may have been in his mid-seventies but he was still the same irascible headmaster she had known and feared throughout her school years.

'I'm sorry to bother you—' she began.

'And you have every right to apologise. This is a bloody Sunday! And it's late in the day at that!'

'My colleague DC Robertson called you earlier to

explain that we need to ask some questions, if you don't mind?'

'And if I do mind?'

'Then I will have to bring you back to Newcastle to help with our enquiries.'

Tobias Patterson had retired to the wilds of Northumberland and the small, picturesque market town of Wooler which boasted the Cheviot Hills as its backdrop. It was an hour north of Newcastle by car, so she was hoping the threat of spending Sunday evening in the city's busy police station might make him reconsider his attitude.

'I'm not happy at being disturbed like this, I can tell you!' With that, he walked off down the hallway, leaving the door open.

'This will be interesting.' Harri steeled herself. It seemed that his temperament had not improved with retirement.

'I did ring him, Sarge. I told him we would be here within the hour. Which we are,' he said checking his watch.

'I have no doubt you did, Robertson.'

Harri and Robertson followed him through the oak-panelled hallway. The walls were covered in black-and-white photographs and awards; memorabilia from his days at Oxford.

'Take a seat if you must,' instructed Tobias Patterson as they entered his study. 'I would ask my housekeeper to make some tea, but it's her day off.'

'We're fine, sir. Thank you,' answered Harri as she

walked into the large room. French doors led out onto a long, immaculate garden.

She sat down on the tan Chesterfield sofa and gestured for Robertson to follow suit. The well-worn leather Queen Anne chair in front of the smouldering open fire clearly belonged to Patterson.

Harri had spent enough time in her old headmaster's office to know she had to bide her time until he was ready to engage. She watched patiently as he threw coal onto the fire, forcing it to splutter and cough its way back to life. He then took his time to sit down, moving various objects out of his way. Harri used the time to look around the impressive room. The walls were lined with bookcases; all full to capacity, dominated by the classics.

'Right. Exactly why are you here?'

Harri turned her attention back to him. He was sitting in his chair, hands poised together, waiting for an answer.

'It is in connection to an incident involving two ex-pupils from Church House School. Elijah Hofmann and Anthony Johnson—'

'I don't see how that has anything to do with me. You clearly have the wrong person. As you can see, I am retired,' Tobias Patterson interrupted. He stood up. 'If you don't mind?'

Harri ignored him.

'Sir, both men left sixth form twelve years ago. Both had been pupils there while you were headmaster.'

'I see,' said Tobias Patterson. He remained standing. 'I still think you have the wrong person. I can't help you. I have no access to school records. I retired over ten years ago.'

'I am aware of that. I have already talked to your successor, Mrs Donaldson. I am looking for something that could have happened while they were at school together, involving another student. There is nothing in the school records that stands out, apart from one pupil, Marcus Fletcher, who was in the same year as Elijah Hofmann and Anthony Johnson. He disappeared on the 2nd April when he was twelve. Mrs Donaldson could not tell me why he left, as there was no explanation recorded. She suggested I contact you.'

Both Anthony Johnson and Elijah Hofmann had exemplary records from their time at the school; neither one had been in trouble. The sudden departure of Marcus Fletcher was the only anomaly Harri could find. She realised she was clutching at straws, trying to find out if someone could have had a score to settle – enough to murder them on the same night. Their only connection with one another, apart from the fact that someone had killed them the same way and on the same night, was their time together at Church House School.

She looked at the retired headmaster and saw a flicker of something in his eyes. She realised he had remembered something. Whatever it was, he didn't want to share it.

'What did you remember?' Harri asked.

Tobias Patterson made an attempt at flattening down his wispy hair. His blue-veined hand was trembling.

'Sir? What did you recall?'

'I'm . . . I'm not sure . . .'

But Harri could see from the way he was trying to avoid any eye contact that he was certain.

'I can take a formal statement from you at Forth Banks station in Newcastle, if required.'

She had his undivided attention.

'Tell me the names of the two boys again.'

'Anthony Johnson and Elijah Hofmann.' Harri waited for a response.

He didn't reply, just sat back down, shakily.

It was clear from the heavy silence that he was considering how to respond.

'Detective . . .?'

'Detective Sergeant Jacobs, sir,' Harri answered.

'There was a rather dreadful incident with that Fletcher boy. He had an "accident" of sorts.'

Harri immediately thought back to the local newspaper article she had found; the only thing that tied together the date, 1st April, and the school in Jesmond.

'Nasty business. Marcus Fletcher never returned to school after the accident. From what I heard, he was helicoptered to a specialist burns hospital in Sussex for treatment. His injuries by all accounts were rather serious.' He paused and looked across at Harri. He gave a dismissive shrug: 'The boy never fitted in anyway. One of those loners who never integrated with the others. Not a team player, shall we say? Not our sort. There was something odd about him. Enough to make the other pupils and even the staff uneasy in his company. Parents had made money and had aspirations, if you understand me. Better for all that he left when he did.'

Harri remained silent.

'Unfortunate business, all the same,' he added.

'What did they do to Marcus Fletcher?' Harri asked, still ignoring his last statement.

'Who?'

'What did they do to him?' she repeated. She could see from the look in his eye that Marcus Fletcher's burns had not been self-inflicted. It was clear that Patterson was prejudiced against the boy, that he was defending whatever actions had been taken against this 'loner'.

He narrowed his eyes. Suddenly: 'I remember you!'

Harri could feel Robertson look at her. She had omitted to tell him that she, too, until the age of twelve, had attended Church House School and had once known the two murder victims. She hadn't recognised either of them immediately, but the connection with the school had jogged her memory. She had known Anthony Johnson simply as 'Ant' and Elijah Hofman as 'EJ'; however, no matter how hard she tried, she could not remember a pupil named Marcus Fletcher.

'I knew I recognised you! DCI Jacobs' daughter. He was quite a man, your father. Why he chose to remove you from Church House School and place you in that bloody convent was beyond me!' Tobias Patterson suddenly sprang up. Harri refrained from informing him that it was her mother, not her father who had removed her and forced her to spend the following six years in an overtly religious all-girls' public school. Instead Harri kept quiet. Not that Tobias Patterson expected a reply.

He walked over to his desk in the corner and started rummaging through what appeared to be an extensive collection of old, leather-bound books.

'Sarge?' whispered Robertson.

Harri shook her head and waited. She wasn't sure whether it was a simple avoidance tactic or if he was going to show them something relevant.

'Come! Have a look at yourself, Miss Jacobs,' he instructed after finding the yearbook.

Harri stood up, followed by Robertson.

'There you are,' Patterson said as his finger stabbed at a scrawny blonde-haired, twelve-year-old girl in a tartan skirt and grey wool blazer. 'Never forget a face!'

Harri could feel Robertson sniggering behind her. She tried to elbow him to shut him up. It failed. She looked at the school year photo. Her eyes scanning the regimented lines for Ant and EJ. She didn't have to look far. Both boys were to one side of her. She understood why Chantelle Johnson would not have recognised the name, Elijah Hofmann. Her husband would have simply referred to him as 'EJ' – that was what everyone, Harri included, called him then.

'Where's Marcus Fletcher?' Harri asked.

'There!' Tobias Patterson pointed him out.

He was standing directly behind Harri, his twelve-year-old face staring blankly at the back of her head.

'That's Jacob, isn't it?' Harri asked. 'I never heard him called anything other than Jacob.'

Tobias Patterson nodded. 'When he started at the age of nine he asked to be called by his middle name, Jacob, didn't like "Marcus" for some reason. So he was registered in all his classes as Jacob, but in any official capacity he was Marcus of course.'

Harri stared at him. She vaguely remembered him disappearing. It hadn't had much effect on her. He wasn't part of her social circle.

'This was taken at the end of March. Just before . . .' Tobias Patterson's voice trailed off.

'What did they do to him?' Harri had a bad feeling that the boys had committed some unthinkable act upon Marcus.

'It was Anthony Johnson. His grades had started to drop. I asked to speak with him. Johnson did come to see me, but with his parents. He thought I had found out about Marcus Fletcher's "accident" and that I was going to expel him and Mr Hofmann. He was rather shaken up by it. I had no idea what he was talking about. He started to explain that he and Hofmann were responsible for what had happened to the Fletcher boy. I suggested that he keep quiet about it. His parents agreed. Father was a District Judge, you see? Deceased now, sadly. It wasn't the sort of ugly mess one wanted to become public. Better to be discreet than have the whole thing blown out of proportion, what with the newspapers and everything. Something like that could have caused incommensurate damage to the school's reputation, let alone Hofmann and Johnson's futures. Anyway, the Fletcher boy never named them, thank God. He stuck to his story that he had accidentally set himself alight. I have no idea why. But I told Johnson and his parents to leave it at that.

Which they did. And no one has said a word about it since . . .'

'Thank you, for your time,' Harri said. She had all the answers she needed now.

'Hofmann and Johnson . . .' Tobias Patterson asked suddenly. 'What has happened to them?

'Again, thank you, sir.' With that, she gestured to Robertson that it was time to leave.

Robertson shook his head when they got back in the car. 'Seriously sick!' he muttered. 'So both Elijah Hofmann and Anthony Johnson doused this Marcus kid in petrol and set him on fire eighteen years back on 1st April. Then they both end up dead, on that exact date. One of them doused in petrol.'

'Exactly. We need to need to get back to the station and track down Marcus Fletcher's whereabouts,' Harri said as she swung the car around and accelerated.

'Make sure you get us back in one piece, Sarge. You know I signed the car out in my name. Any damage and it's me who'll get the blame!'

'Stop being a bloody backseat driver and get on the radio. We've got a murder suspect at large, Robertson. We need to move fast. I want a photograph of him released to the public to see if anyone knows his whereabouts.'

DAY FOUR
MONDAY: 4th APRIL

Chapter Thirty-Five

She had accepted the inevitable. She had to get out. He had not come back yet. It was late now. He had been gone for over thirty-six hours. It had given her enough time to prepare. She refused to become another statistic, to be his punching bag every time he was pissed off or he just felt like it.

Most of all, I refuse to die at your hands.

Then there was the other woman – the blonde-haired, green-eyed woman. The one he had talked about after he had nearly killed her in the hallway. She had distinctly heard him:

'*I will make her relive every moment of the rape. The blade slitting her throat open. Followed by the tip penetrating her chest. This time, I will finish what I started.*'

She had initially discounted it. Too afraid to accept the truth, to process what she was hearing. But she had memorised those words, so that when she felt weak and pathetic – *scared* – she would play them over and over again. If she couldn't save herself, she would do everything in her power to save this woman. She knew better than anyone what he was capable of.

She had broken his cardinal rule and gone up into the

attic. *His attic*. She had wanted to find a hammer – just in case; to protect herself. But what she had discovered had been enough to convince her that she had not misheard him. The boarded-up room was dedicated to *her*. The photos he'd taken of this woman without her knowledge had made her feel physically sick. But it was the crime scene photographs of her body, her face – her neck – that covered the walls that had convinced her. She had the evidence that she wasn't mad. She had even found a beautiful knife she assumed he had used to slit her throat. *He hid it in the attic that he had turned into a shrine. His crime that he could play in his head, again and again.*

She knew she had to get this information to the police before he reached the victim she had read about in the newspaper clippings that he had hidden in the attic; the petite woman with the long, curly blonde hair and green eyes that the newspapers had reported was a Detective Constable with the Met – if he hadn't already killed her.

She looked at her only way of escape. Then raised the hammer and smashed it as hard as she could into the bottom of the double-glazed French doors. It didn't work. But it had weakened the glass. So she raised the hammer again and this time thought of how she had been forced to crawl on the floor to the toilet for fear of waking him, and facing his anger at the fact that she had got out of bed without his permission. She remembered how she would lie on her stomach and hold her breath, waiting, hoping he wouldn't stir so she could edge her way past him to the bathroom; of how sometimes it could take thirty minutes to crawl just a few feet. She thought of the last time he had kicked and punched her out of bed for no reason, screaming at her.

'You fat, ugly troll. Look at you! With your tree-trunk legs and fucking tree-trunk arms. You're disgusting!'

She swung the hammer with so much force the glass shattered, drowning out his words.

Chapter Thirty-Six

Harri turned to Robertson as he came into the office space they shared.

'Tell me some good news.'

He shook his head.

It seemed she wasn't the only one who had hit a brick wall.

'Nothing. He disappeared at the age of eighteen. No trace of him since then.'

Harri contemplated the information on her computer screen.

'We're still checking if Marcus Fletcher changed his name or moved abroad,' Robertson added.

'Grab your coat. And car keys.'

'Where are we going?'

Harri picked up her leather jacket from the back of her seat and pulled it on.

'Sarge?' asked Robertson.

'I'll tell you on the way.'

'Seriously? It's late. I was hoping we could call it quits?'

The look in Harri's eye told him he had no chance.

'Sarge. Wait! Aren't you supposed to clear leaving the station with Douglas?'

But Harri wasn't listening. She was already walking.

She stared at the house. It was a secluded property off Elswick Road. It had belonged to Marcus Fletcher's deceased parents. 'Yep. This is it, Robertson. Pull over just there, behind that wall,' she instructed.

She had told Robertson to use his own vehicle; she knew that if she took one of the unmarked pool cars, it would have to be logged, and word would get back to Douglas. He may have granted her request to interview Tobias Patterson earlier, but she knew for a fact he would not condone her searching an abandoned property at this godforsaken time. It was late: 12:33 a.m. She didn't plan on being away from the station for too long, just enough time to take a look and see if there was anything that would lead them to Marcus Fletcher. She was sure that the man in the baseball cap and long dark coat caught on camera at both 'suicides' was Marcus Fletcher – a man now wanted for the murders of two men.

'Are you sure about this, Sarge?'

Harri turned to him as he killed the engine. She could see his trepidation. 'The house looks deserted, Robertson. But look, if we think otherwise, we pull back and call in back-up. Yeah?'

Robertson nodded, but his eyes told Harri that he still wasn't sure.

She understood why. They had a murderer who had struck twice in an hour late on Friday evening. He was a dangerous and violent suspect; one who didn't think twice about pushing one man under the wheels of a train, or dousing the other one in petrol, setting him alight and watching him choose whether to jump off the Tyne Bridge or burn to death.

'Do I think he's inside waiting for us to turn up?' Harri asked. 'For fuck's sake, no. He tried to make both murders look like suicides. He nearly got away with it. Now his picture is all over the media.'

'Yeah, but his face is hidden. He knows we can't identify him from the image released.'

'But he knows that we're looking for him. Whether he thinks we'll figure out his identity, who can say? Maybe he's a cocky bastard. Even then I doubt he would return to where he was known as Marcus Fletcher.'

'How can you be so sure?'

'Because he may be arrogant, but he's not stupid. His MO has already told us that. This guy covered his tracks. The reason we're on to him is serendipity at its purest level. If I hadn't been removed from the murder investigation, then I never would have taken these two suicides on. Same with you. Who knows if the two suicides would have been flagged as suspicious, let alone premeditated murders? Even if they had made the connection that Elijah Hofmann and Anthony Johnson went to the same school, they would still have to find a name. And a motive. The newspaper ran a small piece about a twelve-year-old local pupil suffering an accident. It never mentioned Marcus Fletcher's name or the school he attended. It was only chance that I found out he'd left the school mid-term, which then led us to the fact that Johnson and Hofmann were responsible for a heinous

328

crime eighteen years back. Their names were never reported, not even by the suspect, and so they went unpunished.'

'Until now,' stated Robertson.

Harri nodded. She had an uneasy hunch that Marcus Fletcher had intentionally bided his time; eighteen years, to be exact. The question was why? Harri thought back to her conversation with the retired headmaster and his candid unease about his former pupil. She thought back to his words: *There was something odd about him. Enough to make the other pupils and even the staff uneasy in his company.*

The words sent a chill through her body.

Robertson's personal mobile rang. He looked at the number. 'Sorry, Sarge. That's the girlfriend, no doubt checking if I'm coming back tonight.'

'Take it,' said Harri. She could tell he didn't want to miss the call. He had surprised her again, as clearly he had feelings for the woman. The bad boy image he wore with pride seemed to be a front. 'I'm going to grab some fresh air and take a quick look around.'

'You sure?' Robertson asked.

'Sure. Five minutes. We need to get back before Douglas realises that I've gone AWOL. Otherwise, the shit will hit the fan!'

She got out the car. Robertson's face lit up as he spoke to the caller.

She assessed the house. It was isolated. It also looked deserted. The high metal gates were locked, so she jumped up and over the old stone wall. The place was shrouded in a heavy darkness. She fought the urge to take out her phone and shine it around in case the suspect was there. Also if someone noticed the light and reported a suspected break-in she would never be able to live it down.

She walked along the grass verge, avoiding the expansive driveway that swung around from the gates to the main house; an imposing old stone building. Harri shouldn't have been surprised; Tobias Patterson had implied that Marcus Fletcher's parents were nouveau riche. Whether it was old or new money, they had lots of it. She couldn't make out any vehicles, suggesting Marcus Fletcher had not returned to his childhood home.

Then why do you feel so fucking on edge?

Harri couldn't shake the feeling that she was being watched.

She continued walking towards the house, deciding that she hadn't come this far not to see whether it was lived in.

Seriously, Harri?

She silenced the unease, pushing it to the back of her mind, and reached the wide stone steps that led up to the entrance. Her legs felt like lead as she willed them to climb towards the ornate double doors. She stopped. Looked up at the first-floor window. She was certain that she had seen something.

Come on, Harri, there's no one there. The place is deserted.

Her hand reached out for the door handle. She tried it.

Just to check. It was unlocked. Both doors swung open in front of her.

Shit! She stood perfectly still, not crossing the threshold into the all-consuming blackness. She waited for her eyes to adjust. They didn't. She pulled out her phone and clicked the torch mode on. The house was set so far back from the main road that no one would see the suspicious light. There were piles of unopened mail on the floor.

Come on, Harri. That's why you came. Make a decision. Do it and get the fuck out of here!

A feeling of unease took hold. Something was wrong. She could feel it. She stabbed the weak torch light into the shadows. Nothing. Apart from her imagination.

She ignored the distinct unease and forced herself to walk into the house. She was being ridiculous. Marcus Fletcher wouldn't be here. He would have tried to get as far away as possible.

Wouldn't he?

She shook her head. She was being ridiculous. She wasn't the type to jump at shadows.

She stepped over the threshold, into the darkness. Every atom in her body felt like it had turned to ice.

She thought she heard something.

'Shit!' she cursed. She called Robertson. Waited and waited as it rang.

Fucking come on!

'Sarge,' he answered. 'I was going to ring you. Just got off the phone from the DI. There's been a new development. They've got a name—'

331

Her phone cut out. She looked at it and realised it had lost its signal. *Shit!*

There was a noise coming at her from behind. She spun round as an old-fashioned wheelchair rolled towards her out of the blackness.

SHIT!

She closed her eyes against the horror of what he had done. Sitting in the wheelchair staring straight at her was ... *Fuck* ... *Fuck* ... *It was her doppelganger.* Harri was staring at some macabre copy of herself.

Louisa McPherson: the remaining victim.

But this time it was different. This time he had completely altered the body. Had left her naked for the horror to be visible to all. The victim's dyed blonde hair had been loosely tied up to match Harri's. But unlike the other murdered victims, her face was hidden behind a white mask. Green glass eyes glinted through the mask's narrow eye slits.

But it wasn't the mask that unnerved her. She was transfixed by the wound across the victim's throat – he had slit her neck open to match her own assault. Her eyes took in the small, misshapen breasts. Above the left one was the unmistakeable stab wound. Numb, she stared at the lifeless body; the killer had removed every piece of loose skin and had stitched what was left back together. *He had completely altered her ... Changed her into ... You ...*

Her skin felt as if it was crawling. She spun round.

She was staring at DI Aaron Bradley, the SIO in charge of her rape case. Until Mac O'Connor had taken over.

'Sir?' she asked, trying to keep her voice as steady as possible.

'You've got nothing to fear. It's over, Harri.'

Harri looked at him. Six foot two. Athletic. Just like Mac. He was twelve years younger and absolutely driven. The job was all he thought about. All he obsessed about.

'I've got him restrained.'

Something in her told her to run. But she put it to one side. She nodded, her eyes never leaving him.

'Where is he?'

'Down in the basement.'

She didn't move.

'Who is he?

'I'd rather you saw for yourself.'

Harri didn't react.

'Don't you want this moment? Just you and him alone before back-up arrives? Before they lock him up?'

She forced herself to nod. She was trembling. Shock. Surprise. Or pure adrenalin.

He flicked a light on. It was simultaneously overwhelming and oppressive. He put his hand on her shoulder and guided her ahead. She slowly walked in the direction he was pointing her, ignoring the empty wheelchairs lined up against the walls, towards the end of the long hallway.

A light was coming from a room at the bottom of the stairs. She had no choice but to face her demons. If she didn't, then she would live with what had happened to her forever. It was simple. She thought of Dr Adams. Of their last session together. This was what he wanted for her; what she wanted for herself – the opportunity to face her rapist, once and for all.

She walked down the stairs. Every sensation was heightened.

What the fuck are you doing, Harri?

But she knew what she was doing. And she knew exactly what she was going to do to him. She would only have a second to appraise the situation. Then she would have to act – without hesitation; without thinking.

Or, you're going to die.

She felt Bradley's hand tighten his grip as she stepped through the open door. One second.

Fuck ... Fuck ... Fuck ...

Harri blocked out everything else in the room and focused solely on the man she wanted to kill. The man who had stalked her, raped her and left her a victim. Not now. Not any more. She had taught herself how to survive.

Two seconds: then she made her move. She spun around, and as she did so she swung her right arm back, taking his hand from her shoulder and securely restraining it. Then before he had a chance to react, she aimed her left elbow straight up into his jaw, followed by her fist. She heard a dull crack as it connected with his nose. Without hesitation, she then struck a blow straight at his throat. Swiftly followed by her knee into his groin. Hard. Twice. As he bent over, she grabbed his head and yanked it down, forcefully headbutting him in the face.

She took a step back. Watched as he staggered, temporarily blinded, as blood exploded from his shattered nose.

Then she came at him with a spinning wheel kick; heel to the jaw. His head jerked backwards. She repeated the action: heel to the jaw. This time, he dropped to his knees.

'You fucking bastard! Why?'

His dazed eyes stared at her.

'WHY?' Harri screamed.

She walked behind him, placed her right hand tenderly under his chin, her left hand holding the back of his head. Then she bent close enough to whisper in his ear: 'Tell me why, or I'll fucking kill you.'

'Because of what you did to me.'

Her fingers dug into his skin, ready to end it.

'What? Can't remember? Or don't want to remember?'

'Remember what? That we went to the same school?' she hissed. 'You left when we were twelve. What am I supposed to remember?'

'You told EJ and Ant to burn the desire out of me.'

Her mind was reeling. Even though she couldn't see his eyes, they still penetrated her. Brutal, menacing.

'No . . .'

'They told me, Harri. They taunted me as they doused me in petrol . . . I begged them not to light the match. I told them I would leave you alone. That I would never look at you again. That was all they had to do. Scare me. Make out it was an April Fool.'

Harri didn't move as she absorbed the enormity of his words.

'They said you had asked them to play the April fool. That you wanted me to be set on fire, to know that I literally burned with desire for you. EJ threw his match first. Then Ant. They chanted "April Fool" before running off and leaving me screaming.'

Her mouth felt dry. The hairs on her body were standing on end.

She shook her head. 'No . . . I never said that. I . . .' She faltered. No matter what she said, he would not believe her.

'I forgave you. Took a long, long time. But I did. I followed you. I joined the Met so you could have a chance at redemption. But even then you ignored me. Mocked me.'

'I didn't,' she whispered.

'But you did, Harri. Remember how I asked if you wanted to meet for a coffee at that staff party?'

She remembered. She remembered how she and Anna had howled about it afterwards. It hadn't seemed such a big deal – not to her.

'You burst out laughing.'

His words stung her.

'I was drunk. I thought you were joking. It was so out of the blue. You had never shown any interest in me before . . . If you hadn't overreacted and stormed out, I would have told you as much. You didn't give me a chance . . . I . . .' But there were no more words left.

She hadn't realised that he had been serious. That he had obsessed about her for years. The insignificant incident – for her – must have been the catalyst for him. It had given him the motive to carry out the most heinous crimes she had ever seen.

She refused to let him pass that responsibility on to her.

She looked up. She ignored the empty metal autopsy table in the centre of the room; focused instead on the girl in the wooden wheelchair, sitting mute and restrained straight in front of her. Alive.

The emaciated girl nodded. Her eyes filled with want. These were the defiant eyes that had stared into the camera; for Harri had realised in the first second in the basement that this was Louisa McPherson. That the body with the mannequin mask in the wheelchair on the floor above had to be another victim that they had not known about.

Before she had a chance to make a decision, he suddenly slashed at her with a knife.

Fuck you, bastard! She pushed his head up, then pulled back; a sudden two-way action. She heard his neck snap. Harri released him and watched his body fall to the floor. As she did so she heard the thunder of footsteps above her as an armed response unit arrived.

Chapter Thirty-Seven

Harri was waiting for Abbi McPherson. She had given Robertson the job of telling her that her sister had been found – alive. It was a nod to him that there were moments that made the shit times bearable. *Just*.

'Hey,' Harri said, as she gently touched Louisa's arm. She couldn't believe the resilience of the young woman. She had somehow survived, both physically and psychologically.

Louisa turned to her. The hostility in her dark brown eyes gradually retreated into some dark recess that would fester until her psychologist tried to exorcise it. 'I'm just thinking about him. You know.'

Harri nodded. She, better than anyone, understood. A nurse walked into the private room, smiled at the patient first, before silently taking various readings from the machines wired to Louisa's malnourished body. The doctors had said that there should be no long-term damage to her body. *But to her mind?*

Douglas had already taken her statement. It was protocol. Not that Harri had needed proof she was fighting for her life; the knife wound to her leg from when DI Aaron Bradley stabbed her was evidence enough. Harri had felt no pain at the time. Nothing, other than the will to survive. Not only for herself, but for Louisa McPherson. Then there was DI Mac O'Connor, and the other three victims he had tortured and murdered – testimony that Bradley would not have spared her. After all, this had all been about killing Harri.

'Why did he pick me?'

Harri looked into Louisa's questioning eyes. She felt compelled to answer her. Not that she was comfortable with it. 'I suppose you fitted his type.'

Louisa shook her head. 'No. I don't mean that. I know he chose me because of the way I looked. Just like the others. Long dark brown hair, brown eyes and . . .' She gave Harri a weak smile. 'Big boned, as my grandmother used to say. And too trusting. That's what she said. Not like Abbi.'

Harri nodded and waited.

'I mean why didn't he kill me like the others? Why keep me until the . . .' She faltered, unsure.

But Harri knew exactly why. Bradley wanted her presence to throw her. When he had dyed Louisa's hair blonde, her uncanny resemblance to Harri became even more apparent. He had placed bright green contact lenses in Louisa's eyes, making the disconcerting likeness even more striking. The only details he had missed were the scar across Harri's throat and the crisscross stab wound on her chest.

Harri could see Louisa taking in the damage to her neck.

'He did that to you, didn't he?' she whispered.

Harri nodded. She understood why Louisa was staring at her throat, assessing what he had done to her, for she had seen the serrated knife lying on her lap waiting to be used.

'Why didn't he do it to me? I knew he was going to. I watched him . . .' Her voice trailed off. Then it came back, stronger, more assertive: 'I watched him cut her throat. The one he called "Subject C". I watched him use the same knife that he left with me when he went upstairs. It was you, wasn't it?'

Harri gave her a quizzical look.

'I mean he heard you arriving. That was why he didn't get a chance to cut my throat. He didn't expect you so soon. You distracted him. And if you hadn't, then . . .' Her eyes drifted back to the scar on Harri's neck. 'I'm sorry. I . . . I don't mean to stare. It's just, he would have done that to me, if it wasn't for you.'

Harri smiled at her. 'It's OK. I don't mind you looking.' She nearly added 'not any more'; for now she had dealt with her past – *with him* – the scar on her neck didn't hold the power it once had.

'"John", he said his name was. He had also said both his parents had died when he was young, like mine. That he had studied psychology. He was lying, wasn't he? To make me trust him. To make me believe we had this unique connection.'

'I'm afraid he was,' Harri answered. Now wasn't the time to go into the details of who this killer was. When she was stronger, Harri had already decided that Louisa deserved to know the truth. She could see that she had already made some of the connections.

'Just like his photograph was a lie. I didn't doubt anything until those electronic gates closed behind me. That was when I saw the white transit van waiting. He had the doors open, a ramp leading up into the back.' Louisa shook her head, as if not quite believing it herself. 'That old, ugly wheelchair was sitting by the side, just waiting. I never got a chance to realise it wasn't the man in the photo. I didn't see his face till later. He had grabbed me from behind and put duct tape over my mouth before I had a chance to scream. He was too big for me to fight back. I . . . I had no chance . . . Then I felt him stab something into the side of my neck. He must have drugged me because I blacked out. When I eventually woke up I was lying on a hospital bed in a ward with the others. I was wired up to an IV drip and I . . . I couldn't move my arms or legs. I didn't know what he was going to do to me. All I could do was lie there and wait . . .'

Harri squeezed her arm. She knew what it had felt like to have been held at someone else's mercy. Not knowing whether they were going to kill you. But unlike Louisa, her experience had only lasted hours; not months.

'Up until the moment I actually met him, I had believed him. Every word. That he owned this huge house in Islington which he had bought with his inheritance. Same deal as me. When Mum and Dad died, I inherited a trust fund when I turned eighteen. I don't know, he just seemed to really know me, get me. It made me believe we had something really special. Sounds crazy, doesn't it?'

Harri didn't answer. She couldn't give her one. Instead, she waited for Louisa to continue.

'Even though we hadn't actually met, I felt like I knew him. That he just might be the one. That we were really going to backpack around the world together and . . .' She shook her head at her own naivety.

Harri refrained from telling her that Bradley had indeed inherited the money from his parents. But nothing else matched the story he had told her. There was no point. Not yet. Louisa still had a lot to process before being told the reason for her abduction – one that was directly tied to Harri. Louisa had no idea yet that Harri was intrinsically connected to the abductions and murders: Louisa had not seen herself in a mirror – not yet. And when she did, she would realise that it had all been about Harri. There was no mistaking the disconcerting likeness between them.

'Will you come back?' Louisa asked.

Before Harri had a chance to answer, she was interrupted.

'Lulu! Oh God, Lulu!'

Abbi McPherson ran into the room and straight to Louisa. She grabbed her sister's head and roughly kissed it repeatedly. Tears fell down her face as she held her.

Harri stood up discreetly and left.

Chapter Thirty-Eight

She looked at Douglas. It was over – for good. It was late Monday evening and they were in The Bacchus with the rest of the team. She still couldn't believe it.

It's done, Harri. You can move on.

With that thought, she looked over at Stuart. He caught her eye. *Fuck, it feels so good.*

Douglas had bollocked her of course, which she had fully expected. Not for what had happened to DI Aaron Bradley, AKA Marcus Fletcher. No. That was self-defence. Douglas had Louisa McPherson's word on that, and she had the stab wound to her leg. She hadn't felt it. She hadn't felt anything, other than a desire to destroy her attacker.

No. Douglas had exploded because she'd left the security of the station. She had put herself into his hands – literally. Marcus Fletcher had been obsessed with her from the age of twelve. He had kept diaries detailing how he had stalked Harri, stolen personal items that she had believed she had lost. Then he had graduated to photographing her while she was unaware. At eighteen he had changed his name by deed poll, then enrolled at Bristol University, just as she had, before following her into the

343

Met. Had proved himself better than her by fast-tracking his way to DI. Then he had copied her keys and replaced them without her knowledge; with the intention of entering her flat, raping and mutilating her. He was even appointed the SIO of the investigation afterwards. His DNA at the crime scene had been dismissed.

Harri vaguely recalled Marcus Fletcher as a lonely twelve-year-old boy desperate for her friendship. A friendship that she didn't need – didn't want. She had discussed his unwanted attention with her friends. The fact that he made her uneasy; *made her skin crawl.* But she would never have believed EJ and Ant would take matters into their own hands; that they would have attacked Marcus in such a horrific way. Nor that her naive rejection of him would result in Marcus obsessing over her to the extent that he killed to get her attention.

No. To punish her for rejecting him. An unknowing, repeated rejection.

That was the intent behind the abductions. He was altering them, trying to show her how much he obsessed about her.

But he had accused her of being responsible for the murders. That if her friends had not poured petrol over him and set him alight as a warning, then none of this would have happened.

She swallowed. Hard.

She had never suggested that Marcus Fletcher needed to be taught a lesson. Not once. She hadn't realised the other pupils had noticed how he followed her. How he had wanted her . . .

She shivered at this thought. At the retribution he had exacted because of what had happened to him in his childhood. He held her – them – responsible, without realising that it had all stemmed from him and his obsession with her. An obsession that others had noted. An obsession that others had decided to end. Their actions had not ended it; had instead become the catalyst for Marcus Fletcher's murderous rampage.

Harri blocked out his voice. Had to – otherwise she would never move forward.

She had to think of something positive: Louisa McPherson; alive, and still with the same defiant look in her eye; unlike the other victim in the hallway. Her name was Ella Taylor and she had once been someone's beautiful daughter. It was the same story; a young woman, physically large, ensnared on a dating app. She swallowed a mouthful of wine. She needed it. The autopsy findings had been horrific. The killer had broken countless bones in Ella Taylor's body; including her neck. She took little comfort in the fact that the toxicology findings had found high traces of the sedative benzodiazepine. Harri took another drink. Thought of the killer and what she had done to him. *Sweet fucking justice, you bastard!*

She remembered her conversation with Louisa McPherson. The things she had seen. How she had been forced to sit for hours staring out the first-floor windows, looking at the tombstones beyond the grounds of the large house. The property backed onto the sprawling and abandoned St John's cemetery.

'You all right?' Douglas asked as he glanced at her injured leg.

Harri nodded. 'I'll be back running again in a few days.'

Douglas didn't look convinced.

'Looks worse than it is,' she assured him. She was lucky; the wound had been superficial. She thought of the women Bradley had tortured and of DI O'Connor.

'Mac will be all right, won't he?'

Douglas nodded. 'Mac O'Connor's made of tougher stuff than you think. A week or so in hospital, followed by a few weeks' sick leave and then he'll be back at work.'

Harri nodded, knowing that Douglas was minimising Mac's injuries for her sake. She would be surprised if he was back at work in a few months' time; even that seemed optimistic. She was relieved that she had not shared her suspicions that DI Mac O'Connor was her attacker. Ironically, it could not have been further from the truth. It was Mac who had first suspected that DI Aaron Bradley was responsible for Harri's attack.

Not that anyone else had any inkling about DI Bradley; he projected himself as a charismatic team player who had everyone's sympathy because six months earlier his wife had been diagnosed with a terminal illness. Her condition had rapidly deteriorated to the extent that work had agreed that he could indefinitely reduce his hours to be able to take care of her. Not that anyone had any idea that he was lying; that instead of caring for a terminally ill spouse, he was in fact holding captive four victims in an unoccupied building he had inherited. But the lie had given him the opportunity to travel between London and Newcastle for the past four months.

346

The only person to suspect DI Bradley was Mac O'Connor. They had been out for a drink together a few months back. When DI Bradley had pulled out his wallet to buy the next round, Mac couldn't help but notice the photograph of Harri he carried. It had taken Mac some time to persuade his superiors that DI Bradley could have been responsible. Finally, they had allowed him to take the case over and undertake a covert surveillance operation – for Mac was convinced Aaron Bradley would attack again. Bradley had discovered that he was on to him, leading to Mac being left for dead in her lift.

Harri then thought of Sarah Bradley, the abused wife. Once she had discovered Aaron Bradley's room in the attic, dedicated to Harri, she had literally smashed her way out of the prison he had built and gone to the nearest neighbours for help. Douglas and the team had been alerted. Sarah was currently in hospital in London after undergoing six hours of surgery. The internal injuries she had sustained from her most recent assault by her husband were critical but not life-threatening – *not now*.

Harri still found it hard to comprehend the strength it had taken, both physically and mentally, for her to smash her way through a double-glazed door. If she hadn't escaped, she would have died within the next few hours from her internal injuries. Harri planned to visit her. After all, Sarah had risked her own life to save Harri's. She had put aside the fear of her husband's physical reprisals to save another woman from the fate she had suffered for two years.

She had talked briefly to Sarah. She'd been adamant that she needed to talk to Harri. *She needed to know. And she had needed to know from the person who had done it.*

'He's gone?' she asked. 'For ever?' Her quiet words trembled.

'Yes, he's gone. I promise you.'

'Thank you . . .'

Harri had known she was crying. Not from sadness at her loss, but gratitude at her gain. She had her life back.

'Thank you . . . For making sure he can never hurt me again. Thank you, DS Jacobs.'

'Harri . . . Call me Harri,' she had replied. 'And Sarah, thank you . . . for risking—'

But the line had then been cut before Harri could finish. She had decided to visit her tomorrow – with Douglas. After all, there were questions they needed to ask of her. And Harri wanted to accompany Douglas to Bradley's house in Islington. Now a crime scene. She wanted to see the attic for herself; the room he had dedicated to her.

She took another sip and turned to Douglas. 'He knew you would remove me from the investigation.' She saw the pain in his eyes. She didn't mean to cause that. 'Sorry . . . I didn't—'

'No,' Douglas said, shaking his head. 'You're right. We played right into his hands. We placed you on what should have been two straightforward suicides, but he knew you would keep digging. He knew how you worked, Harri. Well enough to know he could lead you exactly where he wanted you. Separated from your team. Isolated and alone.' He broke away from her gaze, clearly struggling with what could have happened.

Harri looked at her colleagues around her. Laughing and drinking. Celebrating the fact that the sick, psychopathic son of a bitch had been caught. And their DS had not been killed in the process. She caught Robertson's eye. He shot her a smile as he raised his pint. She returned the gesture. No one had been more relieved than Robertson to find her still standing. Still breathing. Very much alive.

'You say he knew me . . .' Harri mused. 'He didn't. If he had really understood me, he would have known that I would never let him lay a hand on me again.'

She thought about how he had put his hand on her shoulder. How he had gripped it so tight, it had hurt. That was his first mistake. The second was thinking that she was scared of him, or of what he wanted to show her – the metal autopsy table where he had altered his victims so they could become her.

It's over now, Harri . . . It's over.

Chapter Thirty-Nine

She knocked on the door before opening it: 'Sir?'

'Harri?' His voice was weak, unsure. Surprised.

She was taken aback by his condition. 'I just wanted to check for myself that you're going to be all right.' She had decided to call in to the Royal Victoria Infirmary on her way home from The Bacchus.

He attempted to smile. 'In my defence, he came at me from behind with a crowbar. Didn't stand a chance . . .'

Harri didn't know how to reply. The trauma Mac had suffered was extensive. If she hadn't found him immediately, he would have died in the lift.

'I'm sorry . . .' he whispered.

'You did everything in your power to prove it was him, sir.'

He attempted to move his head, but groaned at the pain.

She looked out of the private hospital room, hoping to see a doctor.

'Just a bit of a headache. That's all,' he said, trying to reassure her, but he winced as he spoke.

Harri stared at him uneasily. The drainage tube that fed out from the back of his bandaged head and the countless wires attached to his body told her different. She felt out of her depth with him, but knew she had no choice but to come and see him. To find that 'closure' she had been searching for. DI Mac O'Connor was a part of that process.

'I . . .' She faltered, not knowing what to say. She turned her head away, unable to hold his gaze; the regret in his eyes made her feel awkward. She tried to rein in the tumultuous emotions that had hit her the moment she had cast eyes on him. It was a throwback to the last time she had seen her father alive; unable to breathe on his own as he lay in a medically induced coma after surgery. But it hadn't saved him. He had died shortly afterwards, as Harri had stood, unblinking, unbelieving, while medics failed to resuscitate him.

'Harri?'

She forced herself to look at him.

'I need to apologise . . .'

She waited. Unsure.

'I don't know how to say it, but I need to . . . After everything that's happened, you deserve more . . . I should never have treated you the way I did.' He faltered for a moment. Then forced himself to continue. 'I . . . I was embarrassed about that night at your flat. Ashamed for being so attracted to you and behaving the way I did. Afterwards, I felt awkward around you. I found myself doing everything I could to force you out of the team. So I didn't have to face the guilt I felt whenever I looked at you.'

Harri didn't react. She didn't know how she felt.

'I'm sorry . . .' he muttered.

She knew it was genuine; the sadness in his eyes was clear enough. She realised that he wanted closure, as much as she did. He had had a part to play in what had happened to her.

She looked at him and nodded.

He closed his eyes. Exhaled; slowly.

'Mac?'

His eyelids fluttered. He struggled to open them. Failed. The exertion of what he had said, too much. Too soon.

She reached out. Touched his hand. 'I'm sorry too . . .'

Epilogue

'You've got a visitor, Aaron,' the nurse said as he followed her into the sterile hospital room.

Dr Adams watched as Aaron Bradley's eyes darted in his direction.

He appraised his client's condition. It was worse than he had initially assumed.

He walked towards him, so he could see him. Bradley could not move. Not after she had broken his neck. Snapped it in two. The doctors, himself included, were surprised that he had survived. But he had. Now a prisoner in his own body. Unable to do anything for himself. Whether he would be able to talk again was debatable. The medical profession believed it to be psychosomatic, which explained his presence. After all, Aaron Bradley was a serial killer; a man who had brutally transformed women into the likeness of his obsession: Harri Jacobs. Protocol had to be followed and only physicians authorised to the highest level were allowed access to such a dangerous man.

He nodded at him.

Bradley tried to communicate something to him. After all, he was his psychologist; no one understood the workings of this man's mind better than him.

'Let's start by discussing our plans for her.' He needed to give Bradley some hope. Something to cling on to. If that was slowly torturing the person responsible for doing this to him then so be it. It would offer him an end to his misery. After all, he had helped Harri Jacobs find the closure she had been seeking: the result was lying, immobile, in front of him. He was satisfied with the outcome. Harri Jacobs had not wavered from her decision to end it – by whatever means necessary. However, she had foolishly failed to completely finish it. She had not killed him. Bradley might not be able to hurt her any longer, but he knew clients who would relish the opportunity. He smiled encouragingly at Aaron as his 'Angel' came to mind.

Acknowledgements

I would first like to thank Janette Youngson and Paula Youngson who have continuously and selflessly supported me. Also, Natalie and Scott Ritchie. I would like to thank Keshini Naidoo for all her excellent editorial help. Thanks also to Donna Ferguson for sharing her police expertise. Thanks to Vicki Smith, Karen Knox and Alwyn Williams for their continuous support and advice. A heartfelt thanks to Pamela Letham and Gill Richards for everything they have done for me to ensure that I kept writing and kept my sanity. Finally, Francesca, Charlotte, Gabriel and Ruby, you are the reason I write – always.

Thanks to my literary agent, Euan Thorneycroft of A.M. Heath to whom I am eternally grateful for all his support.

Special thanks to all at Mulholland, Hodder & Stoughton for being such an extraordinary team; especially Cicely Aspinall. Finally, I am indebted, as always, to my exceptional editor, Ruth Tross. Thank you – you truly are one of a kind!

If you enjoyed THE LAST CUT, why not try
Danielle Ramsay's DI Jack Brady series

Turn the page for an extract from

THE PUPPET MAKER

Out now in paperback and ebook

MULHOLLAND
BOOKS
HODDER

Prologue

The basement was dark, damp and cavernous. It suited its purpose as a graveyard of sorts. Forgotten about. Filled with ghostly objects and questionable medical implements. Brady shone his torch across the discarded equipment, some dating back to when the Victorian mental asylum had first opened. The security guard had left him to it. Unnerved by the old psychiatric chairs with their leather restraints and other paraphernalia left to rot in the blackness. Brady couldn't blame him. He was equally uncomfortable down here. Then he heard *it* again. A doleful booming.

That noise . . . What is that noise?

He stumbled over something on the floor. *Shit!* Whatever he had tripped over rolled away, clattering into another item. The sound echoed around him, reverberating off the high brick walls. He flashed the torch into the deep recesses of the basement. Not that he could make anything out: the blackness was impenetrable.

He was starting to get jumpy. He needed to focus. There was a reason he was searching the bowels of an abandoned

359

and boarded-up mental asylum late on a Saturday evening – James David Macintosh; a serial murderer who was still at large. Brady had found himself unable to ignore the gut feeling he had; one that was telling him that the old psychiatric hospital was somehow significant.

He heard it again. A dull thud. It seemed to boom around him. Echoing off the high cold walls.

Fuck!

He turned around, stabbing at the shadows surrounding him. He couldn't figure out the direction of the noise, let alone the nature of it. He listened again.

Bang ... bang ... bang ...

It was then he knew. He was not alone. Something – or someone – was down here with him. His mind raced with thoughts of James David Macintosh as the banging – low, dull and repetitive – filled the chilling blackness around him.

Shit! What if ...

He pulled out his mobile. No signal. What did he expect? He thought of yelling out for the security guard. But he dismissed the thought. It was crazy. He was overreacting. He flashed the torch around the basement again, but the space was so large that he could not make out where it ended. Then the thought came back to him.

What if he is here?

Macintosh. The suspect he was looking for. A serial killer who had axed his victims to death. First, his psychiatrist and his family in 1977. Then, when he had finally been paroled for that crime, he had murdered his probation officer and *his* family. But he had left one survivor. A

360

three-year-old girl, who for whatever sick reason only Macintosh could answer, he had taken with him when he fled the murder scene.

Bang . . . bang . . . BANG.

Cold sweat ran down Brady's back. He held his breath and waited, trying to ignore the loud, accelerated thundering of his heart. He wondered whether he had foolishly walked into a trap. Had Macintosh lured him here? Had he followed unwittingly? Images assailed him of the axe the killer had used so indiscriminately.

BANG . . . BANG . . . BANG . . .

The booming intensified. He had no choice but to find out. He kicked random objects out of the way as he walked into the endless darkness ahead of him. He shone his torch, swiping at the shadows and ominous black shapes. Then he understood. Saw it. At the other end of the basement.

Brady held the torch as steady as was physically possible. He stared at the brick monstrosity that had revealed itself to be an industrial-sized furnace. It was twelve foot wide and ran up the entire height of the basement wall.

The banging began again. Louder. Uglier.

He walked over to the disused furnace, discounting the idea that Macintosh would be in there. Why would he be? No. Brady was now thinking about the infant girl he had taken with him.

He dropped the torch and started struggling with the large furnace door. It seemed to take forever before he succeeded in freeing it. The hinges groaned and creaked in resistance as he swung it open.

It took him a moment to register.

Annabel?

A girl. Thin. Small. Crouched over on scabby knees. Dirty. Covered in dried blood and . . .

Fuck . . . No . . . Brady steadied himself, not quite trusting what he was seeing.

Hair filthy. Matted. Her eyes. Black. Stared back at him. Unresponsive.

Oh Christ! What's happened to her? What the fuck has someone done?

All thoughts of James David Macintosh and the three-year-old girl disappeared. He was too thrown by the young victim facing him. *Someone had locked her in there. With . . . Oh God . . .*

Shocked, he stared past her. Past her undead eyes to the others.

So many of them . . .

He stood still. Mesmerised by the horror. They were dead. All of them – apart from her.

Why were they like that? Identically dressed. Long dark hair. Perfect faces. Painted. Heavy red lipstick – each one of them. All turned to face him. Watching him.

Grotesque. Horrific. Dead.

Then the screaming started. The girl. Her black eyes now filled with terror. Staring and staring at Brady, screeching a cry so inhuman, it was as if she had lost her mind.

DAY ONE
SATURDAY

Chapter One

Shit ... shit ... my head ...

She struggled to open her eyes – to keep them open. The pain in her head was unbearable. She closed them again, willing the pounding to subside. Minutes passed. Torturously slow. Any kind of movement racked the pain up to a level that was insufferable. So she lay face-down on the hard, cold floor and waited. Not moving – breathing as shallowly as possible – she remained there.

She had no idea how long she had lain there for, but finally, she was able to open her eyes and turn her head. The room was so black it was impossible to see anything.

That smell ...

The still, heavy air was nauseating. It smelt of vomit combined with an astringent odour of stale urine. She could feel herself starting to gag. Fear snaked its way through her cold body, coiling itself into a tight knot in her queasy stomach. It brought with it a sudden acknowledgement. A hard slap that jolted her back to reality.

Last night ... Oh God ... what happened?

365

Then she started to remember. First one image, then another and another. Lurid, debasing snapshots assaulted her senses.

Him ...

Her stomach started to churn. He had drugged her. She was certain of that. He had taken her to his place ...

Oh fuck ... where am I?

'Help? Help me?' she suddenly cried out. But her voice was barely audible.

Her throat hurt. It felt raw and swollen. Then she remembered why. She did not need to see the mottled purple and bluish bruising left behind by his hands. She could feel them encircling her neck and squeezing: slowly, surely, mercilessly. Her stomach tightened as she recalled the satisfaction he gleaned from strangling her while he— She stopped. She couldn't bring herself to think about what he had done.

She now understood why the room smelt of vomit. She had been sick, but her stomach could only retch up bile. Not that he had cared. He was only interested in raping her.

She could taste him in her mouth and smell him on her skin. A vile, distinctive odour that reminded her of bleach. She swallowed.

She tried to block out the thoughts. The brutal, sick images that kept replaying over and over again on a self-destructive loop.

She needed to pull herself together. She didn't have time to be weak and self-pitying. If she did, then she wouldn't leave here alive. She had to focus on one thought – *getting out.*

She listened for a noise. Something that could give her a clue as to where he had brought her. But there was nothing but oppressive silence. Then she heard it; a dripping noise. Faint but constant. Scratching . . . Something or someone was scratching. It was barely audible. But she could make out what sounded like nails dragging against metal.

Terror gripped her as she tried to discern the direction of the scratching. But it had stopped. Tears started to spill down her cheeks. She was desperate for a drink. It felt as if tiny shards of broken glass were lodged in her throat. She willed herself to get up. To move. She needed to find that water – *and a way out*. But her body felt as if it belonged to someone else. The smallest movement was an effort. Her head was still pounding and her limbs felt too weak to comply. She tried to push herself up from the mattress.

She cried out. Her knee exploded. The pain, blinding. Then the panic took over.

I don't want to die. Not here. Not like this.

She needed to focus. Get herself thinking straight. He had left her – *for now.*

She forced herself to fight the panic. Managed somehow to pull herself up. Exhausted and light-headed, she leaned back against the cold, damp wall and sat for a moment steadying herself against the screeching pain in her knee.

Had she fallen? She couldn't remember . . .

She breathed out slowly, trying to stop herself from retching. She had no idea what time it was, or how long she had been here. It was then that she became aware that her ankle hurt as well. More than hurt, it was burning with a cold feverish intensity. She pulled her leg in towards her body and heard what sounded like metal being dragged. Something was clasped tightly around it, cutting into the flesh. Panic-stricken, she felt her way down her leg.

Panic took hold again. She tried to fight it. A metal cuff was secured around her ankle. Desperate, she grabbed at the chain attached and yanked as hard as she could. It was futile. It didn't move.

Fuck! I'm trapped ... Oh fuck, why? Why has he done this to me?

Then she understood – *he's planning on coming back and ...*

She stopped herself. She didn't want to think about him coming back. The thought of *him* filled her with dread. Those eyes filled with contempt. No remorse, shame or empathy. Nothing but disgust for her.

The things he had done to her ... He had hurt her in a way that was inconceivable. And that was just the beginning. He had told her he had plans for her.

She tried to stop herself trembling. Whether it was fear or cold that had taken over her body, she couldn't say. All she knew was that she was terrified. Terrified of him coming back. There was no mistaking the fact that he had *hidden* her.

She wrapped her arms around her chest in an attempt to warm herself.

The darkness surrounding her had started to become claustrophobic. She could make nothing out. Fear of the unknown was threatening to unhinge her. She had always been terrified of the dark. It was something that she had never grown out of – that irrational feeling that something or *someone* was lurking in the shadows waiting for you.

For fuck's sake, keep it together and think ... think it through. Try and remember what happened ...

She shut her eyes tight as she tried to recall the events that had led her here. Slowly, pieces of memory, sketchy and hazy, started to come back.

Last night. Then ...

The memory jolted her. Him. The car. What happened next? She couldn't remember.

She couldn't fucking remember!

Then she was here.

Wherever here *is ...*

She had woken up in a cellar of sorts – some underground basement. But she couldn't be sure. All she knew was that it was black in here. So black. She couldn't see anything. Nothing. But she could feel the damp everywhere. The wet cold embraced her bare flesh. Clung to her hair. She used her fingers to feel the ground. It was nothing more than dirt. The wall behind her was stone. Damp and mould-covered.

She shuddered involuntarily as she thought of him. For all she knew he could still be in here, waiting in the blackness for his next move. His touch had been hard, aggressive. His breath sour and filled with longing.

'Help? Help me? Please?' she called out. But her voice was nothing but a whisper. 'Please ... please ... someone help me ...'

For some reason she knew it was pointless. That he had hidden her some place where no one would hear her. After all, how loud had he made her scream out? And no one had come then. So what were the chances of someone hearing her pathetic cries now?

Tears started to fall freely at the realisation of her situation. She had had a crap life. Been through shit, much more than your average teenager, but she had coped. Survived. Even started to make something of the hand that life had dealt her. And now . . . She clenched her fists as anger coursed through her. She was under no illusions. She had watched enough TV crime series to know that her outcome didn't look good. Worse still, no one would realise she was missing. She trusted no one and consequently kept herself to herself. How long would it take someone – *anyone* – to realise that she wasn't around? Terror sliced through her like a searing blade. The likelihood of her ever being reported missing was remote.

An overwhelming sense of alarm took hold. How would the police find her if they had no idea she had been abducted? Did *he* know this in advance? Had he stalked her? It seemed more than probable that he had been watching her; for this was not some random abduction – it had to be premeditated. Otherwise, how would he have known that she was going to be there last night? She hadn't told anyone her plans. No one knew her personal life. And that was the way she operated. She had trusted people in the past – and what had it got her? Nothing but pain. So she had shut people out. And now, it seemed that the isolated sanctuary that she had created for herself had imploded. Because now no one would be aware that she had disappeared.

Oh God!

Then she heard it again. The hairs on the back of her neck stood up.

A rasping, grating high-pitched noise – as if something or someone was trying to claw their way out. But it was not the scratching that scared her. No. It was something much more sinister.

Breathing. Someone was in here with her.